The Forgotten Pharaoh

David Adkins

First published by Endeavour Press Ltd in 2017.

Table of Contents

Introduction

It is the year 1365 BC. Amenhotep III, the magnificent king, is pharaoh in Upper and Lower Egypt. Amenhotep is the ninth pharaoh of the 18th dynasty and under his rule Egypt has enjoyed a period of peace and prosperity. Amenhotep had three sons and four daughters by his great royal wife, Tiye. This is the story of the youngest of these sons, Prince Smenkhkare.

Very little is known of Smenkhkare because later pharaohs sought to erase much of his family from history due to what is known as the Amarna period when the pharaoh turned away from the traditional gods of old Egypt. The story therefore, though sprinkled with possible historical fact, is almost entirely fiction. Indeed, Smenkhkare is shrouded in mystery and though there is substantial evidence to his existence it is often conflicting in nature and disagreed upon by some Egyptologists.

The story begins about 3400 years ago and, though a great civilisation, the world of Ancient Egypt was vastly different from the world of today. When reading the story two things, in particular, should be remembered and that is the early age when a child passed into adulthood and alsothat intermarriage was common within the royal family. Children became adults at an age that might seem scandalously young to us. This was partly due to the short life expectancy in ancient times. A commoner could only expect a life of 40 years, if he was lucky, for his life would have been one of considerable hardship and lacking in the medical help that we now take for granted. Life expectancy in the royal family would have been higher for life was easier for them except that plots, conspiracies and murder were commonplace throughout Egyptian history and sometimes cut their lives short. Intermarriage was commonplace within the royal family even to the extent of fathers marrying daughters and brothers marrying sisters. This was believed to keep the royal blood pure.

The result of this was that with a shorter life expectancy everything was accelerated. Children passed into adulthood between the ages of 12 and 14, and marriage would often take place during these tender years.

With early adulthood came responsibilities as children would begin work at the age of 12 or even before. Marriages, whether it was the commoner or the royal, would usually be arranged by the parents to the benefit of their family. Love would always be a factor but never a major one.

Religion was of massive importance in the Egyptian world as the entire civilisation centred around religious practices. Each individual had to know his place in the religious and social order. The pharaoh and his family, with the priests and other nobles, were the elite in the Egyptian world. In the middle were the soldiers, skilled workers and merchants. At the bottom were the farmers and labourers and below them the slaves. As a member of the royal family Smenkhkare held a great responsibility not only to the continued supremacy of his own family and to a successful war machine for the protection of his country but also for the well-being of his people.

The young Smenkhkare would be well educated and comfortable prior to his entry into the adult world. He would be looked after by his esteemed family until the day came when he would have to fulfil his destiny. This was the world that Smenkhkare entered at his birth about the year 1379 BC. In 1365 BC when the story begins Smenkhkare was 14.

Part 1 – Malkata

Chapter 1

I walked slowly along the corridor of the Royal Palace with a sense of overwhelming dread engulfing me. My father, the all powerful pharaoh, had taken little interest in me since the day I was born and this unexpected summons brought with it a strong degree of foreboding. On the rare occasions he spoke with me it was usually to berate me for some offence that I had unwittingly committed. He treated me with disdain and that was not surprising for most of my family treated me in the same manner. Unlike my two charismatic elder brothers I was a disappointment to my father, Amenhotep, for I was credited with little sense or intelligence. He mistook my shyness for stupidity and my small stature for lack of strength in both mind and body. I knew that I was not as hopeless as most of my family believed but in a family as dysfunctional as mine it was perhaps prudent to appear unobtrusive. If you were inconspicuous then you appeared less of a threat and as I was the youngest of the royal siblings that was probably a good thing.

I hesitated, took a deep breath and then knocked firmly on the door to the royal apartment of the mighty pharaoh and then pushed it open. "Come in, Smenkhkare," my father beckoned.

I entered the sumptuous audience chamber where foreign dignitaries were received and which was one of the largest of the many rooms in the grand palace of Malkata. "Thank you, father," I muttered nervously.

My anxiety grew when I saw that my mother, Tiye, and my two brothers, Thutmose and Akhenamun, sat alongside my father and they were all smiling. I had never seen so many smiles. "Sit down, Smenkhkare," my father commanded and I obeyed and waited for him to speak.

"Your older brother Thutmose is destined to be pharaoh one day when I pass into the next world. Your other brother Akhenamun I intend to make our High Priest in a few years time." He looked at me in conspiratorial fashion. "Of course, that is just between the people in this room, for the moment anyway."

I nodded agreement. "Yes, father."

"That left me with a problem, Smenkhkare. What was I to do with you? You are not intelligent enough to be an administrator. I do not say that in a cruel way but I have to face facts. The only obvious way to make use of you is in a similar way to your sisters, in a useful marriage."

I gasped. "I am to be married, father?"

"Yes and very soon," he replied. "I have officials in the Mitanni capital, Washukanni, even as we speak. They have sent a messenger to inform me that they have reached agreement with the Mitanni King, Shatuarra, that you will marry his daughter, Taduheppa. When they return to Thebes they will bring Taduheppa with them and you will marry immediately. It will herald in a new era of peace with the Mitanni. You will live here in Malkata with your new bride. Do you have any questions?"

I was dumbfounded and stared at him blankly. This had come as a complete surprise to me.

"Well?" he asked again.

"Is she beautiful?" I stammered.

"An excellent and most important question," laughed Thutmose.

My father showed more gravity. "I do not know and that should not be important. The most important thing is for you to do your duty."

"The officials say she is passable," grinned Thutmose.

"Why do you look so astonished?" my father asked, sounding a little irritated.

"I am surprised I am to be married before my two elder brothers," I said.

"I am to be High Priest and so I cannot marry," interrupted Akhenamun.

"And I must eventually marry into our royal family though to whom it has not yet been decided," stated Thutmose.

"Do you have any further questions, Smenkhkare?" my father asked.

"How old is she?" I blurted out.

I could tell my second question had annoyed him as much as my first but he deemed to answer it. "She is 21 years. I know that is a lot older than you." He turned to my mother. "Tiye, how old is he?"

"Your son is 14 years old," she replied.

"Is he that old?" He looked at me with contempt. "As I was saying, she is a lot older than you now but the gap will seem to decrease as you both get older. Now if you do not have anything useful to say you are dismissed."

I was only too glad to leave. I stood up. "Thank you, father, for the truly wonderful news." He did not even realise that I was capable of sarcasm though Thutmose knew I was and grinned.

I left his divine presence and made my way back along the corridor to my own quarters which it now seemed I was soon to share with the Mitanni princess, Taduheppa. Then I remembered that I had promised to meet my sister, Nebetah, perhaps my one true friend, in the palace gardens after my interview with our father. My head was all over the place after the unexpected news he had inflicted on me.

Nebetah was waiting for me and I sat down disconsolately on the bench next to her. "Bad news then," she said and looked at me with tempered eagerness.

I nodded sadly.

"It cannot be that bad surely."

"I am to be married," I said.

"Is that bad news? I thought they would find me a husband before they found you a wife for I am older than you."

"Only by 18 months," I reminded her.

She took my hand. "It is not bad news, Smenkhkare. It had to happen. I will be here to advise you on being a husband."

"I like my privacy apart from when I am with you and perhaps Thutmose. I do not want to share my apartment with a wife and knowing my luck she is bound to be ugly and not beautiful like you."

Her face reddened and then so did mine when I realised what I had said. "I am not beautiful," she said modestly.

"Yes you are, Nebetah. You are more beautiful than our other three sisters and everyone agrees you are. Even our brothers are handsome and nobody is ugly like me."

"Now you are just feeling sorry for yourself. You are not ugly," she reassured me.

"I am small, spotty and often tongue-tied. Almost everyone in the family including mother and father treat me with contempt because they think I am also stupid."

"Mother does not."

"She does," I reiterated. "Father treats me with hostile contempt and mother treats me with kindly contempt. Because they see little of me they think I have no intelligence. They compare me with my handsome, charismatic brothers and find me sadly lacking."

"Stop that," she scolded. "Tell me about your bride."

"I do not know much. Her name is Taduheppa and she is the daughter of the Mitanni King. Even as we speak she is preparing to leave Washukanni and come to Thebes. She is 21 years old. That is all I know except that our marriage is to bring peace between our nations."

"She will probably be given her own apartment in the palace so you may not lose your privacy entirely." She did some calculations. "She will probably arrive within three months. You must be ready for her."

"What do you mean?" I asked.

"You know," she grinned. "You do know what to do, don't you?"

"I am not sure," I confessed, "I may need you to help me with that." I laughed nervously and she giggled.

"What is the big joke between my little sister and my little brother?" asked Thutmose who had approached us unnoticed.

"A private joke and not for older brothers," teased Nebetah.

Thutmose looked disappointed and then laughed. He turned to me. "I came to see how you had taken father's announcement."

"I am worried that I might let everyone down," I admitted.

"Well it will be months before she arrives and so forget about your worries for now. If they persist then you can always come to me with them," he said kindly. "That is what big brothers are for." He turned back to Nebetah. "I have something to show you at the lake." He took her arm. "Would you like to come too, Smenkhkare?"

I shook my head. "No, I am still trying to digest my news."

I watched them as they walked towards the lake. I believed they were possibly the only two people that cared about me. I watched them laughing and chatting and I smiled with them though I could not hear their words. I wondered if my new wife would care about me.

Thutmose was always willing to talk with me and often chided Akhenamun for being abrupt with me. It was surprising that he found the time for he was busy preparing to be the next pharaoh. He was over ten years older than me and it was believed that on marrying, which would probably be soon, my father would declare him as fellow pharaoh and co-regent. My father doted on him for he was handsome, brave and intelligent and a great warrior with already many victories to his name.

My sister, Nebetah, was my greatest joy. She was 15, nearly 16, and we had played together all the time as children and then formed a deep friendship as we grew older. My other three sisters followed the lead of my parents and treated me with disdain. To be fair my sister Henuttaneb had married the vassal Nubian King two years previously and gone to live in his city of Napata, and I had not seen her since. My two oldest sisters, Sitamun and Iset, remained distant to me though they lived in the palace. They, by all accounts, were destined to marry my father and my brother Thutmose to continue the royal blood line. Nebetah, though, was by far the most beautiful in looks and nature, even at her tender age, and she was loved by all, even possibly Akhenamun.

I looked across at the lake. It was an engineering miracle dreamed up by my father and brought to reality by his most trusted architect. The lake was huge and shaped like a broad sword with a large hilt. Fish had been introduced and wild fowl had made the lake their home but there were thankfully no crocodiles. They were to be found in abundance in the river Nile, the harbour to which was on the other side of the royal palace. There were a few small boats out on the lake but I surmised that my brother and sister had gone to view the royal barque which was under construction. This would be used in future for the pleasure of the royal family. I wondered if Taduheppa would enjoy going on the lake with me but more to the point I wondered what she would be like.

It was some time before I wandered back to my apartment only to find my mother had been waiting for me. She was an attractive woman, noble in stature with an air of great authority derived from her many years as the great royal wife. She was still not yet 40 and had given birth to her oldest child Thutmose, my brother at the age of 15. My father had other minor wives, of course, living in the harem at the far side of the temple complex overlooking the great river, but mother was the important one. Father's successor would be born from her body and this gave her a position of much power. Like my father she was a living god and had no rival except perhaps for the beautiful Magente. Among the harem women Magente was my father's favourite and was often by his side, but her lowly birth meant that she was not a rival to my mother

"At last he returns. Where have you been, Smenkhkare?" she asked.

"Sitting in the gardens, watching the lake and thinking," I replied.

"Daydreaming more like or thinking about your new wife," she smiled benevolently.

"I was wondering about her," I admitted.

"I am sure you were. The treaty between the Egyptians and the Mitanni is one of utmost importance. Both of us are threatened by the Hittites to the north and so your bond with the Mitanni Princess is of great importance. It is time you grew up and started to take your responsibilities seriously and so I have suggested to Thutmose that he takes you army training. You need to build a military background for these are troubled times for Egypt. I know you are not as talented as your brothers but I also know that you are not as foolish as you sometimes seem. You must make the most of what you have." With that she turned around and left. I did not know whether I had just been paid a compliment or had received a rebuke.

A few days later I was collected by Thutmose for my first stint of army training. As we left the palace to walk down to the Nile we passed Akhenamun on his way to the temple of Isis, just a short walk south of the palace. He addressed Thutmose. "You cannot be expecting our little brother to learn how to use a sword," he quipped.

"He might surprise you," retorted Thutmose.

"He would not be able to lift it."

"I could," I said angrily as Akhenamun laughed. "You will never have to fight because you will be a priest," I added for good measure.

He took me by surprise and pushed me and I stumbled and fell over backwards. "Leave him alone." It was the voice of my sister Nebetah.

"I hardly touched him," protested Akhenamun.

Thutmose, frowning, pulled me to my feet. "You took me by surprise," I muttered between gritted teeth. It was not wise to antagonise Akhenamun but that did not worry my sister.

"Apologise to Smenkhkare now!" she ordered her elder brother.

"I never apologise to anyone with the exception of when my sweet little sister asks me to. I am sorry, Smenkhkare." He turned to Nebetah. "Am I forgiven, sister?" He kissed her on the lips, a gesture which infuriated me but I said nothing. I knew that half the women in the palace would love a kiss from Akhenamun and my sister did not seem to mind. Akhenamun was even more handsome than Thutmose if that were possible. He had long dark hair, a swarthy complexion and was athletic in build. He often wore black which I suppose was fitting for a future priest but it gave him an air of mystery which seemed to appeal to his admirers.

"Let us go, Smenkhkare," said Thutmose. "We have chariot racing to participate in. You must learn how to handle a chariot. Coreb is waiting for us." He took my arm and hurried us away.

We boarded a boat to cross the Nile to where the military manoeuvres were to take place. Nebetah waved to us but Akhenamun did not. I watched as Akhenamun now joined by his sinister companion, Metos, walked to the temple while Nebetah returned to the palace. Metos was a tall, slim and wiry man with a threatening disposition who was often at Akhenamun's side. He made me shudder and together they seemed even more threatening and sinister, totally unlike my handsome and open brother, Thutmose, who was so often smiling and had a captivating and cheerful disposition. They were alike in many ways but in other ways so different.

I watched as several crocodiles swam close to the boat. They were also threatening creatures with their powerful bodies, long tails and massive teeth. Many a person had fallen victim to these ferocious animals that lived in the great river. It seemed as if they were just waiting for one of us to fall out of the boat so they could pounce. Our oarsmen took us swiftly across and we jumped out of the boat on to the jetty at the other side of the river. It was now not far to walk to the training ground.

"It is chariot riding and sword practice today and so I thought you and I would take a chariot," said Thutmose smiling.

I cheerfully nodded agreement. We were met at the jetty by Commander Coreb. He bowed his head. "Your majesty," he greeted Thutmose who was several strides ahead of me. I was looking in wonder at the line of chariots and the lines of soldiers going through their paces with swords and shields.

"Thutmose and Smenkhkare are just fine as you well know," said Thutmose as he grinned and patted Coreb on the back. They were the same age and had been friends for a long time. Coreb was a proven military commander and a man of considerable ability.

"Your chariot awaits you." He led us along the line of chariots until we reached a golden one with the head of Osiris blazoned on the side. Coreb turned to me. "Have you ever ridden in a chariot, Smenkhkare?"

"Never, I am a little nervous. I ride horses in the palace grounds but I have never ridden a chariot."

"Do not be nervous," Coreb encouraged me. "Your brother is an expert." He whispered in my ear. "He is one of the best but we do not want him to become conceited."

I laughed for I liked Coreb. "That would not do." Coreb watched as we mounted the chariot. Thutmose took the reins and I sat next to my accomplished brother.

"Watch all that I do carefully," Thutmose advised.

I nodded eagerly and Thutmose tugged on the reins and the chariot started to move. There were already many chariots doing the circuit of the vast training ground. As we gathered speed the wind took my long brown hair and a thrill such as I had rarely experienced engulfed me. We made a number of circuits of the training ground and I watched my brother with great attention studying closely all that he did.

"It is time to go a little faster," he shouted exuberantly and my excitement grew. We were now travelling at great speed and overtaking many of the other chariots. As we passed Coreb he waved to us and I waved back. Speed brought added excitement and after about six circuits at what seemed to me an incredible speed we began to slow down until we came to a halt.

"Your turn," said Thutmose handing me the reins. We changed places and he gave me an encouraging look. "Take it slowly and do a few circuits."

I did as I was instructed and to my surprise I was able to handle the horse and chariot quite successfully, though on my first circuit another chariot had to take quick evasive action to prevent a collision. I completed five circuits and I was really now enjoying myself after getting over my initial anxiety.

"Bring it to a stop," my brother instructed. "That will have to be all for today. We need to get back to the palace."

I could not hide my disappointment. "Why is that?" I asked.

"I have an interview with father and he does not like to be kept waiting."

"He would not mind if it was you," I offered.

He laughed. "He would, so bring the chariot to a halt."

I quickly did as he asked and he climbed out of the chariot. Coreb helped me out. "Are your legs fine, Smenkhkare?" he asked. "Sometimes your balance can be affected when you are not used to it."

"I am fine," I smiled.

I walked back to the boat with Thutmose. "Thank you for taking me today. I enjoyed it greatly."

"It is something we must do regularly. You must learn to be an excellent charioteer and I also want to teach you archery, but combat can wait until you put on a bit more weight."

We climbed into the waiting boat and the oarsmen started rowing as we began our return trip across the mighty river. "As the passenger on the chariot, little brother, you would have been firing your arrows at the enemy as I controlled the horse and chariot. It is a team effort." The term 'little brother' would have sounded derogatory to me if said by anyone else but Thutmose.

"I understand," I said.

When we reached the opposite bank Akhenamun was waiting for us. He seemed to sneer at me as he spoke to Thutmose. "Father is waiting for us." And with those words they hurried off leaving me to make more sedate progress to the palace, daydreaming about firing arrows from the chariot and defeating Hittites.

I passed my sister, Iset, as I entered the royal palace. "I hear you are getting married," she said. "I hear it is a Mitanni princess."

"That is so," I replied.

"I never did like the Mitanni. It serves them right," she laughed but it was a mirthless laugh. "I feel almost sorry for her."

Iset was reasonably attractive but was rather tall and gangling which was a trait in our family that I had avoided. Unfortunately tall was good but small, like me, was bad, at least as far as my father was concerned. However, she did take the time to insult me which was rather more than my very plain oldest sister Sitamun did. She simply ignored me and pretended I did not exist. It was generally assumed that Sitamun, as the eldest, would marry my father and Iset would marry my brother Thutmose. Perhaps I was lucky to be marrying a Mitanni princess. "I hear she is a great beauty who will put my sisters to shame except, of course, Nebetah. It seems I am very lucky," I hit back and surprised her. I think driving that chariot had given me more confidence.

"You little brat," she muttered but also laughed and she strode away with her head in the air.

I almost warned her not to hit her head on the palace door as she exited but that might have been going too far and I was not yet quite that confident. She would have probably complained to father and I would have been in trouble. There was one thing the great pharaoh Amenhotep always did and that was to take the side of my siblings against me. This was not surprising for I was sure that he was ashamed of me. I wondered if my Mitanni bride would be a great beauty. I would be happy and satisfied if she just proved to be a good friend.

"Did you have a good time?" asked Nebetah emerging from behind a pillar, grinning.

"Did you hear?" I asked.

"I did but honestly you must try to get on with Iset for she is not so bad."

"Let us go for a walk into the town," she suggested. "We can put on some old clothes and nobody would know and we would not be recognised."

I was horrified. "Get such notions out of your head, Nebetah. We are forbidden to go into Thebes alone as you well know. It is a dangerous place even during the day." I did not want to antagonise my father even more and he would probably find out. He seemed to know everything that went on in Thebes.

She sighed. "I would love to go shopping at the great market, the clothes and the jewellery are all very colourful, but you are right. I am sure father would find out because he has spies everywhere and one of them would be sure to see us."

"How do you know that he has spies?" I asked.

"I listen to what others say," she replied.

"Like you did when you were behind that pillar?"

She grinned. "Thutmose and Akhenamun often talk of spies and I have heard Akhenamun speaking with Metos of such things but I do not really take much notice."

"In that case we should certainly not go into town alone. It would get us into trouble and inevitably I would be in more trouble than you. We are allowed to walk down to the harbour and there is a small market there," I suggested.

"Then the harbour it is," she said taking my arm.

The harbour was always interesting and Nebetah was always good company. We wandered around for a couple of hours or more watching the ships go back and forth on their journeys up and down the great river. Nebetah bought a bracelet at a stall which seemed to please her greatly. At last, feeling tired and with night starting to close in, we returned to Malkata.

"Will you mind being married?" she asked.

"I do not know but it makes me nervous," I admitted.

"You are younger than me and they have already found you a bride so it will probably not be long before they find me a husband."

I nodded. "That would be difficult to bear."

"Yes, it would mean me leaving Malkata like Henuttaneb had to when she married the Nubian King."

"And I would miss you so much," I sighed.

"No you will not, for you will have your wife by then."

"I will but I will still miss you," I smiled.

"And I would miss you, Smenkhkare, but I may have a handsome prince for compensation though I doubt it. I think father intends to marry me into the Hittite royal family, probably to their old king," she sighed.

"He would never do that. The Hittites are our enemies," I reassured her.

"Father likes to turn enemies into friends and maintain peace."

"He loves you and will only marry you to a young prince and eventually you will become the beautiful Queen of a great nation," I added.

"Like our mother," she happily agreed, but then more solemnly declared: "I hope I never have to leave Malkata."

I nodded and we entered the palace. She kissed me on the cheek and returned to her apartment. I watched as she disappeared down the corridor and then I returned to my apartment where the servants would be waiting for my return. Tonight I would dream of my beautiful wife-to-be and no doubt Nebetah would dream of her handsome prince. The problem is that dreams have a habit of not coming true.

Chapter 2

It was indeed about three months later that the news that the Mitanni caravan was approaching the city brought great excitement to both the people of the city and the residents of the palace. It was rumoured to be quite a spectacular sight as it travelled across the barren desert towards Thebes. By the time the caravan reached the city multitudes had lined the streets to see the wondrous sight. For once the great market had been abandoned as news spread that the new member of Amenhotep's family had arrived.

The royal family assembled in force in the gardens of Malkata for the pharaoh had decreed that every honour should be given the Mitanni princess as she was the glue that would bind our two great nations together. I was experiencing a strange mixture of fear, excitement and wonder as the caravan drew ever closer. It was almost beyond my comprehension that I was playing a significant role in the union between the people of Upper and Lower Egypt and the people of the Mitanni and the Arzawa – such was the joint inherent fear of the Hittites.

From the noise outside the palace walls I knew that the caravan was approaching at last. Progress through the city streets had been slow and laborious due to the encroachment of the crowds resulting in the route having to be cleared by soldiers. At last the great, ornate gates to the glorious Malkata palace opened and the Mitanni caravan appeared like a gift from the gods. I was amazed at the sight that met my eyes. I could see the Theban officials at the head riding with armed Mitanni guards and three caravans behind the escort, but it was the caravan at the rear of the convoy that most took my eye.

It was covered with a canopy of gold and flower petals were being thrown by several handmaidens into the gardens. My nose picked up the aroma of exotic perfume emanating from the caravan. The front of the canopy was open and my bride to be could be seen lounging on a couch covered with coloured silks while sweet music could be heard coming from a flute in the second caravan. I could only stand and stare in amazement. The Mitanni princess knew how to make an entrance.

My father met the Mitanni ambassadors, who emerged from the first caravan and he spoke with them at some length. The slow-moving third caravan carrying the princess at last drew to a halt and I could see her more clearly. I really could not believe my eyes. She was more beautiful even than Nebetah or Magente. She had a serpent crown on her head that only partly covered her long, flowing raven black hair. She had mesmerising dark eyes that matched her hair and the most beautiful, bewitching face. She wore a long, plain, deep green gown but the plainness only seemed to make it even more exotic. It flowed all the way down to her ankles but hugged at her slim figure. Finally on her feet she wore brown sandals that were studded with silver jewels. I could only continue staring in disbelief.

"She is wasted on our little brother," I heard Akhenamun say to Thutmose. "I will marry her instead."

"You are to be a priest," my older brother reminded him.

"I would rather have the Mitanni woman as a wife and be a warrior." There was resentment in the tone of Akhenamun.

"We cannot always be what we wish to be, not even us," Thutmose rebuked him.

We turned our attention back to the caravan for my wife-to-be, Taduheppa, was stepping out with a little help from one of the Mitanni ambassadors. My father stepped forward to greet her and embrace her as his new daughter. One of her female servants placed a chest at my father's feet which no doubt was a gift from the Mitanni king. My father turned around and called to my sister: "Nebetah, take Smenkhkare back to his quarters. I have allowed him to witness the arrival of Taduheppa but now we must conform to custom. He will not see her again until their wedding day." Nebetah took my hand and led me into the palace and I followed her in a daze.

As I left the wondrous scene I heard the words of Akhenamun to Thutmose. "The custom is one day before, not a week before. The pharaoh is frightened that if she sees Smenkhkare up close she will run back to Washukanni in fright and there will be no wedding."

I ignored his hurtful words and spoke to Nebetah. "Did you see her?" I said as we walked along the corridor to my apartment.

"I did." It seemed that even Nebetah was amazed. "She is lovely."

"I think lovely is an understatement, sister," I retorted.

I opened the door and we went inside, dismissing the two servants who were tidying my rooms. "When will we be married?" I asked, not expecting Nebetah to know the answer.

"I heard father saying it would be in one week. He wanted it to be as soon as possible but needed some time to prepare."

""You know everything, Nebetah. Will she live here in my apartment?"

"I suppose so, but I am not sure for I think she will also have her own rooms."

"I cannot believe it," I said.

"Nor can I," she replied. "I will return to the gardens for I do not wish to miss anything. I will be your spy and tell you everything about her in the coming week."

"Thank you," I said as she eagerly hurried out of the room leaving me with my hopes and fears and a week of anticipation and trepidation.

****

The next morning I had two surprise visitors and I was not pleased to see them. Vizier Ay was father's highest official and supervised the local running of the government – from palace security to taxation and the courts. He was a cold man full of his own importance and a relative for he was cousin to the pharaoh. The man who stood alongside him, Ramose, was a sycophant who stuck to his superior Ay like a leech. I had to admit, though, that Ramose was a handsome young man with a striking persona.

Ay seemed to look down his nose at me as he addressed me: "Smenkhkare, your marriage will take place in five days' time at the Temple of Isis in the palace grounds. It will be a small affair attended by the Mitanni ambassadors and members of the royal family and there will be a feast in the royal palace afterwards to celebrate the nuptials." He seemed to sneer at me and then continued: "You will remain in your quarters until then as your bride, with the help of my daughter, Nefertiti, will be acquainting herself with the palace and gardens and the layout of our great complex. It would not do if you were to bump into one another." He smiled mirthlessly.

I shrugged. "I might embarrass everyone and the intended bride might run from the palace screaming," I said, remembering the words of Akhenamun. I pictured Taduheppa and Nefertiti together – two goddesses walking the palace grounds for Nefertiti was also a great beauty. Her good looks must have been passed down to her by her mother. I sneered at Ay.

He ignored my words. "Ramose will look after any requirements you may have during the five days and your sisters will be instructed to visit you so you are not lonely."

"I have servants and therefore have no need of Ramose, and I only require one sister to visit me, Nebetah, and she would do so anyway," I pointed out. "Why is the ceremony taking place at the Temple of Isis? Why is there a ceremony at all?"

"The Temple is a suitable place because it is a small family temple in the palace grounds. Akhenamun will bind you together with a few words while Taduheppa's servants will move some of her belongings to your apartment to seal the union. It is better that way."

I nodded, accepting the explanation. In most marriages there were no ceremonies, but my wedding being a royal one was I suppose a little different.

"As you wish with Nebetah, but Ramose will call on you daily to see if you have any special requirements. We will leave you now." They both headed for the door but before they left Ay turned to me again. "Remember, Smenkhkare, stay in your room."

****

Having to stay in my room seemed to me to be absurd and left me feeling like a prisoner in my own quarters. I supposed that I would feel that way until the wedding had taken place. I could see the injustice of the situation but I did not care. Most of the time I was happy with my own company and Nebetah was sure to visit me and perhaps Thutmose too.

Nebetah came every day and sometimes twice a day and we played many games of senet. I won most of the time for it was not just a game of chance but one of skill and strategy and I was good at it. We gossiped as we played and the time passed quickly with much enjoyment and fun all the time that Nebetah was with me. Ramose also visited me daily but it was a visit of duty and we had little to say to each other and so he did not stay long. The day before the wedding he came early in the morning and stayed with me for over an hour giving me instructions on my behaviour during the ceremony. He told me he would collect me late the next morning and escort me to the Temple. In fact I had a number of visitors the day before the wedding.

Next came Nebetah and we had another game of senet and wiled away the rest of the morning. She gave me a sisterly hug and told me not to worry, and she teased me about my wedding night but it was all good fun. My next visitor was Thutmose who apologised profusely for not coming earlier in the week, making the excuse that father was keeping him very busy. I knew that it was true for my brother was a very busy man. He offered me some brotherly advice on the ceremony and told me not to worry. He also told me that he would take me army training again as soon as he had the time. He then wished me well and left.

My final visitor was my mother, Tiye. She also gently embraced me and smiled a sad sort of smile. "I hope you are ready for this," she said.

"I know what I have to do," I assured her.

"Many get married as young as you," she said, "but you seem extra young."

"Do not let my size fool you mother," I said. "I will conduct myself properly during the ceremony and not embarrass my family."

"You are not that small and you will grow. Your brothers are such tall and powerful men and your father tends to make comparisons between you and them. I know your introversion makes you seem dull at times, but I also know you have intelligence and so I am not worried. I have confidence in you."

It was probably the kindest words my mother had said to me in years. I involuntarily hugged her and she returned my hug. "I will not let you down," I said.

"I know," she smiled. "I must go now."

"Does Taduheppa wish to marry me?" I blurted out. It was a question I had kept suppressed all week.

She shook her head sadly. "It does not matter what you or Taduheppa want, for you must both do your duty." She left without answering my question.

Sitamun, Iset, Akhenamun and my father, the great pharaoh did not visit me.

****

I did not sleep well that night as there was so much going on in my mind. The next morning the servants dressed me in my finest clothes and soon after Ramose appeared at my door. I was feeling nervous but I was ready. "The guests are assembled in the temple and they are waiting for you," he informed me. We walked along the ornate corridors and exited the palace through the grand doors. We walked through the gardens under the midday sun and down the shaded path that led to the Temple of Isis and all the time I was in a daze. The time had come and I did not really feel ready for it but I was determined not to let my family or my nation down. Egypt must embrace the Mitanni and secure the future of both nations against the threat of the ever increasing power of the Hittite Empire.

Taduheppa was waiting for me with her chief ambassador, who was actually her uncle, at the Temple doors. It was fitting that we entered together for we were of equal rank: I was the son of the pharaoh, Amenhotep, ruler of Upper and Lower Egypt; and she was the daughter of Shatuarra, King of the Mitanni and ruler of Arzawa.

I looked nervously at my bride. She wore a long blue dress made of linen which stretched right down to her sandalled feet. The dress was simple but her neck was covered with necklaces of gold and precious jewels. The bangles on her wrists were both gold and silver and jewels were studded into her sandals. I wore simply a shorter red tunic. She put her arm around my waist and in return I put my arm around her. I could only see her black eyes for she was wearing a veil. She realised that I was searching for her face and briefly pulled back her veil for a second. I was captivated by that one enticing glance at her beauty. She gave me a slight tug and together, followed by her ambassador, we walked into the Temple.

My family and the Mitanni contingent were standing, awaiting us and they broke into spontaneous applause. I was sure the reception was for Taduheppa and not for me. We approached my brother, Akhenamun, who was standing by the statue of Isis in his signatory black tunic. He would say a few brief words and it would all be over and we would return to the palace for the feast. I managed to approach him in a dignified manner without falling over, which had been a recurring nightmare these past few nights.

He began: "We are here to acknowledge that the marriage of my brother Smenkhkare, son of Amenhotep King of Egypt to Taduheppa daughter of Shatuarra, King of the Mitanni is binding. Taduheppa has moved in with Smenkhkare and they are man and wife." Taduheppa handed me the lotus flower that she had been carrying in her right hand to indicate that I was her husband. I accepted it to show that I accepted her as my wife. Akhenamun then spoke again: "I ask for the blessing of mighty Aten for this happy union." He put his hands in the air beseeching the blessing as the sun's rays poured in through the open doors. There was a slight murmur of disapproval for this was the Temple of Isis. I was pleased that so far it was my brother and not me who had provided the only controversial moment of the day. "The blessing has been given," he announced. "Now we must make merry."

All the guests filed quickly out of the Temple and we made our way back to the Palace for the celebrations. I walked hand in hand with Taduheppa though I could not help feeling that we probably looked ridiculous as she was much taller than me. I felt tongue-tied but I managed to blurt out a question: "Are you happy here in Malkata?"

"Yes, very happy," she replied. "Your family have been most kind and Malkata is much grander than my palace in Washukanni."

"My family have been kind," I repeated.

"Yes, they have." She looked at me quizzically.

"Do you mind me being your husband?" I inquired.

"No, but then you are hardly my husband," she replied.

I wondered what she meant but I could not see the expression on her face for it was still covered with the veil. Silence then ensued as we entered the palace and made our way to the large central hall where the banquet was waiting for us. "Your things have been moved into my apartment," I reminded her as we sat down at the long, exotically furnished table.

"Not all of them," she replied. "Many are still in my own apartment."

"Does that mean we are only half married?" I asked her.

She removed her veil and looked at me. "What do you think, Smenkhkare?"

She was dazzling. I took a deep breath as I drunk in her matchless beauty. I knew what she meant. She was a woman, a Goddess, perfection. I was a boy, unattractive and immature. I could hardly be her husband. As she chatted to Sitamun, who sat the other side of her, I felt a great sadness engulf me. I saw Akhenamun smirking at me for he must have heard her words. I wanted to leave for I felt inadequate even though the day had gone well up to now.

I felt a hand on my shoulder. It was Nebetah. "It has been an excellent day. Congratulations, brother." Her smile was warm.

"Thank you, Nebetah." At least I still had my sister, but I wanted my wife. My sister returned to her seat further down the table and I was left next to a wife who did not even want to talk to me and found the dull conversation of Sitamun preferable to mine.

The servants began to bring in vast quantities of food. The music began to play. Everyone looked happy except for me. I wanted to run from the scene but I remembered the words of my mother and did not move. The musicians were playing their flutes and lyres and the guests were eating the exotic meals placed before them. I did not feel hungry and just nibbled at my food. I decided to once again speak to Taduheppa who had so far paid very little attention to me.

"Why are you ignoring me?" I asked.

"I am not, but I must talk with our guests. I need to get to know the people who live in the palace, your family. My ambassadors and officials will return to Washukanni tomorrow and I will be left with just a few Mitanni serving girls. I am alone and a long way from home."

Her explanation made me feel bad. "I will help you fit in as best as I can."

"Thank you, husband," she smiled. "But you cannot do that by yourself." She stood up and walked gracefully around the table and I watched her elegant strides in awe. This incredible creature was my new wife. She started a conversation with Akhenamun and Thutmose and I watched as she chatted and laughed, and for some unaccountable reason I felt overwhelmed with jealousy. It was plain to me that she would not find it at all difficult to fit in.

Then the dancing started and Taduheppa was dancing with Akhenamun. They made a stylish couple, my wife and my brother. Nebetah took my hand and pulled me to my feet. "They are just dancing and they are a similar age. It is understandable, for you must seem young to her."

My sister understood my feelings perfectly. "That may be so but she is my wife," I countered.

"True, but do not make a fuss," she warned.

"I do not intend to." My dancing was clumsy and lacked finesse unlike my accomplished brother, and so I returned swiftly to my seat and waited for my wife to return. I had to wait a long time, for after Akhenamun she danced with Thutmose and my father.

At last she returned to her seat next to me. "Will you dance with me now, Taduheppa? " I asked.

"I am now too tired."

I felt anger well up inside me. "Will you come to my room tonight?"

"Of course, I am your wife. I will pay you a visit."

I did not know whether to be pleased or angry with her reply and so in order to calm down I moved around the table myself and talked with some of the guests and family. It was not a situation I was comfortable with, but I think I did what was expected of me. As the evening drew to a close I knew that the onus was on my wife and me to leave the festivities and go to our apartment. I stood and nervously looked around me. "It is time for me to retire."

I looked down at Taduheppa and she did not move. A few seconds passed and then she stood up. "You will wait for me, husband?" she beamed. I swear every man and boy in the room must have been envious of me, at that moment, and by the gods they did have cause. I nodded and a few moments later she joined me. We left the banqueting room and made our way along the corridor towards the royal apartments.

As we approached my apartment she stopped. "I must go to my rooms first and prepare," she said. I was reluctant to release her but she deftly freed her arm.

"Please do not be too long, Taduheppa." I was certain there was pleading in my eyes.

"I will not," she said. I watched as she glided gracefully down the corridor back to her own rooms. I was fraught with nerves but also eager with anticipation.

I waited for many hours and just when I had become certain that she would not come there was a knock on my door. My heart raced as I rushed to the door and opened it, and it raced even harder when my wife stood before me. I ushered her in. She was dressed in a long yellow robe and yellow matching slippers, but there was no sign of gold or jewellery. She strolled nonchalantly into my chamber showing none of the anxiety that was threatening to overwhelm me. "The bed is in the adjoining room," I blurted out.

"Why would I want the bed?" she asked. "I do not feel tired."

"You are my wife," I exclaimed. "I thought you had come to …" My words faded away into nothingness.

"You thought I had come to consummate the marriage," she laughed. "You are just 11 years old."

"I am 14 and will be 15 soon," I corrected her.

"You only look 11."

Her words hurt me to the core. "Then why did you come?"

"It has to look as if we are man and wife and therefore I and some of my belongings must enter your room. I made very sure that I was seen entering your room for effect. I will stay here for a while and then return to my own quarters."

"Please, Taduheppa, I am sorry I am not older but I will try to be a man."

"Smenkhkare, where I come from males do not marry until they are 17 and maybe not even until they are my age. Women do marry earlier but you are not a woman. We are married for the purpose of bringing peace between our nations and no other."

"That is not so." I was feeling downcast.

She laughed. "Wait a few years and I will consider it. Is that a senet board I see over there? Egyptian travellers taught my brother the game and he taught me. Shall we play to while away an hour or two?

"Yes," I reluctantly agreed.

She was surprisingly good, but senet was my forte and eventually I overcame her stout resistance. "You were lucky," she smiled.

"I am skilful," I corrected her, pleased to be able show her that I am at least intelligent.

"Then you should have let me win," she admonished me.

"I am sorry, Taduheppa."

"Did you really expect us to make love, Smenkhkare?"

"I hoped," I said feeling embarrassed.

"So even at your tender age you want me."

"I suppose I do," I agreed.

She shook her head. "Perhaps when you are a little older," she said as she leaned over and kissed my forehead. "Goodnight little husband, I will see you tomorrow."

I was speechless as she left my apartment. Not only was I a little brother but now I was a little husband.

****

I did not see my wife the next day and I assumed she was avoiding me, and the next night she did not visit me. I thought about visiting her apartment but decided against it for now. I needed a strategy for dealing with her. Nebetah was occupied with her two sisters which was unfortunate because I needed to talk with someone. The morning after that Thutmose came to see me and I was very pleased to see him.

"You do not look very happy, Smenkhkare," he observed.

"I am not very happy," I confirmed.

"You can tell me the cause, though I think I can guess, but for now there are more important things to deal with. A caravan has been attacked by a large gang of bandits not very far from Thebes. I intend to leave immediately with a large force to hunt them down. Do you want to come?"

I was amazed that I should be asked. "Yes, I will come, Thutmose." I felt it would be something to take my mind off my wife.

"It will be a good experience for you, but I will make sure that you are never placed in danger."

"Do not worry on my account." I tried to sound brave.

"You are too young to fight and you have little training. You will be in a chariot in the rear but you will be able to watch proceedings. These raiders must be eliminated. Now we have no time to waste. Can you leave straight away?"

"I am ready, Thutmose," I said, strapping on my bow and quiver.

"You will not need that," he smiled. "Let us go."

****

We left the palace and climbed into his waiting chariot. Another chariot containing two soldiers fell in behind us. We moved quickly south keeping close to the great river until the large force of nearly 200 chariots came into view under the command of Coreb. It was all about speed, for the ambush on the caravan had happened the day before and we had to catch the fleeing bandits before they disappeared into the desert. Our large force continued at great speed south towards Kom Ombo. The ambush on the caravan had taken place close to Thebes but the bandits were reported to be heading south along the west bank in the direction of Kom Ombo. I had hardly had time to catch my breath and we had already left Thebes well behind us.

"Relax, brother," advised Thutmose. "It will be some time before we catch up with them."

"Do you think we will find them then?" I asked nervously. I had never witnessed a real battle before.

"We will catch them and we will rid Egypt of their pestilence. They robbed and murdered almost everyone on the Nubian caravan. Just two escaped to bring us news of the deed. They must be caught and punished or preferably wiped out."

"We cannot have peaceful traders living in fear of being attacked by outlaws," I agreed.

"Just think, Smenkhkare, they could have attacked the Mitanni caravan carrying Taduheppa."

I nodded. "That would have been terrible."

"While we speak of Taduheppa, brother, I was wondering if she could be the reason you were looking sad this morning."

I had wished to speak to someone of my dilemma and this was my opportunity. "She is the reason," I confirmed.

"Do you want to talk about it?" he asked.

"She only came to my apartment for a couple of hours on our wedding night and we played senet and she has not returned since. She is supposed to be my wife." I may have sounded a little bitter.

"And you wish her to be a wife in every meaning of the word," he mused.

"She is ..." I was lost for words.

"She is very beautiful, I have noticed, Smenkhkare. Have you told her what you desire?"

"I have and she said that I was too young."

"You are young and it is not uncommon for children to marry and for consummation to follow years later."

"I am not a child. Would you take a child into battle?"

"A fair point, Smenkhkare," he said thoughtfully. "You are not a child and you want Taduheppa. However, you must consider that she is most definitely a woman and a very beautiful one. She is probably experienced and has had other men and is not prepared to consider a boy – and you are still a boy. Can you try to see it from her point of view? Perhaps it would be best to give her time."

"Giving it time will not work if she refuses to see me or avoids me, Thutmose."

He laughed. "You are eager little brother. It has only been a few days. Make sure that she is not able to avoid you. She will come round. She has to."

"It is her duty," I reiterated.

"It is probably best not to call it her duty unless you are determined to force the issue now."

"What should I do then?" I asked.

He considered. "You probably have a few options. You could force the issue now and demand your dues as her husband. You could try and coax her with gifts and compliments and give her time to get to know you and come round. You could wait until she considers you an adult."

"She said that would not be until I am 17."

"That is a long time to wait, particularly as you are so smitten," he said smiling.

I reddened but did not deny it. "That is too long, Thutmose."

"Then I advise the second option. Be kind and generous to your wife and give it a little time. That can be fun and I am always here for advice on how to go about it."

"Thank you, Thutmose I will take your advice."

I had hardly noticed that another chariot had drawn up alongside ours. "I have sent some scouts on ahead," Coreb called out. "If we can take them by surprise so much the better and I do not want them getting the opportunity to ride off into the desert where it would be difficult to follow them."

"I am sure they will stick to the river but when they are spotted it might be better to divide our forces," Thutmose yelled back. "If we are able to cut off any possible escape into the desert then it will make our task easier. Of course the desert is a dangerous place and they may not wish to take that risk. They may prefer to stand and fight."

"I hope so," shouted Coreb as he turned his chariot and rode off.

Thutmose turned back to me. "Now, Smenkhkare, we will turn our attention to the matter in hand – the destruction of the bandit horde."

Chapter 3

It was only a few hours later that Coreb once again brought his chariot alongside ours. "Our scouts have spotted the bandits and they do not believe they were seen. They have set up camp a little more than 10,000 cubits ahead of us."

"Excellent, take 100 chariots and outflank them so they cannot escape into the desert. I will take charge of the rest and advance down the river bank towards them. Once they are trapped we will wipe them out." Thutmose gave his orders.

"Agreed," replied Coreb and pulled away again.

"We are very close to having action, Smenkhkare. You will stay at the rear at all times. I want you to be able to watch from a safe position." He called over another chariot which stopped alongside us. He jumped down, as did a soldier from the other chariot. They had a conversation which I could not hear and then Thutmose turned to me. "Menes will ride in your chariot and take the reins. He has his instructions and I will now ride in the other chariot." I watched while my brother took his chariot to the head of our column while Menes steered my chariot to the rear.

"What did my brother say to you?" I asked Menes.

"He said that we were to stay at the rear and not engage the enemy."

"Is that all? You spoke for longer," I observed.

"I am not sure that I should ..."

"Tell me," I demanded.

"He said that in the unlikely event of things going wrong I was to take you back to Thebes at high speed and that you should not be allowed to fall into enemy hands. However, do not worry young master for that will not happen. Victory will be swift and easy."

I smiled, for Thutmose was watching out for me.

The enemy soon came into sight as we quickly bore down on them. They were thrown into a state of panic and retreated hastily towards the desert. The bandits were composed of about 100 riders, half on horseback and the rest on camels. They thought it was a race to reach the desert which came up close to the river bank in parts and where they believed our chariots would be less speedy and less manoeuvrable. Their hopes were dashed when Coreb's chariots appeared blocking their way. They then turned north towards a hillock which was partially covered in drifting sand. It was obvious that they hoped to defend the hillock knowing that it would eliminate the use of chariots. It was a desperate measure for they were totally outnumbered.

They abandoned their horses and camels, gathered up their weapons and scampered up the hillock. They had little cover and so they had gambled that we had few archers. They had made a miscalculation in their desperation. We surrounded them and then Thutmose ordered his archers forward. We had almost 100 archers and Thutmose ordered them to make ready to release their arrows. At his signal the bolts flew skyward like a flock of birds towards their targets on the hillock. I watched as many of the enemy were killed by the flurry of shafts, and their lifeless or wounded bodies rolled down the hillside. We waited but there was no reply. Either they had few arrows or few archers or both.

"Shall we attack now?" asked Coreb.

"Let us give them one more volley and make our task even easier," replied Thutmose. Another volley of arrows was fired at the hillside but it was difficult, amidst the dust, to see how many more bandits had been eliminated. There was still no return fire.

"We shall now attack, for I think there are very few left who can put up a fight," ordered Thutmose.

"Archers shoot over our heads and give us cover for they may have a few archers still alive," added Coreb.

So the assault on the hillock began. Thutmose and Coreb led the attack and our archers provided cover. A few arrows from the defenders killed some of our soldiers as they came close to reaching the hillock top, but it was obvious they had few archers to rely on. It was now only a matter of time before the enemy were overwhelmed and annihilated.

It was exciting to watch and I was happy that we were suffering few casualties. My pride in my brother as I watched him climbing the hillock at the head of his forces was suddenly turned into bone-shaking horror. I saw Thutmose go down and Coreb rush to his side. I tried to jump out of the chariot and rush to his aid, but Menes grabbed my arm and pulled me back.

"He has probably slipped," he said but there was no conviction in his words.

"I must go to him," I said.

He hesitated. "No, stay here until our forces have mopped up the few bandits left." I waited for what seemed an eternity as Menes held firmly on to my arm.

"They are all dead," I cried. At last he released my arm and I jumped down from the chariot and went racing up the sandy hillside. I was horrified as I hurried and stumbled past numerous blood-stained corpses, making my way up the hillock towards my brother. Some were still alive but had been injured by rocks thrown down by the bandits. The excitement, which I had first been feeling at the start of the battle, had now been replaced by panic at the sad fate of some of our soldiers and my concern as to my brother's fate.

I reached him at last and then stopped in my tracks in fear of what I had found. Coreb was kneeling over him and he turned to look up at me. "He was not just my lord, but he was also my friend." A lone tear rolled down his cheek and he wiped it away.

I too fought back the tears as I also knelt before the corpse that just a short time ago had been my full of life and caring brother. "He was not only my brother, but he was also my friend too." I looked at his stricken body with an arrow protruding from his neck and I could not hold back the tears.

Coreb put his hand on my shoulder. "I was with him immediately after he fell. He was probably dead before he hit the ground and could have felt no pain for it was all so quick." Coreb broke the arrow that had brought about my brother's death and I leaned forward and kissed Thutmose on the forehead. "We will put his body on a litter and take him back to Thebes where his body can be prepared for a funeral that befits his rank as the pharaoh's eldest son."

I nodded agreement and stood up. I felt numb and grief-stricken. My family would be devastated, for Thutmose was a favourite with all because of his generous personality and his love for life. I put my head in my hands and wept. Menes, who had appeared behind me, led me back down the hillside to the waiting chariot. Coreb was shouting orders to his men who lifted the body of Thutmose and followed us down the hillock.

The wounded were helped back to the chariots and the litter which was to carry my brother back to Thebes was prepared.

****

We left the battle site in almost silence for the whole army felt the immense loss of a popular leader. It would be a terrible blow for my ageing father and for my dear sister Nebetah who loved her big brother. We travelled in sombre fashion and at a slow and dignified pace. It was already like a funeral procession. Coreb drew up alongside me. "Shall I send some messengers on ahead to the palace to let them know what has happened? It would be such a shock if we arrived without giving them some advance warning of the terrible tragedy."

I nodded. "Yes, that would be appropriate," I agreed, surprised by the fact that he asked my consent.

"I will send them off immediately then." Coreb barked out some orders but I barely heard them such was my despair. I watched as the messengers rode off at a good pace in the direction of Thebes. I shook my head for everything was going to be so difficult. Death came easily in this uncertain world, but the loss of my brother was so hard to take and so unjust. I glanced back at his litter and the tears welled up again. I wiped them away for I knew I had to be strong.

When we entered Thebes it was obvious that news of Thutmose's death was not yet known in the city, but when we entered the grand palace of Malkata it was a very different matter. The bulk of the army had been left on the outskirts of Thebes and just four chariots had entered the Royal Palace, one of which pulled the litter of the dead prince. We entered the gardens in great solemnity and all my family and almost all the palace servants were also waiting for our arrival. Coreb jumped down from his chariot to give a quick report to Amenhotep and then led the king to his son.

I watched as my father broke down and wept and then was joined by my mother and my brother and sisters. I jumped down from my chariot to join them as they surrounded the body of Thutmose. My family was devastated, with perhaps some more devastated than others, but my father was particularly distraught and collapsed. His health had not been quite so good in recent times and the death of his eldest and favourite son and heir was a severe blow to him. He had to be carried into the palace where he went into a deep morose, not wishing to see anyone and for the most part simply staring into space. The rest of us paid our respects and homage to the body of Thutmose before it was taken down the great river where the lengthy process of preparing it for his journey to the afterlife would begin.

A great cloud had descended over Malkata and I felt the loss of my brother deeply for he was also a dear friend and I had been with him when he died. The main source of comfort to me was my sister Nebetah who came to me regularly and we shared our grief together. Even my wife visited me on occasions and attempted to comfort me, but it seemed more out of duty and pity than genuine affection.

It was the day after the body of Thutmose had been taken to the burial grounds that I had another unexpected visitor, the general Coreb. The servants showed him into my apartment and I offered him a seat and a cup of beer. I had not seen him since the fatal day when my brother fell to a bandit arrow.

"It is good to see you, Coreb," I welcomed him. Surprisingly he looked uncomfortable and was searching for words. "What is it?" I asked, believing that his grief was hampering his words.

He clasped his hands and took a deep breath. "I do not know if I should burden you with my thoughts but I had to talk with someone in the royal family. Your father is in poor health and understandably not his usual self. You are the only person I feel that I can trust, even though you are young in years."

"What do you wish to say?" I was now starting to feel concerned.

"We are alone?" he asked.

"Yes we are," I confirmed.

He leaned forward. "I believe that the arrow that killed Thutmose was not fired by the bandits on the hillock."

I could not contain my shock. "What are you saying, Coreb?"

"I was close to him when he died. I saw the trajectory of the arrow and tried to warn him but it was too late. I am sure the arrow came from behind and not from the bandits on the top of the hillock. I would have told you sooner, but the palace was in a state of sorrow and pain and so I waited for as long as I could."

"You mean the arrow was fired from our own ranks?" I asked incredulously.

"I believe it was," he confirmed.

"Was it an accident?" I asked, wishing to disbelieve that my brother was murdered though I realised an accident was unlikely.

"If it was an accident then he would have been hit by one of our arrows. He was killed by an unidentified arrow."

"Then it was probably a bandit arrow," I offered.

He shook his head. "I know what I saw. Somebody within our own ranks wanted us to think that it was a bandit arrow."

"Thutmose was murdered by an Egyptian!" I gasped.

"Yes, one of our own men," he said with conviction.

"Do you know who?" I asked.

"No. I have discreetly asked around but without any luck ,and unfortunately nobody has come forward to volunteer any information."

"We must find out who and why," I said firmly.

"I intend to. I will not let this go until I find out who did it. I am convinced this was no accident. We have a conspiracy here and I mean to get to the bottom of it."

"A conspiracy," I gasped.

He nodded. "If one of my men did fire the arrow then he must have been working for somebody and that is where you come in, I hope."

"Where I come in?" I muttered. "What do you mean, Coreb?"

"I mean I want revenge. Do you want revenge, your majesty?"

I thought about his words and their implications. "I do."

Coreb continued. "If I can find out who fired the arrow I will get the truth from him, of that you can be sure. However, the truth will probably lead to the palace, though the murderer will not have left an easy trail to follow, of that I am certain."

I mulled over his words. "So you believe the killer was working under orders and those orders probably came from the palace."

"It is within the palace that we will find those who have most to gain from the death of Thutmose."

"Are you accusing my family?" I asked with some agitation.

"It would not be the first time that members of the royal family were murdered by their own kin. There are also many who live in Malkata who are not close members of the family. I am asking you to work from this end while I work from my end. I will visit you regularly for updates and nobody will suspect, for we have become friends since the start of your military training."

"I usually stand aloof from palace affairs."

"Then take more of an interest," he suggested. "Who would most gain from the death of Thutmose?"

I shook my head for it was not something that I wished to think about.

"Be impartial and just say who has the most to gain."

I gathered my thoughts. "Well the new heir will now be Akhenamun, Sitamun or me. Akhenamun is going into the priesthood and my father wants him to become chief priest to gain greater control of the priesthood because they have become a law unto themselves. I suppose that could now change, but if Akhenamun did become chief priest then either I or Sitamun would become pharaoh. Of course Sitamun is a woman and I am a fool."

"If your father considers you a fool then he is mistaken. Thutmose knew that and said it often enough."

"Then why do you trust me?" I asked.

"Because you loved Thutmose as I did. I know that. How about Tiye or Ay? Could they take power?"

"My mother would certainly have no such ambition." I sounded a little indignant. "Ay is ambitious but surely he could not hope to seize power for himself."

"Keep your eyes and ears open, Smenkhkare. Discreetly talk to people and find out what they hope for or expect with regard to the next pharaoh. Your father is ill and so it is a subject that will be discussed, particularly by those with ambition. Be careful though, for we are obviously dealing with a ruthless person who may have spies. Do not put yourself in danger. Are you with me in this undertaking?"

His words made me shudder and think of Akhenamun and his henchman, Metos. "I am with you. Whoever ordered my brother's death will pay," I assured him.

"Good, I will ask more questions of my men. If I have to interrogate every man in our army who was there on that fateful day I will. I will find out who drew his bow and fired at Thutmose. Farewell, Smenkhkare, I will see you in a few days."

"Farewell, Coreb."

****

The conversation had stunned me. I remembered that the arrow had protruded from the back of Thutmose's neck but I had simply assumed that he must have turned around to issue orders to those behind him. I felt both great sorrow and great anger but like Coreb I was determined to find the truth behind my brother's death. I did not have much time to dwell on this when there was another knock on the door.

"Come in," I called.

Nebetah entered looking sad. "How are you today, Smenkhkare?" she asked smiling sweetly.

Perhaps it would be wise to start my investigation with her. She knew more than me about the goings on in the corridors of power. "I am well though still distressed," I replied.

"Much the same with me," she volunteered. "We must soon go south to the valley of the dead and visit our poor brother. We must go regularly until the burial. It makes me shudder to think what they are doing to him."

"His body must be preserved so that his soul can go to the afterlife," I said.

"I know that, but removal of his organs is difficult to think about. He was such a handsome man."

"His body must not decay. This way he will remain handsome. He will always be our brother and he will live by the side of Osiris."

She sighed. "But it has all come too soon."

"What do you think will happen now?" I asked.

"What do you mean, Smenkhkare?"

"Who will now be father's heir? Who will be the next pharaoh?"

"I did not think you worried about such things. I have not thought about it."

"I thought you might have heard something, sister. You normally know what is going on in the palace."

"I expect it will be Akhenamun. He is now the eldest son."

"But he is destined for the priesthood," I reminded her.

"He never wanted to be a priest. I expect he will press father to allow him to take Thutmose's place as heir and leader of the army."

"I have never heard him say that he wanted to lead the army either," I mused.

She shrugged. "No doubt he will talk to father about it when he is well enough."

"Have you not heard anything else?" I inquired.

"I have not heard anything else for we are all too busy mourning. You are showing an unusual interest in palace affairs, brother."

"Think about it, Nebetah. We will all be affected by whoever it is that wields the power. Let me know if you hear anything."

"I will," she smiled. "Do you want to play senet to take our minds off things?"

"Of course, I do."

We played four games of senet and I won three and Nebetah one.

****

I had a restless night and another lonely one. Mother announced the next day that the family would be going to the tomb complex to see Thutmose in four days' time. My wife still avoided me most of the time and I took to wandering around the place corridors and gardens listening to snippets of conversation. I heard nothing of interest and the day before we were due to visit the valley of the dead Coreb visited me again.

I ushered Coreb quietly into my apartment and dismissed the servants. "Have you any news?" I asked eagerly.

"Indeed, I have. I set about questioning large numbers of men without any luck until I came to a soldier named Hesu. He was obviously very scared and it was clear to me that he was hiding something. I had to promise him my protection before he would talk. I believe him to be an honest man but a frightened one. He said that he saw an archer called Antosh fire the arrow at Thutmose. When I pressed him he was sure that the act was deliberate. It seems that Antosh has a reputation for violence and Hesu was terrified. Once I had put a watch on Hesu to ensure his safety I went to find Antosh."

"Did you find him?" I asked.

"This all happened yesterday and much to my exasperation he was nowhere to be found. I asked around and nobody had seen him that day. That same night a half-devoured body was washed up on the river bank and despite the attentions of the Nile crocodiles there was enough left to be identified as Antosh. Now I find myself inquiring into the death of Antosh which was clearly not accidental for that would be too much of a coincidence.

"It seems to me that we have a conspiracy and Antosh was murdered to keep him quiet but it is not clear how I will find out who is conducting the conspiracy. Have you anything to report on this, Smenkhkare?"

41

I was staggered that there now seemed irrefutable proof that Thutmose was deliberately killed by a dead archer working for a person unknown. I shook my head. "I have little to tell you except that Akhenamun probably intends to persuade father to release him from the intended career of chief priest and make him his heir. Apparently he was never interested in the priesthood."

"It seems then that Akhenamun has most to gain from the death of Thutmose," he mused.

"That does not make him the murderer," I pointed out.

"We must both keep working at our separate ends," he said. "Stay close to Akhenamun but do not put yourself in jeopardy. The perpetrator of this crime is very dangerous."

I nodded agreement.

"I will return in a few days," he added and headed for the door.

"Coreb, what do you intend to do when you find out who is responsible?" I asked.

"I will avenge Thutmose." He closed the door behind him.

Once again I was left pondering on the words of Coreb. It now seemed clear to me that Coreb intended to kill the person or persons responsible for the murder of Thutmose. If it was Akhenamun then he intended to deprive me of another brother. It was difficult to contemplate but if Akhenamun was responsible then I would back Coreb.

****

The next morning the family set off for the valley of the dead to the south of Malkata. My mother, Tiye, led the way followed by her five offspring. Also in the party was my wife, Taduheppa, who was now considered one of the family and for some reason, Vizier Ay. I could not help thinking that all the chief suspects were assembled. We took two boats down the river with four in each boat. In my boat were Akhenamun, Iset and Nebetah. In the other boat were Ay, Tiye, Sitamun and Taduheppa. It seemed my wife even avoided being in the same boat as me. Akhenamun took charge and guided the boat down the great river towards the valley of the dead.

Iset was the first one to break the silence. "Did you all have a nice day yesterday?" she asked. Her question took me by surprise for it was not the sort of question that you would expect from Iset. Akhenamun scowled and Nebetah stared across the river almost seeming not to have heard the question.

I felt obliged to answer as nobody else did. "Thank you sister, I did." I answered inanely.

She smirked. "Did you all have some pleasant visitors to help pass the time?"

I grimaced. Had she seen Coreb visiting me, and did she wonder why he had come to see me?

Akhenamun simply glared at Iset and Nebetah continued to focus on the far bank of the Nile. I decided, however, to brave out the question for I was sure it was aimed at me. "Coreb came to see me. He wants me to continue the military training that I started with Thutmose. He has also become a good friend and reliable friends are always good to have."

"What a waste of time," observed Akhenamun. "I would not have you in any army under my command."

"The army that you will command will be an army of priests and that is not an army I wish to be in," I goaded.

I thought for one minute that he was going to toss me in the river. "Do not be so sure about that, tiny brother." Little had become tiny. I must have rattled him. He continued: "Look at the Mitanni princess in yonder boat, ravishing and waiting to be ravished and she ended up with you."

Now I was furious. "She could have done worse and ended up with the likes of you, but fortunately for her priests do not marry," I retorted.

"What exactly do you mean by 'the likes of me', Smenkhkare?" His words were cold and iced with anger.

Nebetah intervened. "Brothers it is not comely to argue at this moment. We are going to visit our dead brother."

"You are right sister. The family must stand together at this sad time," Akhenamun conceded.

I nodded agreement but could not help thinking that it suited Akhenamun if the family were of one mind as long as it followed the dictates of his mind.

Iset grinned and continued her questions. "Smenkhkare was visited by the valiant commander, Coreb, so how about you two?" She turned to Nebetah and Akhenamun and I realised that it was not me she had been probing.

Nebetah stopped staring at the approaching bank. "How about you, Iset?" she said. "What have you been up to recently?"

Iset went silent for a moment and I realised that there were things going on in the palace that I did not know about. She recovered her composure. "I do not know what you mean, Nebetah."

I had the distinct feeling that something was being hidden from me. The boat arrived further down the east bank of the Nile at the land of the dead. Akhenamun jumped athletically from the boat and helped out his two sisters though he seemed to be quite rough with Iset which seemed to amuse her. He ignored me and I made my own way out of the boat. A few minutes later the other boat pulled in alongside ours and Akhenamun offered his hand to all the occupants as he helped them out one by one. I then took Taduheppa's arm and made sure that we walked together.

"It is good to see you again, wife. We must meet more often." I was becoming quite sarcastic. Others had heard my words and some found them amusing but Taduheppa did not for she frowned and tried to free her arm. I did not let her go for I was stronger than I looked.

My mother, Tiye, came over and put her arms around both us. "I hope everything is well in the land of the Egyptians and the Mitanni."

Chapter 4

We made our way solemnly through the valley of the dead towards the tomb of my brother. Each of us carried a gift that Thutmose would take with him into the next world. I carried an emerald-studded dagger with which he could protect himself during his journey. Many of the items that Thutmose had used during his life had already been assembled in the tomb and many more still needed to be placed there. More items would have to be made for his use in the next world and by the time this was all finished he would have all that he needed for his final journey.

The tomb was cut from the rock face in the great valley. It had been begun many years ago for my father, Amenhotep, and had numerous chambers for the old pharaoh and members of his royal family. Nobody would have believed that the first chamber to be sealed would contain the body of Thutmose. It was with some trepidation that I entered the tomb containing the chambers intended for my family. I had never been there before, not even during the period of construction. It was gloomy but lit by candlelight and lanterns. A steward led us to the chamber containing the body of Thutmose and at last we stood before the entrance.

Each of us went in alone to pay our own private respects. When it was my turn I could barely hold back the tears. It was spacious and well decorated with scenes of everyday life in Malkata and with the exploits of the Gods. The body of Thutmose was on a table and it was apparent that he was in the process of being prepared for his final journey. On one side of the table was a brightly painted wooden coffin with symbols of rebirth painted on the sides plus figures of the great Gods and Goddesses. On the other side was a wooden boat, put there in case he needed it on his final journey, for the Gods themselves travelled in boats across the heavens.

It would be another 60 days before the funeral rites and the sealing of the chamber and then he would receive the final honours and the chamber would be sealed. The body needed to be dried which would take about 40 days and Anubis would watch over him during this process. There was no doubt that my brother would be judged by Anubis to be just and good and would take his place alongside Osiris in the world of the afterlife. I looked down at my unfortunate brother. The process of organ removal had begun, but he seemed at peace.

I leaned down and kissed him on the forehead as I had done on the battlefield. "Thank you, Thutmose, for watching out for me when I was a boy and for being one of the few people that treated me well. I am a man now and with the help of your great friend, Coreb, I promise I will avenge you. Your soul will once again unite with your body. Your enemy will be defeated. You will have peace for eternity at the side of Osiris in the next world." I kissed him again. I would not return again until the final funeral ceremony.

As I left the chamber I turned for one last look at my brother in his earthly form. Soon, when all his organs except for his heart had been removed, my brother would be a semi-divine being. He would be washed with wines and oils and then wrapped in linen strips. Amulets would be placed within the bandages and last of all his burial mask would be applied. My brother would then be transformed and ready for his great journey. "Farewell, brother, I will share a chariot with you in the next world when I join you." I wiped away a tear and finally left his chamber.

When all my family had paid their respects to my brother we left the chamber and the tomb and made our way back to the great river. Taduheppa made a point of not walking with me but instead she walked with Akhenamun. For once I did not care, for my brother's murderer was on my mind. I had made a solemn promise to Thutmose that I had to fulfil.

My thoughts were interrupted by Nebetah. "Smenkhkare, I have been talking to Nefertiti. She has been telling me about Taduheppa who has become her good friend."

"Really?" I asked, my interest having been sparked. "What has she said?"

"Look at her," suggested Nebetah. "You say that I have beauty, but I am plain beside Taduheppa." I looked at my wife. "What do you see?" asked Nebetah.

"I see a dark beauty with olive skin, full lips, black stunning eyes and a fine nose. I see long flowing dark hair cascading down her shoulders." My words oozed with appreciation.

"Exactly brother, she was adored by all in the court at Washukanni. She was indulged from an early age and she is well used to getting her own way. Nefertiti says that the choice of her adolescent Egyptian husband is the only exception. Her entrance into Malkata showed her flamboyance and her inflated self-esteem. Men fall at her feet and so you, little brother, never stood a chance. You are a head smaller than her and to her just a boy-husband. You need to grow both in size and stature before you can take your rightful place as her husband. That is how she sees it. You need to be patient, brother."

"And even if I am, how can I be sure that I will ever be successful?" I asked.

"Nefertiti tells me that Taduheppa is not only just a beauty but that she is also very intelligent. She can be charming and understanding as well as fiery, distant and aloof. She will come to see your qualities if you are patient and forthcoming."

"She sounds a bit like you, sister?" I joked.

"I wish I had her good looks," she mused.

"You have and you do not have to be so modest with me."

She smiled. "I hope I have helped a little."

"Taduheppa was right, for when she came to Thebes I was a boy but now I am a man and she will come to see that," I mused.

"Why do say that?" asked Nebetah.

"I have to be," I said and offered no further explanation.

****

We went back up river back to Malkata not speaking. It seemed fitting after our visit to the tomb of Thutmose that we travelled back in silence. As we walked through the exotic gardens I took Taduheppa gently by the arm. "I will come to your room this evening."

"Why would you do that?" she asked.

"You are my wife," I offered.

She shook her head. "It is a union of convenience."

"I will come anyway. We need to talk."

She sighed. "Very well, but I will come to you. It is better that way."

I nodded. "Good, there are certain things to be sorted out."

She walked away and began talking to Sitamun. I watched them as they entered the palace along with the rest of my family. I then headed down to the harbour where I bought a silver necklace at the market for

Taduheppa. I was aware that she already had much jewellery but she seemed to like such precious trinkets though my allowance did not stretch to gold. I was going to heed the advice of my poor brother, Thutmose. How I wished he was still with me now.

That evening I waited for hours for Taduheppa to come but she never appeared. My frustration was growing rapidly for I felt that she could at least do me the courtesy of keeping her word. At last, fed up with waiting, I resolved to go to her room. I suppressed my rising anger as I walked down the corridor clutching my gift. I knocked at the door of her room but there was no answer. I knocked again even louder but there was still no answer. "It is Smenkhkare," I called at the unresponsive door. At last it opened a little and I was looking at one of the Mitanni servant girls. I brushed past her and into the chamber where two more of her servant girls were seated. "Where is Taduheppa?" I demanded. They looked at each other but I received no answer. "Where is she?" I asked again.

"She has gone for a walk in the gardens," the one who had opened the door replied.

"At this time in the evening?" I commented.

"Egypt is hotter than the Mitanni lands. She needed to take some cool air."

I walked out of the room and made my way out of the palace into the gardens. I walked around for some time in the darkness but I saw no sign of Taduheppa. I then returned to my room. I did not sleep well that night.

The next morning I took an early morning walk in the gardens to clear my head and there was Taduheppa sitting on a bench close to the lake. I sat down beside her. "Have you been here all night?" I asked.

"I love the gardens," she said not answering my question.

"We have something in common then. The royal barque is almost finished. When it is will you come for a ride on the lake with your husband?"

She looked at me for the first time, since I had joined her, with those dark, intoxicating eyes. "I will," she said.

"And will you really, unlike last night?" I asked. "I came to your room with a gift. I did not bring it with me this morning for I did not expect to see you here."

48

"I know you came, Rana told me. You must understand that our marriage is one of convenience and is no more than that, and for the present it will remain no more than that."

"I could demand otherwise. I am your husband."

"You could but you will not." Her stunning eyes sought my acquiescence.

I could not resist her even in this. "I will not," I confirmed.

"We have been married to each other to bring about peace and unity to our countries in the face of a greater threat."

"If we are to do that then it is important our marriage is not a sham," I countered.

She shrugged. "We are pawns in a greater game and you are still not much more than a boy."

"In the past few weeks I have become a man." I repeated the words that I had spoken to Nebetah. "If we are to unify our nations then we need to show the world our personal union is not a sham. We must meet regularly even if it just to talk. We must not live as strangers."

"As you wish, husband," she said and smiled that captivating smile and stood up. "I will seek you out regularly to talk." With that she walked away leaving me to ponder on her words.

Then my thoughts went back to Thutmose and his untimely death. I needed to make some progress before Coreb returned to the palace. I remembered the words of Iset on the boat. She had goaded Akhenamun and perhaps Nebetah too. She knew something that might be useful or at the very least interesting. I needed to speak with Iset.

****

I knocked at the door to Iset's apartment and waited tensely. The door was opened by her young companion, Zeta, who looked at me in surprise. "It is your brother," she called out.

"Akhenamun," I heard Iset say.

"No, your other brother, Smenkhkare," Zeta called back.

"Then show him in and tell him to wait."

Zeta ushered me in and indicated that I sit on a couch in the large, plush lobby. "She will not be long. She has been taking a bath."

"Get him a beer and one for me too," Iset yelled out.

Zeta placed two beers on the small table alongside the two couches and left the room presumably to tend on her mistress. I sat back and considered what to say. I thought I would confront her first with the question I had asked Nebetah. Iset entered the lobby wearing a long yellow robe, her dark hair dripping wet droplets on to the floor. She sat down on the couch opposite to me. "This is a surprise. Have you ever visited me before, Smenkhkare?"

"Only once that I remember. You bought me a birthday present three years ago and I came to thank you for it."

"I remember. I must have been in a generous mood at the time. What have you come to thank me for this time?"

"I have come to ask you a few questions," I answered.

"This is intriguing, brother. Ask what you wish but I may not answer," she laughed.

"Who will be the next pharaoh?"

"Is my little brother taking an interest in politics? The big question is not who will be the next pharaoh but who will be his chief wife."

"So who will be the next pharaoh?" I repeated my question.

"Why Akhenamun, of course," she replied smiling.

"Why are you so sure, sister?"

"There are only two unlikely alternatives. You, Smenkhkare, but you are too young and lack ambition and you are seen as a fool," she teased.

"And the other," I asked.

"Why Vizier Ay, but he seems content to serve and though he is an ambitious man he does not have quite the necessary royal credentials and probably accepts that. So it will most definitely be Akhenamun. Father is likely to join Thutmose in the valley of the dead quite soon and who could possibly stand in Akhenamun's way? He will discard the priesthood and declare himself pharaoh. It is written in the stars and that is why the more interesting question is who will be his chief wife."

"Is father really that ill?" I was staggered by her words.

"They do not bother to tell you, brother. They all keep it from you. He is not much longer for this life."

I quickly regained my composure for I realised I had little feelings for my father after all the years of neglect that I had suffered at his hands. "Who will be his chief wife?"

She smiled. "Is my brother growing up fast? Is he asking himself if he can seize power?"

I ignored what I took to be her jibes. "Who will be his chief wife?"

"Let us examine the candidates. First there is the most logical candidate, Sitamun, but I think not her. Akhenamun likes beautiful women."

"He would have his harem, no doubt," I suggested.

"True, but Sitamun despises Akhenamun and he despises her. She is stuffed full of morals like a giant moral moth fluttering over the palace looking down with disgust at all the lewd behaviour. Akhenamun, on the other hand, has no morals at all. Even joining the priesthood was a sham for he has no truck with the old gods. He looks only to Aten for guidance. He wants to be the next pharaoh."

"Did he have Thutmose killed?" I asked.

For once I had shaken her. "I never suggested that for one minute. Of course not and be careful with what you say. What has happened to you, Smenkhkare?"

I ignored her question. "If not Sitamun then who would it be? Would it be you, Iset?"

She sighed. "I am neither the eldest sister nor the most beautiful sister. It will not be me."

"You are intelligent."

"When did a man ever value intelligence in a woman? I am not a candidate and you can be sure of that."

"Then who are the candidates, sister?"

"There are three strong candidates and they are all beautiful; sadly far more beautiful than me. I have said enough on this subject, but with your new-found sense of awareness you should not find it difficult to work out who the three are."

"Who are they?" I pressed.

"I am saying no more," she resisted.

I changed the subject slightly. "On the boat returning from Thutmose's tomb, I recall, you asked if we had had pleasant visitors to help pass the time. I rather think that your question was mischievous and I volunteered Coreb, but I do not think your question was aimed at me."

"You are waking up from your slumber, brother. If you became pharaoh would you take me as your chief wife?"

"What about Taduheppa?" I retorted

"What about Taduheppa?" she replied.

"You have already said that is hardly likely to happen," I reminded her.

She grinned. "You do have a powerful friend."

"What pleasant visitors did Akhenamun have?"

"You assume I meant Akhenamun, but then you think Nebetah can do no wrong."

"I saw the expression on Akhenamun's face when you asked the question."

She laughed. "I have said enough. It would not be a good idea for me to annoy Akhenamun any further, after all we have both agreed that he will become the next pharaoh."

"Will you not answer my question?" I felt a little agitated.

"I have said enough and to be fair, brother, you did not answer my question. But think on my words and you may even work things out for yourself. I do not have the natural gifts of the three candidates and so I must return to my handmaidens and let them try to enhance what I do have."

"You are attractive, Iset."

"My little brother now tries flattery. Am I attractive enough to be your chief wife? Show yourself out, Smenkhkare, and be careful." She left my presence and returned to the inner chamber. I did as she suggested and showed myself out.

****

I went back to my apartment and lay down on my bed and pondered on the words of Iset. If Thutmose was murdered, and Coreb was sure of that, then Akhenamun had much more to gain than anyone. He would not enter the priesthood which it seemed he despised and he would gain the reins of power virtually unopposed. He had always seemed ruthless to me and there were unsavoury rumours that circulated the palace occasionally about his night-time antics with Metos in the city. If Akhenamun was behind the murder of my brother Thutmose, how could I prove it?

My mind wandered to another of Iset's deliberations; if Akhenamun assumed power who would be the chief wife who shared this power with him? Who were Iset's three candidates? It was probably of no significance with regard to the murder of my brother, but it was fascinating. The obvious candidate was Nebetah, for pharaohs more often than not married within the immediate royal family to maintain the royal blood line. Iset had ruled out herself and Sitamun, so Nebetah was the only sister left and she was certainly beautiful. I also knew that she seemed at times to be the only person Akhenamun actually liked. So who were the other two? I would think probably Nefertiti for she was the most beautiful member of my family until the arrival of my wife. She was not a sister but she was a half-cousin and therefore did have Egyptian royal blood flowing in her veins. She was also the daughter of Ay which could have the effect of gaining the support of the powerful vizier.

These were two likely candidates but who was the third? The answer did not come to me and so I turned my attention to another of Iset's assertions. She said I had powerful friends. She could only mean Coreb for he was effectively leader of the army. I gasped, for it had never occurred to me that my friendship with Coreb might make me a threat to Akhenamun. She asked me, if I were pharaoh would I take her as chief wife. She told me to be careful. I felt alarmed but it did not stop me from falling asleep.

****

The next morning I decided to visit Taduheppa. She had told me that she would speak to me regularly but there was no sign of that happening. Once again I stood outside the door to my wife's apartment and I was about to knock when I heard voices from within. It took me a few moments longer to realise they were arguing. I put my ear to the door and strained to listen to what was being said and by whom. There were two female voices and one was that of my wife. I listened a bit longer and managed to identify the other voice. It was Nefertiti.

I heard Nefertiti protesting that my wife had betrayed her. I heard Taduheppa claiming that it was not a betrayal. I heard a bang and wondered for a moment whether to barge in. Then I heard their voices again but this time softer so I could not hear what was being said. It seemed the argument was over. I heard footsteps fading into the distance. They had moved away from the door and were crossing the apartment. I dashed into the gardens and took up a position where I could see Taduheppa's balcony. I had been right for that was where they had gone. I slipped behind a bush where I was certain they could not see me spying. I looked up and saw Nefertiti put an arm around Taduheppa. Whatever the argument had been about it seemed it was most definitely finished and they were reconciled. I was relieved because it would have been a shame if a quarrel between Taduheppa and her new-found friend brought lasting enmity.

"Are you spying on your wife now?" I turned abruptly to see Akhenamun grinning at me and alongside him stood Nebetah.

"I was walking in the garden and I happened to see them on the balcony." That was my explanation.

"They are certainly worth spying on." He smiled lasciviously.

"You are talking about Smenkhkare's wife!" Nebetah scolded her older brother.

"And he just happened to walk into a bush," Akhenamun laughed.

We had now been seen by Taduheppa and Nefertiti who waved down to us. We waved back. "I have important matters to deal with and so I cannot stay here gossiping with you two," said Akhenamun and went on his way leaving me with Nebetah.

"Let us sit by the lake," I suggested. "I would like to talk with you."

"That would be a pleasure, brother," she replied.

We sat down by the lake and looked across at the water fowl that had now made it their home. I looked at my sister intently. "Nebetah, we have been together nearly all our lives. We played together as children and we have always got on very well. You and Thutmose were always my greatest friends. Now that Thutmose is dead I trust you more than any living person."

"That is really something you are putting on me." She tried to lighten the mood.

"If I tell you something, sister, will you promise me to tell nobody – absolutely nobody?"

She looked both worried and intrigued. "I promise."

"Thutmose was murdered."

She looked stunned. "You must be mistaken; our brother was loved by all."

"I am not mistaken; he was murdered by an arrow which came from our own ranks."

"It must have been an accident then," she offered.

"The soldier who fired the arrow has since been murdered to keep him quiet."

"He was working for someone else?" she gasped disbelievingly.

I paused, letting my words sink in. "You are exactly right, sister."

"Who would order such a thing?" she asked.

"That I do not know but I have my suspicions, and I know who has most to gain from the death of Thutmose."

Her eyes opened wide. "You mean Akhenamun, don't you?"

I nodded. "He will be the new pharaoh by all accounts."

"You must not say such things, brother. Akhenamun would never murder Thutmose. It is unthinkable and you are totally wrong. You must never say such things again." I was shocked by how adamant she was.

"He was murdered on the orders of somebody," I said.

"Not on the orders of Akhenamun," she retorted.

"Then who?" I asked.

"It could be anybody. Never repeat such accusations again, Smenkhkare. We must all stick together at this sad time." She stamped her tiny foot.

I knew she would be shocked, but I was quite surprised by the vehemence of her response and I quickly realised that I was getting nowhere with this current conversation and so I changed my approach. "I did not mean to startle you Nebetah. I would never wish to do that. Ever since I knew that Thutmose was murdered it has been eating away at me. I am sorry, sister."

She put an arm around my shoulder. "I understand, but I am sure you are mistaken. You must forget this idea that he was murdered. Grief can play some strange tricks on us."

I nodded, seeming to accept her words, and I laughed. "That was a funny incident on the boat the other day."

"What incident do you mean?" she asked.

"You know the incident where Iset asked if we had any pleasant visitors and I offered Coreb and you and Akhenamun did not answer. I wonder what our dear sister meant by that. She was obviously being mischievous."

"I cannot imagine," she said. "I have to go, Smenkhkare, for I have things to do, farewell." She stood up and started to leave.

"Why did you not tell me father was so ill?" I asked.

"I did not wish to worry you for you were so busy grieving for Thutmose."

"Farewell, sister," I replied. I was puzzled by the reaction of my sister to some of my questions, and it was not like her to rush away so abruptly. I put my head in my hands. What was going on in mad Malkata?

Chapter 5

I returned to my apartment and spent the remainder of the day there. I was feeling defeated. So far I had not been successful in my inquiries regarding the death of Thutmose and though I had my suspicions they were just that – suspicions. I could not think what to do next and my conversation with Nebetah had deflated me. I did not wish to upset my sister and greatest friend. Who else could I speak with? My mother and Sitamun would treat such accusations with scorn and contempt. I could hardly confront Akhenamun who would certainly deny involvement, and if he were guilty, as I strongly suspected, I would place myself in danger. It seemed like a lost cause and yet I had made Thutmose a promise and I had to carry it out.

I did not even go for my usual walk in the gardens the next morning such was my depressed state. I decided to wait upon the return of Coreb and see if he had anything worthwhile to report. I could even ask Coreb for his advice on what I could do here in the palace. While I was contemplating my course of action there was a knock at my door. I opened it and was delighted to see my wife standing there like a vision from Aaru. "Greetings, Taduheppa," I said with enthusiasm. I needed a welcome distraction from my difficult deliberations.

"Queen Tiye, your mother, instructed me to come and get you. It seems we have a family meeting." She led the way down the corridor towards my mother's spacious apartment. I hardly had time to think what this may be about. As we passed through her antechamber and entered her large, plush reception room I quickly realised that we were the last two to arrive. Perhaps I was just an afterthought.

I looked around at my brother Akhenamun and my three sisters. Sitamun was engrossed in conversation with my mother. Iset and Nebetah both smiled at me while Akhenamun only scowled. And there in the background was Ay. Why was Ay always there, hovering like a large bat?

"Thank you all for coming." My mother began to speak. "I wanted to bring you all up to date on your father's condition and to talk about what the future may hold for us. Your father is gravely ill and has now lost consciousness. Our doctors who have been attending to him night and day are saying that he will be lucky to last out the week. We must not give up hope but we must also be prepared for the worst."

"Why was I not told, mother, that he was so gravely ill?" I asked, and my siblings all looked at me in surprise that I had spoken out.

"You did not go to see him and you did not ask." It sounded like a rebuke.

"That is because I did not know he was gravely ill," I pointed out.

"Well all of you can go and see him in his final days but I warn you that you must not expect a response. Now we must be prepared for our future when the pharaoh undertakes his final journey." My mother looked around at us all sadly but we all remained silent and so she continued: "I have been having talks with my son, Akhenamun and Vizier Ay. We have arrived at certain conclusions which I will acquaint you all with."

Vizier Ay is always involved, I thought somewhat bitterly, but did not give voice to my thoughts.

My mother continued: "Akhenamun will renounce his dedication to the priesthood and will be announced as successor to his father, Amenhotep. We hope that the great pharaoh survives but if not then Akhenamun will be declared pharaoh immediately to avoid any period of uncertainty. After a short period of a few months Akhenamun will take a chief wife for he must quickly try to make the succession secure by producing an heir."

Akhenamun allowed himself a slight smile and I sighed for it had all been settled without any regard for me. It would be nice to feel part of the family, and it seemed to me the death of Thutmose had almost been forgotten.

"Who will be the new chief wife?" asked Iset.

"That is yet to be decided," replied Tiye.

"I will make all the arrangements that become necessary," added Ay.

"Then that is all for the moment. You may all visit your father whenever you wish, but for those who have not seen him in recent days be prepared for a shock." We were dismissed.

As we left I took Taduheppa by the arm. "I was concerned about you," I said.

"Why would that be?" She seemed surprised.

"I know that since you came to the palace Nefertiti has been your greatest friend. I was concerned that you had argued with her."

She momentarily looked shocked but then gathered her composure. "I can assure you, Smenkhkare, that I have not argued with her. Whatever gave you that idea?"

"I saw you," I hesitated.

"When we were on the balcony and you were in the garden. We were not arguing. Now, husband, I must return to my room."

"I will come tonight. Perhaps we can play senet again," I suggested. "And I still have that gift to give you."

She nodded and hurried off. It seemed I would just have to ask Nefertiti.

Nefertiti was not in her apartment and so I decided to walk in the gardens and see if the royal barque was finished. It was and so I could now invite Taduheppa to that trip on the lake I had hoped for. I smiled as I thought about us paddling across my father's last great venture and did not notice that somebody had sat down next to me. The man moved with such stealth that I had not detected his presence.

"Good morning, young lord," said Akhenamun's henchman, Metos.

My skin crawled for I could not stand the man. He was above average height and of a wiry, athletic figure. He always carried a number of blades dangling from his belt which I had heard him refer to as his 'little beauties'. It was not acceptable to carry such obvious weapons in the royal palace but with Akhenamun's approval this obnoxious man defied etiquette. He was also a feared figure, for apart from his great skill with knives he was abnormally strong. I had once seen him easily disarm a man who was much larger than he was. He also had a reputation for being ruthless when it came to looking after his master's interest. How much of this reputation was deserved I was not sure but he was obviously a man not to cross lightly.

I edged away from him a little. "Good morning, Metos," I replied.

He moved closer and grinned at me like a palace cat eying a mouse, which made me feel even more uncomfortable. "I see you are admiring the royal barque."

"Yes, I was contemplating taking a trip out on the lake," I replied.

"You need to be careful, young master. Boats can easily capsize and the occupants drown. In fact it is so easy for accidents to happen."

My blood ran cold for I could not help but think this dangerous man was threatening me. "I know how to row a boat," I assured him.

"It has come to my notice that you have been asking indelicate questions and even making veiled accusations. In the present climate it is not wise to be doing such things or even to be talking to the wrong people."

He was trying to intimidate me. "It is not wise to be menacing a member of the royal family either," I retorted.

"By the gods, I would never do such a thing. You misunderstand. Your brother is concerned about your safety and wishes to protect you."

I saw Nefertiti walking in the gardens and I needed to get away from this foul man. "Is that Nefertiti I see, I wanted to have a word with her." I stood up. "Thank my brother for his concern." I walked away from this frightening man, feeling shaken and vulnerable.

I quickly joined Nefertiti as she wandered through the flower beds. "I wanted a word with you, if I may," I said. Nefertiti, like my wife, was a great beauty but what always struck me about her were her stunning hazel eyes. The way they seemed to switch from brown to green was quite bewitching. I almost felt that you could lose yourself in her matchless eyes.

"Of course you may, Smenkhkare" She was always polite but at the same time distant. "Are you all right? You look as if you have had a shock."

"I have been talking to Metos and he always unsettles me."

She smiled. "He is rather frightening but do not worry for he is not as bad as he seems. It is just his nature to be scary for he is a sort of bodyguard to your brother."

"I am sure you are right," I smiled back.

"Now what did you wish to speak with me about?" she asked.

"I am concerned about Taduheppa. You have been her greatest friend since she arrived at the palace. The argument you had with her has distressed her. Please tell me what it was about and I will do my best to make things right between you both."

"You are mistaken, Smenkhkare. We have had no argument."

This was very frustrating. "Then why is she distressed?" I asked.

"I was not aware she was. Do not worry. I think it is all in your imagination for these are stressful times for all of us. I was just plucking up courage to visit your sick father. He was always kind to me and I think I should pay my respects. Would you like to accompany me?"

I nodded. It had also been something that I had been meaning to do. I could not help remembering a rumour that my father had once been besotted with Nefertiti though whether it was any more than an old man's fancy I did not know.

We returned to the palace and we were walking along the corridors towards my father's room when Nefertiti stopped. "I am puzzled, Smenkhkare. Why did you think I had argued with Taduheppa?"

"I just had a feeling that something was wrong between you." I avoided the question.

"I was speaking yesterday with your sister Nebetah and she was concerned that you were making assumptions. Was this one of your assumptions?"

"I suppose it was," I agreed.

"What were your other assumptions?" she asked casually.

Now I was the one being questioned. I realised that she had asked me to accompany her to my father's chamber to interrogate me. My family were unbelievable, and it was all so frustrating for I had made no progress with my investigations. Instead I just seemed to be placing myself in danger.

"I am not aware I made any other assumptions." I started walking once again towards my father's chamber and Nefertiti followed close behind me. As we entered the chamber Magente, my father's favourite minor wife from the harem, was coming out. I saw a tear glistening on her cheek and I wondered if she was distressed because she was fond of my father or because her privileged position in the harem was in jeopardy. I found it hard to believe that this beautiful woman had genuine feelings for my aged father.

The great Pharaoh, Amenhotep, was at rest on his copious bed and I called to him as we both slowly approached him. We received no reaction though it was obvious from his laboured breathing he was still living. I kissed him on the forehead while Nefertiti took his hand and squeezed it gently. Was this really the man who not long ago had greeted Taduheppa on her arrival in Thebes? He now looked so much older as he fought for breath and his skin had taken on a yellowish tinge. He was insensible and totally unaware of his surroundings or his visitors. I knew my mother had been right and the end was very near. He would soon be joining his eldest son in the tomb that had been built for him on the other side of the great river. We did not stay long for we received no response to our words or gestures. We left in silence and went our separate ways.

****

In the last few days I had begun to trust no-one. I was even having doubts as to whether I could believe everything that Nebetah and Coreb told me. Yet I never doubted that Thutmose had been murdered and that Akhenamun was implicated. After my chat at the lakeside with Metos I was also a little frightened for I was sure that he had threatened me. I was not making progress with my enquiries at Malkata and so I decided that I could not wait for Coreb to visit me. The next day I would get a boat across the river to the training grounds in the desert south of the valley of the dead and visit him. I needed to tell him my thoughts and fears. I needed him to confide in me his complete plans and not just tell me he wanted revenge. I had to convince myself that everything he had told me was true. My instinct told me it was but I had to be absolutely certain and I needed to question Hesu for myself.

The next morning I got a boatman to take me across the Nile as planned. I left early for I was starting to get the feeling that, of late, I was being watched and I wanted to avoid prying eyes. The waters of the river sparkled in the dawn sun and the crocodiles lazed idly on the far bank. The world seemed at peace but I was in turmoil. The boatman despatched me on the other side and I made my way quickly to the camp where I hoped to find Coreb. I was met by a group of soldiers and one of them ran on ahead to inform Coreb that I was approaching and the others escorted me to my destination. By the time I reached the centre of the camp Coreb was standing outside his headquarters ready to greet me.

He bowed. "Your majesty, you should not have come for I intended to visit you tomorrow in the safety of your chamber."

"Do you think I am in danger?" I asked.

"Perhaps you are and perhaps I am too," he offered. "But come in and have some refreshments for though the day is still young the temperature already rises."

I sipped at my beer. "Coreb, you said you wanted revenge. Please expand on that to me."

"I strongly suspect that Akhenamun had Thutmose murdered. I just need you to confirm that."

"And if I were able to confirm it, which I cannot at the moment though like you I have strong suspicions, then what would you do?" I asked.

"That is a big question and could depend on what you have to tell me. I imagine you did not risk coming to me unless you had some important information for me."

"I just felt we needed to talk," I responded.

"We are actually very honoured," he smiled. "To have two members of the royal family visit our humble camp in two days is an honour indeed."

"Who came yesterday?" I asked.

"Vizier Ay. He said he wanted to view the camp and the military, but there was more to it than that."

"What do you mean?" I inquired.

"He asked me many questions, discretely of course as is his manner. He has a way with words, the chief vizier. What he wanted to know was would I be loyal to Akhenamun if your brother was shortly declared to be the new pharaoh."

"How did you respond?"

"I told him that I am the general in charge of the army and that I would be loyal to the next pharaoh whoever he might be as I am loyal to the present one."

"Did he accept that?"

"Not entirely, for like all good politicians he wants to keep his options open. He went around the camp talking to some of my commanders. I think that by means of bribery and promises he wants to bring some over to his side in case I am not compliant."

"Would you be on his side?" I asked.

"Not if he is working for the man that murdered Thutmose."

"That brings us back to my big question."

He sat back in his chair and studied me. "You are young, but we are allies and friends and we both want revenge. If Akhenamun had Thutmose murdered then I will assassinate him, and with the army behind me I will back you to be the next pharaoh."

I was staggered. "It would not be easy to have Akhenamun assassinated and there is always the powerful chief vizier."

"He would have a choice to either support the new, young pharaoh or go the way of Akhenamun," he mused.

"You are talking treason," I gasped.

"We are talking treason and we are also talking about what is best for Egypt. I have another reason for believing that Akhenamun was behind your brother's murder."

"What is that?"

"I will tell you, Smenkhkare, and then you can tell me any news that you have from the palace. There was a visitor to my camp the day before Thutmose died. I was unaware of it at the time because he did not make himself known to me. In fact he must have avoided me. I have found out from eyewitnesses that he was here but I have not found out what his business was, but that is hardly surprising."

"Who are you referring to?" I inquired.

"Metos, the henchman of Akhenamun," he answered. "To my knowledge that is the only time he has ever set foot in the military camp."

"It is a bit of a coincidence then," I offered.

"It certainly is. He lives at the palace, so I wondered if you would feel confident enough to question him as to why he was here."

"Metos is a man who inspires fear. He has a menacing nature and he has already threatened me. I would rather not make my suspicions known to him."

"He dared to threaten you!" gasped Coreb. "What did he say?"

"It was along the lines that accidents happen to those who ask too many questions. They could end up in the Nile."

"Like Antosh," he grimaced. "It is best you do not confront him then. I would like this man to fall into my hands."

"That would be very difficult," I surmised. "He lives at the palace and is beyond your reach."

"There must be a way. We will both think on it. This man is the key to us making progress. A confession from him implicating his master is what we need."

"I know Metos. A confession would not be easy to come by. I would also like to speak with the man who saw Antosh fire the arrow that killed my brother."

Coreb looked surprised. "I will fetch him."

He left me to drink my beer. A few minutes later he returned with a nervous-looking individual. "I have kept him close by after what happened to Antosh," explained Coreb. "It is for his protection. You understand?"

I nodded. "So you are Hesu and you saw my brother murdered."

He fell to his knees. "Yes, your majesty, I saw it with my own disbelieving eyes."

"Tell me exactly what you saw," I encouraged.

He looked at Coreb. "Tell Smenkhkare what you told me."

He turned back to me. "The ranks of archers were firing arrows high into the air over the heads of our advancing soldiers at the bandits on the top of the hillock. We were providing cover for our troops, your majesty. Antosh was a few paces from me and I saw him take a strange arrow from his quiver. I noticed it because it was not one of our normal issue arrows used by our bowmen. I watched as he lowered his bow and took careful aim. He deliberately fired it at our men climbing the hill. I did not realise, at that moment, exactly who his target was. Antosh had seen me watching him and he warned me in no uncertain terms that I was a dead man if I said anything. I was shaken, for Antosh was not the sort of man you argued with. He had a fearsome reputation among the men and so I said nothing at the time. When we got back to the camp I came to my senses. He would, no doubt, kill me anyway and so I went to Coreb to tell my story and seek protection. When Coreb showed me the arrow that had killed Thutmose I knew for sure what I had already strongly suspected, that Antosh had murdered Thutmose."

"Did you see Antosh speaking with an unfamiliar, tall, wiry-looking man the day before?" I asked.

"I did not for I always kept out of the way of Antosh when possible."

"Who were Antosh's friends?"

"He had no friends except possibly for Re," he replied.

"I questioned Re and he knew nothing," interjected Coreb.

"Thank you Hesu, you are dismissed," I said thoughtfully. He bowed and left.

"This is why I have come to a full stop at this end," said Coreb looking at me quizzically.

"Then you are right and we must both think on it," I said.

"Yes, I believe Metos may have the answers we seek. I will come to the palace in a couple of days when we have had time to ponder on how Metos might fall into my hands," said Coreb.

I stood up. "I will see you in a couple of days then."

"Does your father have long left?" he asked.

"It might only be days or weeks," I replied. "He is very weak."

"Then we have to act quickly. Once Akhenamun is installed as pharaoh he will be untouchable. I will see you in a couple of days, Smenkhkare." He bowed and had me escorted back to the boat.

As I crossed the Nile back to Malkata I tried to think of a way to capture Metos, but this was Metos we were talking about – the man everybody, including myself, feared. However, there was one thing which I was now certain of and that was that I could trust Coreb. The man had been dedicated to the service of my brother and now that loyalty had been transferred to me.

Chapter 6

Night had fallen and I entered my inner chamber and climbed on to my bed deep in thought. I had heard rumours that Metos and Akhenamun made regular trips into the city at night and I needed to know their destination. It would be far easier to apprehend Metos in the city than at the palace. Once I had the information I could then pass it on to Coreb. I was sure that one of my sisters, either Iset or Nebetah, would know more of these clandestine trips than I did. I decided that the next day I would seek out Iset and ask her for she had been more forthcoming the last time I had questioned her.

My inner chamber was quiet and my servants had been dismissed and I must have fallen asleep even though the hour was still early. Perhaps the day at the military camp and the fear relating to what I needed to do had got the better of me. I lay on the top of my bed covers for the night was warm and finally fatigue had overtaken me and I slept soundly.

I had not slept for long when my eyes suddenly opened and I felt strangely nervous. Was there someone in my room? I felt the hairs on the back of my neck prickle and stand up. I ran my hand down the back of my neck flattening the bristling hairs and wiping away the sweat. I reached out for the flints by the side of my bed and lit my oil lamp. I looked around but my room was empty. I could see no one and nothing seemed amiss. Why did I still feel so nervous?

I heard a faint rustling which seemed to come from the far end of the room. I lifted my lamp and held it in the direction of the sound. I saw nothing and it was such a small sound that I wondered if I had imagined it. I shivered though the night was warm. I sat up and then I heard a hiss and I was overwhelmed with terror. I looked down the bed at the frightening creature that had somehow entered my room. The cobra struck and buried its fangs in the bed covers just a thumb's width from my bare left foot. Fear overtook me and I jumped up throwing my pillow at the deadly snake. It had freed its jaws and was lashing at me again but the pillow diverted it from its target.

I was gripped with fear and my head was pounding. I jumped from my bed, inadvertently dragging the bed covers behind me which also deposited the snake on the floor. The cobra now barred the way to the door from my room and safety. The noise of my frantic activity echoed around my bed chamber and the cobra lifted its head and showed me its striped hood and white underbelly. Its body seemed to glow in the light from my oil lamp. I looked into the ferocious eyes of the snake and knew that the vile creature had only one objective and that was to kill me.

I retreated as far as I could until my back stopped against the wall of the room. I had no further to back away. The cobra slithered towards me and I was mesmerised by the thousands of undulating scales on the creature's back. I had no weapon with which to defend myself and I knew that I was its trapped and doomed prey. It lifted its head once again and I was certain it was about to strike. I still had the oil lamp in my hand and I threw it at the snake. My chamber descended into darkness for a few seconds and then my door burst open. Murat, one of my male servants rushed in wielding a sword. The snake turned towards the light and the new intruder but Murat was quick and with a powerful slash the head of the snake departed from its body. Nebetah was only a few paces behind Murat and she threw herself into my arms weeping with relief.

"Did its venom enter you?" she asked.

I was shaking but I managed a reply. "No, sister, I have survived."

She hugged me again. "I had come to visit you for a late game of senet before bedtime. I was shown into your outer chamber and then I heard a noise from your room. I was frightened for I knew something was wrong and I sent Murat in and he took his sword with him in case it was needed, and it is just as well he did." She mumbled the words out quickly and she looked down at the dead but once deadly creature and shivered.

I was getting over my shock and managed to force a smile. "I was having an early night and did not realise that I was about to dance with death and my partner would be the king of snakes."

Murat dragged the dead snake from my room. "How did it get in here?" Nebetah asked.

"That is a good question, sister."

"It must have got into the palace somehow from the gardens and slithered its way into your room," she suggested.

"Nebetah, we both know that is impossible."

"Then how?" she asked.

"It could have been put there."

She was aghast. "Why would anyone do that?"

"To murder me," I proposed.

"Do not be silly, no one could have a reason for harming you."

I gave her a knowing look but took it no further as she seemed horrified by what had happened and what I was suggesting. "Well, I am fine so for the moment no harm has been done."

"We should tell your wife what has happened," she recommended.

"Would she care?"

"Of course she would, Smenkhkare. Let us go and see her together and get out of this room until the mess is cleared."

I agreed, for it would be good to see Taduheppa and perhaps receive a little sympathy from my wife. We made our way grimly down the corridor to my wife's apartment in silence. The enormity of what had happened rendering us both speechless.

Once again Rana, Taduheppa's Mitanni servant, told us that her mistress was not there. This time I did not even bother to ask where she was.

As we walked away Nebetah turned to me. "I am feeling great fatigue and not myself, brother, after what has happened this evening. I must return to my chamber." I could not help noticing that she appeared a little embarrassed. I watched as she hurried down the corridor back to her apartment then I returned to my own chambers in time to see Murat dragging an empty basket from underneath my bed. "It must have been in the basket," he offered.

I nodded. "Thank you Murat."

I could not sleep for I kept seeing the cobra opening its hood and preparing to strike.

****

The next morning I decided to stick to my plan and visit my sister, Iset. Zeta let me into her apartment but this time I did not have to wait long for Iset to appear. She came almost immediately and reclined provocatively on the couch on which I also was seated. "Have you come to tell me that when you are pharaoh I will be your chief wife," she teased as she prodded my leg with her foot.

"No I have not. I will never become pharaoh." Perhaps I did not say the words with the conviction I intended for she smiled.

"I had a hunch you would soon be back," she said.

"Why did you think that?" I asked.

"I suspect I am the only one who even listens to your questions let alone answers some of them."

"As you are so forthcoming I will ask you more questions and I expect answers."

"My little brother has become so dominant. When did that transformation take place?" She was still mocking me.

"The day my brother was murdered," I answered.

"Are you still insisting it was murder?" she sighed.

"Let us for one minute suppose he was murdered. Who would you believe had done it?"

She thought for a minute. "As we are being simply hypothetical I would say Akhenamun."

"Do you think he is capable of having his own brother killed?"

Again she thought carefully before answering. "Our brother has a violent and ambitious streak. It is difficult to know what he is capable of. You really seem to believe he had Thutmose killed."

"Thutmose was murdered and Akhenamun had by far the most to gain."

"This is becoming a dangerous conversation, little brother."

"I know that only too well, sister," I retorted.

"If that is what you believe then what do you intend to do about it?" she asked.

"First I will try to stay alive."

"That seems to be a bit dramatic," she mused.

"It may be that the only way I will stay alive is to avenge Thutmose."

"I do not mean to be rude to you, little brother, but look at you and look at Akhenamun. He will soon be pharaoh and then his power will be total."

"It was you who told me I had a powerful friend, Iset."

"Are you beginning to flex your muscles, Smenkhkare?"

"I will flex my muscles further and ask you the names of Akhenamun's three prospective chief wives."

"Have you not figured them out for yourself?"

70

"Just tell me and cease the games," I suggested.

She pouted. "If I give you the three names will you promise to question me no further on this subject?"

"I promise," I agreed.

"Nebetah, Nefertiti and Taduheppa," she answered.

I felt surprised but not as surprised as I should have done. Perhaps my brain had worked it out but my heart had refused to believe it. "I see." These were the only words I could manage.

"This conversation cannot be repeated. If it were, then an enemy might get the idea that we are partners. They might think that we were plotting together to use the army to snatch power and that I was going to be your chief wife."

"It will not be repeated," I assured her. "One more thing, Iset before I go; is it true that Akhenamun and Metos leave the palace regularly at night to journey into Thebes?"

She smiled. "It is true and I dread to think what they do in the city."

****

I returned to my apartment deep in thought. I opened the door and walked casually in. The cobra should have taught me never to be casual. Standing with his back to me looking out from the open window across the gardens was my brother Akhenamun. "Who let you in?" I gasped.

"One of your servants," he replied without turning round.

"They should not have done. I have had enough unwelcome visitors of late."

"I should not be unwelcome. I am your brother and as pharaoh no doors are closed to me."

"You are not pharaoh yet," I reminded him.

"Father has very little time left," he mused.

"What do you want, brother?" I asked.

"I thought it was time we had a little chat." He turned round to face me with a fierce expression on his face.

"Then go ahead," I suggested, blanching slightly at his show of aggression.

"It has come to my attention that you have been spreading hurtful and vindictive lies about me. This has got to stop."

"Who would have told you such a thing?" I asked.

"That does not matter."

"It does," I corrected him. "Only if I know the identity of the culprit can I help you do something about it. My name is being blackened as well as yours." I amazed myself at how I was standing up to him and how convincing I sounded.

"I have told you it does not matter."

"I believe it does. If I knew who was bringing false accusations against me then I might begin to understand why."

"You have been saying I murdered Thutmose."

"Answer my question Akhenamun or I cannot comment."

He strode across the room towards me and raised his gloved hand but the blow never materialised. "This is not the end of the matter, Smenkhkare," he warned and started to leave.

He had not struck and I was growing braver. "Who will be your chief wife when you become pharaoh?"

He turned again towards me. "That is none of your business."

"I hope you are right," I countered.

"I did not murder Thutmose." He slammed the door behind him.

He had been furious but he had just about controlled his temper. I felt that I was getting stronger and more resilient by the day. The loss by murder of a protector, Thutmose, and my escape from the venom of the snake had shaken me but also strengthened my resolve. But did I believe Akhenamun? I thought about it and I did not.

****

That afternoon I called Murat into my chamber. "Murat, you have been a loyal servant to me for several years. I want to thank you for saving my life. You put your own life at risk when you bore down on the cobra. It could have struck before you did and one of us would not be alive now."

"I did my duty," he replied.

"How do you think the cobra got into my apartment and inner chamber?"

"Someone put it there in that wicker basket," he replied with a degree of certainty.

"My conclusion too," I agreed. "Who could have done this?"

"Only someone who could move about the palace freely and not raise any suspicion," he responded. "Someone who would then have slipped into your rooms unnoticed, carrying their deadly delivery."

"Like Akhenamun did this morning," I said.

"Akhenamun was noticed but he could hardly be challenged. He is the pharaoh's heir and may very soon be pharaoh himself."

"I take your point." I rubbed my chin. "Who do you think might have slipped the snake into my room?"

"I cannot say. I have asked around among the servants but nobody saw anything suspicious, or at least they are not saying if they did."

"Akhenamun has most to gain by my death. I believe he probably had Thutmose murdered and he knows I suspect him. I am the only possible alternative pharaoh and I pose a threat because Coreb the general is my friend and supporter. Then there is my wife." I said no more.

Murat did not look surprised by my words. "Then your life is in continual danger for whoever planted the cobra in your room will probably try again."

"Exactly. I trust you Murat. Will you help me?"

"Of course, your majesty," he replied.

"Metos does the dirty work for Akhenamun. I am aware that together they make regular trips into Thebes at nightfall, or so it is rumoured. If that is so I intend to follow them and see where they go. The city is a dangerous place to go alone at night. I want you to accompany me."

"I could go instead of you," he offered. "There is no need to place your person at risk."

"We will go together, but keep a nightly eye on Metos and let me know when they are leaving the palace and then come immediately to me. I will be ready to leave."

"It is said they go usually just before the hour of midnight when the palace sleeps. Some of the servants have observed them. It is a matter of conjecture among the palace staff as to what they may get up to." A grin almost passed his lips.

"So it is more than just a rumour," I observed.

He nodded but did not ask why I wished to follow them or why I wanted to see where they go. "I will attend to it and if you are ready just before the midnight hour then we will go and I will protect you with my life in the dangerous streets of the city, but we must dress accordingly."

I nodded and smiled. "That is what I was hoping for."

****

I did not have to wait long for that very evening he returned to me. "They are on the move, your majesty." I was ready and dressed in long mediocre robes with a hood to disguise my royalty and I saw he was dressed in a similar fashion.

"Excellent, and I am ready. I have placed a dagger within my robes. Are you armed?" I asked.

"I have a sword about my person. Now we must hurry for we do not want not lose them."

"Indeed," I replied. We rushed out of the palace into the gardens. In the moonlight I caught sight of them exiting the palace gates. They took the road into the city and we stayed close behind, being careful to stay out of sight.

The city of Thebes was situated a short distance to the south of Malkata and had spilled on to both banks of the River Nile as it expanded in size during the reigns of my father and grandfather. We had no idea whether Akhenamun and Metos were bound for the smaller and newer part of Thebes on this side of the river or for old Thebes on the other side. We continued to follow them at a safe distance right into the heart of the city. This part of Thebes was relatively safe compared to its counterpart on the other side of the river and so I was a little dismayed when they headed towards the river and the place where boats plied back and forth. If we were to cross the river it would make it more difficult to follow them and the whole mission would be far more dangerous.

We made our way past the large villas of the wealthy for this part of the city on the western bank of the river was the city of the nobles, priests and merchants. It was an area of wide streets and exotic gardens and an area of relative safety. We kept to the shadows as we followed Akhenamun and Metos down to the pier. We watched from behind some sycamore trees as they boarded a boat for the trip across to the east bank of the river.

"It will be dangerous on the other side of the Nile," warned Murat. "I can go alone and you could wait here for me."

"I need to see the places that my brother intends to visit."

"There are those among the wealthy who cross the river to partake in clandestine pleasures," he added.

"Do you think my brother is doing that?" I asked.

"It does look likely, your majesty."

"Their boat is leaving, we must be quick or we shall lose them," I warned. We hurried down to the pier and hastily hired a boat and urged the boatman to leave quickly. I was amazed at how many boats were still plying back and forth on the river even at this late hour. The boatman, sensing our wish for speed, moved his boat swiftly across the river. We quickly caught up with my brother's boat and moved quite close to them. I pulled my hood over my face so I would not be recognised and Murat did the same.

"Do not worry, we wear old robes and it is dark. They will never recognise us," he reassured me. Akhenamun and Metos were deep in conversation and did not even look in our direction.

Our boat pulled into the pier on the eastern bank as my brother's boat pulled in almost simultaneously further down the pier. We jumped from the boat and once again withdrew into the shadows. We watched as they jumped from their boat and headed for the centre of this part of the city. We had to follow more closely in this labyrinth of alleys and narrow streets so as not to lose them, but we were fortunate that even at this time there were still people on the streets and we were not observed. I was amazed by the number of people and wondered what business they could be conducting at this time at night for the great market was closed and the stalls shut down for the night. This part of Thebes was the city of craft workers, metal workers, artisans and slaves and their homes were hovels compared to the luxurious buildings on the other side of the river.

We were now in the crowded and notorious crime and prostitute-driven area that formed the heart of this part of Thebes. A foul smell of burning from the metal works and from the waste deposited in the streets was now filling our nostrils. This was a densely populated and poverty-stricken district with beggars on every corner pleading for bread or coins and others who looked more likely to try and take what they wanted. Fortunately our cheap robes and hoods made us look like ordinary east bank dwellers and therefore not worth robbing.

"I did not realise such a place exists and I wonder what my brother is doing here," I asked, looking around me cautiously at our grim and dangerous surroundings.

"I think you probably know," he answered.

We continued to follow Akhenamun and Metos until we came to a slightly more prosperous area known as the Magisa district with larger dwellings though still rife with dilapidated houses. They stopped at one of the largest of these which was a building painted with wide black and white stripes that made it look distinctive. They paused for a moment and then they entered through the dark stained door.

"What is this place?" I asked.

"A slightly more upmarket whorehouse, I think," replied Murat.

We waited for a short while and then we ambled up to the door and entered. There was a reception area in which sat two men on chairs chatting and on two couches in the corner three scantily dressed women reclined. I assumed the women must be the wares. Fortunately there was no sign of Akhenamun and Metos.

We approached the two men and rather nervously I spoke. "A short while ago two men entered your establishment and no-one has entered since. Do you know who those men are?"

"Who they might be is not my concern," the larger of the two men replied.

"He is only concerned with what they pay him," the other man interjected smiling.

"We will pay you well," encouraged Murat.

I continued. "Then tell us how regularly they come here," I encouraged.

"People who ask questions make me nervous. I never ask questions of my customers and never answer questions about them. That way I ensure my safety, for some powerful people sample my merchandise."

Murat intervened smiling. "We fully understand that and it was just that we thought we recognised those two as high-ranking officials. We will forget our curiosity and get on with what we came here for. My young friend needs to be educated in the ways of the world and we wondered if you had a girl that would take him in hand. We will pay well for such an education."

"Lana here will be the right one for such a delicate job." He grinned and Lana stood up smiling.

I was not sure where this was going but I decided to play along. I assumed that Murat had decided that if the man was reluctant to talk then the girl might be more willing. Lana took my hand and kissed me on the cheek and turned to Murat. "Leave him with me, sir."

Murat handed the larger man some silver coins and then said gently in my ear. "Be ready to pay her for the information you want for I am certain she will be more willing to talk – and remember the pox."

"My brother does not seem to remember the pox," I whispered back.

"Are you coming?" Lana was beckoning me up a staircase to the upper floor of this large establishment.

I followed her up the stairs and down a corridor to an empty room covering up my face completely. "I am right behind you, Lana."

"No-one will see you or recognise you here," she assured me. "We are most discreet." She urged me into a room and closed the door behind us.

I hurried in and sat down on a rickety chair. I was relieved as she closed the door behind us for I had half been expecting to bump into Akhenamun or Metos in the corridor. "Thank you," I said as she looked at me with curiosity.

"How old are you?" she inquired.

"I am 15," I replied.

"Are you sure, you look small for 15. Is that your older brother downstairs and is he seeking to educate you in the ways of the world?" As she spoke she let the flimsy garment she was wearing drop to the floor and she stood before me naked.

"I have come here to ask you some questions, nothing else," I gasped as I looked at her naked body.

"Do you like what you see, strange young man?"

"I do, but I did not come here for that. How old are you?" I asked, trying to fight my desire and trying to remember to heed the warning from Murat.

"I am 17. Not much older than you in years but in experience I suspect there is a much wider gap."

"I am sure, but now those questions."

She sighed and advanced towards me. "You could have a great time for just two more silver pieces." She stood over me smiling and touched my cheek with her hand and then playfully slapped my face. "Did you like that, strange young man?"

"Please put your clothes back on." I felt in a panic because I wanted to reach out to her naked body so badly.

She laughed. "That is an unusual request."

"Do as I say and answer my questions and you will still have your two silver pieces – and answer the questions well and it will be three," I bribed her.

She shrugged and put on her flimsy robe and then much to my anguish she sat on my lap. "You do like me," she commented and grinned. Then she put her hand inside my robe.

"Please just answer my questions." I was almost begging but I was not sure for what.

"Well ask them then," she suggested and withdrew her hand and wiped it on her robe.

"Please sit on the couch, Lana," I pleaded.

She got off my lap and did as I asked. "Toss me the coins," she demanded.

"You have not answered the questions yet and you do not know what I am going to ask."

"I heard your questions at reception. I know what you are going to ask so toss me the three silver coins if we are to go any further."

I did as she bid. She looked at the coins greedily. "This is a good night's work."

"You have not earned them yet," I reminded her.

"That old robe does not fool me. You are from wealthy Thebes like the men you want to ask me questions about and the men you were afraid might see you in the corridor."

"You are observant. They are indeed from wealthy Thebes."

"I may sell my body but I am not stupid," she retorted.

"Tell me if they are regulars and everything you know of them."

"They are regulars and they pay huge sums of money, but most of the regular girls will not see them. I saw one of them and I have regretted it ever since." She showed me a bruise on her arm. "This is a memento from the occasion. The others have healed. I got out quick before it got worse and we fobbed him off with another girl. Now we do not supply regulars for them but bring in girls specially, girls that are expendable."

I was shocked. "Which one did that to your arm?"

"The handsome one, but I hear the other one is even more violent."

"What did you mean by 'expendable'?" I asked.

"Once or twice the girls have been beaten so badly by the ugly one that we have had to dispose of them afterwards."

"You mean they were dead," I gasped.

"No, not dead. but we have to send them to a place where they can recover."

"You have a dangerous job," I observed.

She shrugged. "Most men are fine but there are always some violent ones. That will always be a problem in my line of work."

I was not sure I wanted to continue this line of questioning. "Are these two men regulars?"

"Yes, they come every week on this same day."

"Do they always come to this establishment?" I asked.

"Yes, because we fulfil their requirements and they pay exceedingly well for our services," she replied.

She had told me what I needed to know. "Thank you, Lana, you have earned your reward."

She smiled. "You are just a boy. Be careful with these men. They are cruel and dangerous."

"I am a boy who is fast becoming a man."

"I could help," she suggested.

"Perhaps another time, Lana," I laughed.

"Do not say that you have asked me questions and that I have answered them," she requested. "Just say you had a fantastic time and do not say you gave me more money."

I nodded and I went to the door and opened it. I looked up and down the corridor but there was no sign of anyone. I walked down the stairs back to the reception area with Lana behind me.

There was now just the large man and one of the girls. "Your friend is waiting for you outside. I trust you had a good time," he said.

"I had a fantastic time." I turned and blew Lana a kiss and she responded in kind.

"We will see you again soon then. Lana is here most evenings."

"Indeed you will." I walked out into the fresh air where Murat was waiting for me.

"Did she answer your questions?" he asked.

"She told me what I needed to know,"

"And that was all?" he inquired.

I laughed. "And that was all, Murat."

I was soon shaken out of my euphoria at a mission successfully accomplished as we made our way through a Theban alley. A robber sprang from the shadows and attempted to snatch my purse. I managed to sway out of the way as he clumsily thrust his blade towards me, missing by a distance, and his other groping hand did not find the purse that he was seeking. I stumbled backwards and Murat drew his sword and chased the drunken thief away. It was a reminder that from now on I must remain alert at all times.

"Are you all right, your majesty?" He was most concerned.

"I am fine. It was just a clumsy attempt at robbery." In truth though I had been shaken and it confirmed that East Thebes could be a dangerous place at night and I did not know when I might have to return.

We found a boatman to take us back across to the west bank. We did not speak much because I could not help thinking of my brother still in that whorehouse and the violent reputation that he and Metos had built up. All my suspicions about Metos had been proved justified. He was a vile man and I relished the prospect of him being Coreb's prisoner. We made our way back to Malkata through the more gentle suburbs of West Thebes. I was very grateful to Murat and it was reassuring to know that there was someone I could trust implicitly.

As we reached the palace gates I turned to my servant. "Thank you for the help you have given me this evening."

"It is almost morning," he smiled.

"Then it is time we both went to bed and rested," I suggested and made my way back to my apartment.

Chapter 7

It was almost dawn when I eventually climbed in to my bed. I was going to bed when most of the world was getting up and I could even hear the start of the dawn chorus. Though tired I still found it difficult to sleep as my brain continued to analyse recent events. My world had changed considerably of late, of that there was no doubt. Gone were the days when as a boy I felt secure and protected. I might not have been much loved but at least in those days, that now seemed so far off, I had felt safe. The cobra and the hapless thief had emphasised my life had taken an ugly turn particularly in the case of the snake, for then my life had been in extreme jeopardy. It was a sobering thought especially as there seemed every prospect that there were still great dangers to face.

I was still determined to avenge Thutmose and that seemed to mean making enemies of Akhenamun and his extremely dangerous assistant, Metos. After the whorehouse I was left in little doubt how vicious and violent these two men could be. I was now taking the warning of Metos very seriously and I knew that I needed to speak to Coreb as soon as possible. I was sure Akhenamun was behind the murder of Thutmose but I would have to prove it and I needed Coreb for that. When that was done I would have to ask myself if I would agree to Coreb making me pharaoh. With this heady thought I fell asleep.

I was awoken by my sister, Nebetah, entering my inner chamber with Murat close behind her. I vaguely wondered if Murat ever slept.

"Greetings brother." Her smiling face was a tonic to my beleaguered mind. "Why are you still in bed? It is almost midday. Are you well?"

I glanced towards Murat. "I could not sleep."

"I looked for you in the gardens because you are always there in the mornings but there was no sign of you."

"Let us walk in the gardens now," I suggested.

"What a good idea," she beamed.

The gardens were beautiful, full of exotic, colourful flowers kept alive by the water that the gardeners channelled in from the River Nile. We walked among these flower beds, making our way slowly towards our father's grand lake. "I am worried about you, Smenkhkare," she said. "You have not been yourself recently."

"The business with the snake shook me badly, and I have been fretting about recent changes in the palace hierarchy," I explained.

"The snake was unfortunate but there is no need to worry about who is pharaoh. It will pass to Akhenamun without incident."

I sighed. "Thutmose is dead and father is close to death and I do not entirely trust Akhenamun."

"That is nonsense. It is terrible about Thutmose and father but Akhenamun has the interests of our family at heart. There will be no problems when he becomes pharaoh."

"I wish I had your optimism, Nebetah. Now tell me what Nefertiti and Taduheppa have been arguing about."

She suddenly looked embarrassed. "I must return to the palace."

I gripped her wrist. "No, sister, please do not dash away this time. I have spoken to Nefertiti and my wife and neither will tell me what is going on. It is disturbing me considerably and I need to know. It is obvious you know so please tell me."

She sighed. "Very well, Smenkhkare, though I think it should not come from me. They are arguing about who will become Akhenamun's chief wife when he becomes pharaoh. I think he made the mistake of making a promise to both of them."

"Taduheppa is my wife." I spoke the words with little feeling and little surprise.

"That is why I did not wish to speak of it with you."

"How could he marry Taduheppa when she is married to me?"

"They both consider you just a boy. It would be easy to annul your marriage on the grounds that it was never consummated."

"The marriage was supposed to bring peace between Egypt and the Mitanni," I said.

"The Mitanni would hardly object if their princess was to marry the pharaoh rather than a younger brother. It would bring greater prestige to them and make the alliance even stronger."

"I see," I said coldly.

"Are you angry?" she asked.

"No, and I am not even surprised. Is this settled?"

"I do not think so because Ay and Nefertiti are not happy about it. I think that when Thutmose was killed Akhenamun had made a promise to Nefertiti."

"I see," I said again.

"Accept the situation, Smenkhkare, whatever the outcome. If you need to you can always find another wife when you are older – a proper wife."

I nodded. "I suppose I can."

"Say nothing," she urged.

I nodded again but did not make any promises.

"Are you sure you are all right, brother?"

Once again I nodded. "Thank you, Nebetah, for telling me. I see Murat at the far side of the gardens. I need a word with him, so will you excuse me sister?"

"Of course," she replied in a concerned fashion.

I walked away from my sister towards Murat. I was really fed up with being the little brother who could be manipulated at will. I joined Murat at the lakeside. "Are you keeping an eye on me?" I asked.

"I am concerned about your safety, your highness. The snake was put in your room to kill you and I trust no-one."

"Not even Nebetah?" I asked. "I noticed how quickly you followed her into my chamber this morning."

"I trust no-one," he repeated. "It is the only wise way forward."

"I want you to go to the army camp on the other side of the river and tell general Coreb that I wish to see him tomorrow. Do not mention the cobra."

"I would prefer to make sure you are safe. Can you not send someone else?"

"Like you, I trust no-one else and so you must go. Do not worry Murat I will be careful and I will stay safe. You will be back by nightfall."

He nodded. "I will make sure he knows the meeting is urgent."

"Good, now I need to go and see my wife for we have things to discuss."

****

This time Taduheppa was in her chambers but then this was daytime and not the middle of the night. I was ushered in by Turet, the Mitanni serving girl. I noticed immediately that Taduheppa was on edge and I also noticed a bruising on the side of her face that she had done her best to cover up. We sat down on couches opposite to one another. "We need to talk." I said.

"Do we?" she replied.

"Did you hear about the cobra?" I did not know if Nebetah had told her.

"What cobra?" she replied looking disinterested. "Is this important because I have much on my mind at the moment and wish to be left in peace?"

"What do you have on your mind?" I asked.

"I do not wish to discuss it," she repulsed my question.

"A cobra appeared in my room and I was lucky to survive."

She looked shocked. "That is terrible. It must surely have got in by accident."

"I know that certain people look on me as being stupid. but I am not that stupid. It was no accident and I nearly died."

I saw a look of anxiety cross her face. Her normal composure was being tested. "I am pleased you survived though I cannot imagine anyone would wish to hurt you."

"Are you?" I asked.

"Surely you do not think I had anything to do with it?" A flash of anger crossed her face.

"I do not know what to think? Do you wish to have our marriage annulled?"

She looked momentarily shocked. "I do not know. I told you when you first came in that I have much on my mind and I need to think."

"I will give you a day to think about what I have said. I will return tomorrow evening. Make sure you are in your chamber and please be more forthcoming." I always seemed to be making concessions to her.

"I will be here," she confirmed.

"Taduheppa, that bruise on your face, that you have tried to hide, how did you get it?"

"I was silly. I walked into the gates at the entrance to the gardens."

"Really" I said. "I will see you tomorrow evening."

I walked down the corridor and waited. I did not have to wait long. The door to her chamber opened and Taduheppa left. I stepped out of sight and then followed her at a distance making sure that I did not get close for I did not want her to see me. I watched her turn a corner and walk surreptitiously down another corridor before entering an apartment off that corridor. It did not surprise me that it was the apartment of Akhenamun. I walked back to my apartment to await the arrival of Murat.

****

Murat arrived back at the palace just after dusk with the information that Coreb would leave the army camp at first light and be at Malkata in the morning. It was now just a question of trying to sleep and being patient until the morning.

Coreb was even earlier than I expected and Murat showed him into my inner chamber. I indicated to Murat that he could leave. Coreb bowed and greeted me informally. "Good morning, Smenkhkare. I came as early as possible for I sensed from Murat's words that my presence was required urgently."

I replied in kind. "Greetings, Coreb, and you are right. You see that wicker basket over there. I have kept it as a souvenir."

He looked at it curiously. "A basket?" he inquired.

"It was left under my bed with a sleeping cobra within. The cobra emerged from the basket while I slept. It struck but missed my foot by this much." I held up my thumb and forefinger to show how close I had come to an agonising death.

He gasped. "You must come with me back to the army camp where you will be safe."

"I belong at the palace," I contradicted him with a bravado that I did not feel.

"The murderer of Thutmose obviously believes that you are also a threat," he argued.

"My place is here," I said firmly.

"How did the perpetrator get the cobra into your room?"

"I have wondered this. Obviously it is someone in the palace who moves about freely."

"Probably a member of your family. Have you questioned the servants to see if they saw anything?"

I nodded. "I have but with no success."

He paced up and down, his anger welling up. "They dare to try to murder you in the palace and they attempt to undermine my authority in the army and all this after assassinating my friend and your brother, the rightful heir to the throne, Thutmose."

"Who do you think they are?" I asked.

"I imagine Akhenamun and whoever is working for him," he offered.

"We have to prove it," I suggested.

"And then what?" he asked.

"Take the evidence to my mother who, while my father is close to death, rules Egypt in his name. If she can be made to believe that Akhenamun murdered Thutmose she will act against him with our help."

He seemed doubtful. "Does she have the power, and will the palace guard follow her or Akhenamun?" he pondered.

"They should follow her for she is the ruler and she could have Akhenamun arrested."

He was not convinced. "It is a course of action, but the army must be our safeguard, and how do we get this proof?"

"The night before last I followed Akhenamun and Metos into the old town of Thebes on the east bank. They went to an upmarket whorehouse in the Magisa district. It was quite distinctive with wide black and white stripes painted on the front of the building. They go there apparently on the same day each week. They have an arrangement whereby the establishment bring in girls that are suitable for the entertainment they require."

Coreb looked perplexed.

"They are violent and they pay well," I explained.

"You took an enormous risk following them to such a place," he rebuked.

"I took my faithful servant, Murat, with me."

"Even so, that part of the city is very dangerous at night. I take it you were both wearing suitable disguises for it is not a good idea to display wealth in such a place."

"We did and we stayed safe. We were not seen by Akhenamun and Metos. I did what I had to do if we are to capture Metos and make him talk." I did not tell him I was attacked by a drunken robber.

Coreb nodded. "You did well, your majesty, but I hate to think of you putting yourself in danger. So in five days time we can expect them to once again visit this whorehouse. My men will be waiting for them."

"What will you do? Akhenamun must come to no harm. He is my brother and we are not yet absolutely sure that he is responsible for the death of Thutmose. He did deny it."

"You asked him?" He was incredulous.

"No, but he heard that I had been asking my sisters questions and he came to see me."

"Did he threaten you?"

"He sort of threatened me," I replied.

"And then the snake ended up in your room," he mused.

I could see his logic. "We still do not know for certain."

"We will not harm Akhenamun. We will somehow part them and take Metos prisoner. I will find a way of doing that you can be sure, Smenkhkare. If Metos put that snake in your room he will pay for it."

"I want to go with you," I said.

"It is better that you do not go. It is dangerous in the city and we do not want you to be seen. Even I will remain in the background for I do not wish to be seen either. I have good men who will carry out the task but it is a precaution we need to take if, in the unlikely event that anything goes wrong, we do not want to be implicated. Akhenamun is the heir to the throne and therefore powerful."

I nodded agreement. "Then when you question Metos I wish to be there."

"As you wish," he replied. "Keep a very low profile over the next five days until we have achieved our objective. Say nothing to anyone about Thutmose or his murder and they will think you have accepted that it was an accident. When I have Metos prisoner I will get word to you and you can visit your friend at the army camp for more training if anyone asks."

"I will be 15 tomorrow and so I can talk to people about my birthday and my crossing into manhood."

"Congratulation, Smenkhkare – but you are already a man," he smiled.

As he opened the door to leave Vizier Ay appeared to be waiting outside. I joined Coreb as he seemed to be confronted by Ay. "The pharaoh was not expecting the pleasure of his esteemed general visiting the royal palace," he said coldly.

"I was visiting my friend, Smenkhkare, informally and not the pharaoh and so there was no need to inform the pharaoh of my visit," retorted Coreb.

"When the general of the army visits Malkata there is always a need to inform the pharaoh in advance," Ay replied.

"The pharaoh has a bad illness," I reminded Ay.

"Then Akhenamun or myself as head of affairs at the palace should be informed."

"My mother is ruler and not Akhenamun or you, Ay."

"I must politely remind you, Smenkhkare, that I am in charge of palace affairs," stated Ay firmly.

Coreb gave me a look that said 'take this no further' and I remembered that I was supposed to be keeping a low profile. The arrogance of the Vizier was, however, difficult to take.

Coreb replied: "I will keep that in mind, Ay, but as I am instructing Smenkhkare in the ways of the military as his brother, Thutmose, had started to do I thought that our meeting, for such a purpose, was of no interest to others."

"I think it is better if you do not visit the palace again without permission. I would not wish to have you arrested." The audacity of the man took my breath away.

"I hear you visited the army camp without my permission," Coreb replied. "Do not do so again without authority or I might have *you* arrested."

They stared at one another for a few moments. "I am the Head Vizier," Ay responded and walked away.

"He has always been insufferable," I commented.

"Until five days time," Coreb said quietly and left.

****

The next day I was 15 years of age and Amenhotep III, pharaoh of Upper and Lower Egypt died in his bed. I did not have to keep a low profile for the coming days because I was completely forgotten as Egypt, Thebes and Malkata were all in mourning. Akhenamun was now just weeks away, and even possibly just days away, from being declared the new pharaoh. I did not visit Taduheppa the next day as accusing her of plotting to leave me for Akhenamun was not keeping a low profile.

We all took our turns to pay our respects to the deceased pharaoh. My mother Tiye now officially ruled Egypt until the new pharaoh was declared. I knew that Akhenamun would waste little time in bringing this about. Two days after his death, my father's body was taken to his tomb

88

at the valley of the dead to be prepared for the journey to the afterlife. Four days after his death we once again assembled in my mother's apartment for a family meeting. I had kept to myself during that time and apart from brief visits by Nebetah and Tiye I had seen no-one.

Tiye looked at us all sadly. "These are very sorrowful times. First I lose my first son and now my husband. You have lost a brother and now a father. Thutmose will soon be ready for his final journey to join Osiris, and my husband, Amenhotep, is just beginning the same process. We have a funeral to attend in seven days' time and another to attend in 70 days' time. It is difficult for all of us, but life in Egypt must go on and life in Malkata must go on. We urgently need a new pharaoh and we have already agreed that Akhenamun should renounce the priesthood and become the new pharaoh that we need. I will hold the reins of power for two short weeks and then in a ceremony at Malkata Akhenamun will be declared our new pharaoh. There will be rejoicing in our great city of Thebes and throughout all of Upper and Lower Egypt."

"I will make the arrangements," said Ay.

"And I will do my best to be a good successor to my father," stated Akhenamun.

This time there were no questions asked and we all filed out of my mother's chamber in silence. I could not help noticing how angry my wife, Taduheppa, looked but I had other things on my mind and for once I was not concerned with her grievances. I continued to avoid contact with members of my family and they probably put it down to my sorrow at recent events. I had lost a much-loved brother and also a father.

****

The day had come when Akhenamun and Metos were due to visit the Magisa district in Thebes and I wondered if, under the circumstances, they would still go. I instructed Murat to keep an eye on them and let me know if they left the palace.

He returned to my chamber close to midnight. "They have left," he informed me.

89

Chapter 8

I waited all morning but I received no word from Coreb. I discreetly inquired if Akhenamun had returned to the palace but found he had not. My patience was wearing thin and so I sent for Murat.

He came into my presence and bowed. He could see the concern on my face. He obviously knew that something was afoot but was not clear what it was. "Is everything all right, your majesty?" he asked.

"I need you to go back to the army camp now and ask Coreb if all is well, and request that he contacts me immediately. He knows I am waiting for word on an important matter."

"I will leave right away," he said for he understood the urgency of my request.

"Good, then go and try to be back as soon as possible."

I walked on to my balcony and waited for a few minutes and then I saw Murat hurrying off towards the palace gate as he set off on his mission. The height of the sun in the clear Egyptian sky signalled that it was midday. If all went well then Murat would be back with news before midnight.

I dwelt on the balcony a little longer and I saw a dishevelled Akhenamun returning to the palace after his furtive night adventures. He was alone and there was no sign of his henchman, Metos. I could not help smiling, for Akhenamun normally looked so grand in his flowing, black tunic and robes; he had obviously had a bad night. I wondered if I would hear from him but as the hours passed I did not. I decided that now was, perhaps, the time to confront Taduheppa. I now felt a growing coldness towards my wife that I had never felt before, but talking to her and confronting her would pass the time until Murat returned.

I knocked at her door and Rana, her Mitanni servant girl, ushered me into her quarters. "My mistress is taking a bath," she informed me.

"I will go through," I said, and barged my way past her as she tried to block my entrance to the inner chamber of my wife's apartment.

I sat down on a chair close to Taduheppa's bath and studied her. She was, of course, beautiful but I could not suppress my hostility towards her. She did not object to my presence but lowered herself under the milky fluid of her bath. I stared intently at her red eyes and realised that she had been crying.

"Why have you been crying?" I asked.

"I am trying to wash away the shame," she replied. Her small, pert breasts appeared above the mixture of milk and warm water. They were small but perfect. I felt the warmth of the coals that had heated her bath and it seemed to heat my loins though perhaps that was more the effect of my wife. Her breasts once again disappeared under the liquid.

"I have done something stupid," she added.

"Where did you get the milk?" I asked.

A slight smile pierced her agonised features. "I had my maid steal it from Nefertiti's donkey stables." She indicated, with a glance, a churn at the other side of the room.

"Is that the stupid thing you have done?" I asked, returning her smile without thinking.

"If only it were," she said sadly.

"Then what else have you done?" I inquired.

"I have twice shared a bed with Akhenamun."

This cold admission bit through me like a knife into the pit of my stomach even though I had half expected it. Now it had been said I felt the pain even more. "You are my wife," I reminded her.

"You are a boy and Akhenamun is a man, and we had no marriage. Our marriage is a sham." Her words were cruel but it was true that in reality we had no marriage.

"Did you really have to seek comfort in my brother's bed?"

"I was a fool and believed his lies," she admitted.

"What lies did he spin you, Taduheppa?"

"He told me that he was about to become pharaoh and that he would make me his chief royal wife. I was a fool and believed him. He had also promised the same to Nefertiti. " Her matter-of-fact tone astonished me.

"How do you know he does not intend to keep his promise to you?" I asked.

"After I had twice been to his bed he told me that Nefertiti would be his chief wife and I should stay with his little brother." Her words were spat out with great bitterness and her breasts appeared again above the liquid in her bath.

"Perhaps he is right and you should stay with his brother," I suggested.

"He has used me. I am a princess of the Mitanni and cannot be treated this way. He has humiliated me and I want revenge."

"You are not in a position to exact revenge," I reminded her. "Akhenamun is about to become pharaoh and to become the all-powerful leader of his nation. If he has chosen Nefertiti as chief wife then you must accept it. Is that why you argued with her?"

She nodded. "He had already made the same promise to her and she thought I was usurping her position. Yesterday he made it clear to me that she is the chosen one."

"Who struck you and bruised your cheek?"

"Akhenamun – I struck him and he hit me back," she answered.

"It seems you are stuck with me," I said.

"Are you willing to forgive my transgressions, Smenkhkare?"

"What you have done has made me very sad, but I can understand your motivation. You are still my wife and who knows you might become my real wife in time."

She smiled and brushed away a tear. "Who knows, Smenkhkare? You are very forgiving. Now I need my towel and so leave me and send in Rana."

"I could fetch your towel," I suggested.

She smiled again. "Fetch it then."

I walked over to her towel which was draped across another chair and picked it up. It was soft to the touch as I was sure Taduheppa's skin would be. I walked over to the bath and held it open for her. She quickly emerged from the mixture of donkey's milk and warm water. I had never seen her naked before. Her beauty and perfection took my breath away. I delayed in wrapping the towel around her for I did not want to hide her nudity from my admiring eyes. "My towel please, Smenkhkare," she reminded me, and I reluctantly wrapped it around her.

"Please be my wife." I was almost begging.

A fleeting triumphant smile crossed her beautiful features. "When you are a man," she responded and her promise was enticing though seemingly distant.

"I am," I pleaded.

"No, you are not. Now leave me, Smenkhkare. We will talk later."

I obeyed her without thinking and walked out of her apartment in a daze. My mind had certainly been taken away from the worry of whether Coreb had been successful. I did feel sad, as I had told Taduheppa, but I also felt anger. Akhenamun seemed to think he could do whatever he liked. I had seen Akhenamun return to the palace alone and I still wondered if I would hear from him but still I did not.

****

The hour was late when Murat returned to Malkata and he immediately came to see me with his news. "I have spoken with Coreb and he told me to inform your majesty that he has his prisoner and that they have already begun to question him. He recommended that you come to the army camp in the morning and that I should accompany you to ensure your safety. He suggested we go early before the palace is awake so we are not seen."

I smiled with satisfaction. Akhenamun had lost his henchman, Metos, and may just be feeling a little vulnerable. "We will go early in the morning, Murat," I agreed.

That night I could not get the image of a naked Taduheppa from my head and my body responded to it.

We took a very early boat across the great river just as the rays of the early morning sun were peeking over the horizon and glistening on the Nile like small droplets of gold. Once again Coreb sent a troop of guards to meet us and escort us to his camp. It was already hot and I wiped the sweat from my brow as we marched towards the encampment. I thought of Thutmose and the happy hours we had spent together here riding chariots. If Metos was part of the plot, as I strongly suspected, could he be persuaded to tell us who was responsible for the death of my dear brother.

Coreb was waiting for me as I entered the military headquarters. "Greetings, your majesty." He bowed his head in front of his troops in acknowledgement of my position in the royal family.

"Greetings, Coreb," I responded. "Where is the prisoner?"

"He is in that hut yonder." He pointed to a dwelling formed of sun dried mud about 20 cubits away. "I think we should talk in private." I followed him into his headquarters. "We started to question him last night but so far he has not been forthcoming."

"That does not surprise me," I replied. "The man is known for his strength. How did you capture him? Did you harm Akhenamun?"

"Akhenamun unwittingly played into our hands. He was still having his violent fun at the brothel and he sent Metos on ahead to secure the boat for the crossing back to the west bank. The hour was very late and he must have wanted to be sure of a quick boat back. We overpowered Metos as he was approaching the pier. If anyone saw it they turned a blind eye but there were a few people about at that time. He was strong as you say but there were many of us and his resistance was quickly overcome. He was blindfolded and brought back to the camp and bound and put in that hut. I am not sure whether he knows where he is or not."

"What of Akhenamun?" I asked.

"When he made his way to the pier he was shocked to find that there was no Metos and no boat waiting for him. I had him watched. He waited for the rest of the night and some of the morning in a state of extreme agitation and then secured a boat to take him back across the river."

"I saw him arrive back at Malkata," I confirmed.

"I have had some men question Metos and they have tried to persuade him to be forthcoming, but to no avail. He is a stubborn man but he must have a weakness and I will find it. The problem is whether to make myself known to him for I dearly wish to question him myself."

"Have you decided on this?" I asked.

"I think I will," he mused.

"Should I?" I asked.

"If I make myself known to him then you know what must happen and so you can also do so if you wish."

I realised the enormity of his words. If Metos learnt the identity of his captors then he had to die. "If he knows he is to die anyway then surely that might ensure his silence."

"Not if death is a release or if I promise him his life for his co-operation. He must realise that with the army behind us we have every chance of success."

I blew into the air. It seemed that if Thutmose was to be avenged then I must become pharaoh. "Give me time to think about this. We are plotting the overthrow not only of my brother but my mother too."

"Either way Tiye will still be the pharaoh's mother," he reminded me. "It is only Akhenamun who will die."

"What if our interrogation of Metos suggests that Akhenamun is not guilty?"

"Then we will not kill him but instead kill whoever was responsible." He spoke the words but they did not ring true.

"And Metos will have died," I said.

"Metos deserves it, we both know that."

I nodded. "He is a vile and vicious man. Give me a short time on my own please, Coreb. I need to think on this."

"Of course, Smenkhkar. Sometimes in this world we have to do things that we do not like. You will find that even more true if you become pharaoh." He patted me on the back and left me to my meditation.

I sat there for some time staring into space. Was this what I wanted? It seemed I would be virtually challenging Akhenamun for the throne of Egypt. He was the older brother and legitimate heir. I would split my family, though I thought most of them would support Akhenamun. I was sure my mother and Sitamun would side with Akhenamun. I was not sure about Nebetah who loved everyone. Perhaps Iset would be the only one to support me because she had designs on being chief wife and that would be the price of her support.

This had initially been about revenge on the killer of Thutmose, but the death of my father had changed everything. I still wanted to keep my promise to Thutmose and send his murderer to the bottom of the Nile and deny him entry into the afterlife, but it was not that simple. I had envisaged dragging Metos to my mother where he would confess his guilt and the guilt of Akhenamun and she would disinherit Akhenamun and charge him with murder and then my job would be done. I had been naive and now I knew that this was not going to happen. Coreb had seen all along that if Akhenamun was guilty he would have to dispose of him and I would then be declared pharaoh with Coreb as my general.

I wondered, if Akhenamun's guilt was proven, whether he really could be discreetly murdered as Thutmose had been. That way my mother would be left in charge and could make whatever regime change she wanted. This course of action was risky and would be challenged by Coreb, of that I was certain. My dilemma was insoluble and so I decided to bide my time. We would see what Metos had to say and I would make my decisions after that. There was still the slim chance that Akhenamun was not responsible for the murder of Thutmose.

I rejoined Coreb. "I am ready to interrogate Metos."

"Are you sure, for he will not break easily?"

I flinched. "I am sure."

"I intend to make myself known to him right now," he said.

"Then so will I," I replied.

We entered the hut and I looked at Metos sitting bound to a chair, bloodied and beaten.

After a few moments he looked up. "I might have guessed that you two reprobates were behind this madness." He grinned defiantly through reddened teeth as blood trickled down his chin from a swollen lip.

Coreb went over to him and kneeled down in front of him and they locked eyes. I watched in fascination. "You came to my camp and recruited Antosh to murder Thutmose and so pave the way for your lord and master, Akhenamun, to cede to the throne of Egypt."

"That is not true as I told your thugs last night," retorted Metos.

"Then why did you make a rare visit to the army camp just before Thutmose was murdered?"

"Akhenamun sent me to get a feel on how much support you had among the men. He was worried that when he became pharaoh he might not be able to rely on your loyalty. He was right," Metos scowled.

Coreb sighed. "It is too much of a coincidence that you were here the day before Thutmose was murdered."

"I understood it was an accident," said Metos.

"The death of Thutmose was no accident," sneered Coreb. "You will have found out from your snooping that the army is totally behind me." He looked at Metos for confirmation.

Metos did not reply.

"In other words the power is with Smenkhkare. The army will make Smenkhkare pharaoh."

"A puppet pharaoh with you pulling the strings," Metos smiled contemptuously.

"A strong pharaoh backed by a strong general. Akhenamun has no chance against the army."

Metos shrugged. "We will see."

"You need not die. You have one chance to live. Admit your guilt and Akhenamun's guilt to Queen Tiye and Smenkhkare will guarantee your safety."

"And will you guarantee it?" asked Metos.

"I will guarantee it too," replied Coreb.

"I do not believe you."

Coreb drew his face closer to the bruised and battered face of Metos. "You are a tough man, Metos. I accept that we cannot break you. I know that only too well. We tried last night but you gave nothing away. You are very loyal to Akhenamun and you even accept death rather than tell us the truth. However, there are many ways to die and one death may scare a man more than another. I wonder what death scares you the most, Metos." He paused and grinned. "I think I know."

Coreb called over one of the guards and whispered something in his ear. The guard left our presence and for the first time I sensed that Metos was frightened. "Is there anything you would like to ask Metos, your majesty?"

I walked to towards Metos and paused. I had seen the fear of this unknown death on his face and I decided to play on it. "A short time ago, Metos, we sat by the lake at Malkata and you threatened me. Do you remember?"

"I did not threaten you."

"Ah, but you did," I corrected him. "You warned me that people fall out of boats and into the Nile. You implied that my fate lay in the jaws of a crocodile. I wonder if that is what Coreb has in mind for you."

I read his fear.

"You could be dangled over the great river and eaten bit by bit by jumping crocodiles." I was surprising myself, but I hated this man with a vengeance. He was a beater of helpless whores.

His eyes widened with fear and even Coreb looked surprised at my words.

I continued. "Of course I could spare you that fate if you do as Coreb has requested."

"I know nothing of the death of Thutmose," he insisted. "I really do not know anything about it. I am telling you the truth." He was starting to sound desperate.

I shook my head. "I am afraid I do not believe you."

Coreb joined me. "Do you not agree, Metos, that Smenkhkare has described an awful death? The idea of being eaten alive by crocodiles certainly seems to frighten you. It is certainly one option if you do not tell us the truth, but I think I have an even more frightening one in store for you."

Metos was deeply worried. His composure under stress had vanished. "I have told you everything I know. To my knowledge Akhenamun did not have Thutmose murdered. I played no part in the death of Thutmose. It is the truth. I have told you the little that I know."

The guard returned with a wicker basket and placed it on the floor several palms away from Metos. The lid hid from our eyes that which was contained inside the basket. "Do you recognise this basket?" asked Coreb.

Metos shook his head. "No, I do not," he said hesitantly.

"They are very cheaply bought in the market at Thebes. Smenkhkare showed me one just like it."

Metos did not reply.

Coreb continued. "I have this theory, Metos. It is that the death one fears the most is the death one wishes to inflict on one's deadliest enemy."

Again Metos did not reply.

"Does the fact that you work for Akhenamun mean that you have easy access to all parts of the royal palace?"

"You know it does," Metos replied.

"Smenkhkare showed me a basket just like that one. It was left under his bed in his inner chamber. I think we have just agreed that you could gain easy access to his inner chamber."

"I have never been in his inner chamber," Metos protested.

"What do you think is in that basket?"

Metos looked terrified at the question. "I do not know."

"I think you do," continued Coreb. "The same thing is in that basket as was in the basket left under Smenkhkare's bed."

Metos looked at the basket in horror.

"Why are you looking so scared, Metos. Do you know what is in there?"

"I do not," he croaked.

"What I intend to do is to remove the lid and then we will wait outside and leave you bound to the chair and the basket and its occupant will keep you company. What do you say to that?"

"I say you are mad," he swallowed. "Take the basket away."

"Let me tell you a story before I go. I was talking to two of my guards the other day and they had been out walking with a third guard. They had been on duty at the valley of the dead and they were returning to the army camp. Suddenly a snake jumped from behind a rock and bit one of them. The poor fellow was unlucky because the snake was the king of snakes, a large cobra. Well, of course, he died but what really struck his two comrades who watched his prolonged death was the awful amount of pain that he suffered. It is said that the most painful of all deaths is meted out by the king cobra."

By now Metos was white with fear. "I know nothing. I did nothing," he pleaded.

"That was the death you intended for Smenkhkare. It is funny how things come back to bite you." He grinned and shook his head at Metos. "Of course if you change your mind then give us a shout and we will try and save you."

"You cannot do this. I work for Akhenamun the new pharaoh."

"Everybody out!" ordered Coreb and I left the hut with the guards. I caught sight of Coreb kicking the lid off the basket as he quickly followed us.

We waited outside and there was silence within. "If the snake kills him then he will not be able to talk," I said to Coreb.

"He is terrified of the creature for it is his weak spot. If this does not make him talk then nothing will. The cobra will probably slumber in the basket for a while before it emerges. If it does it will give him time to think about his impending death. I am confident he will break and tell the truth."

"And if he doesn't?" I asked.

"Then he dies."

I grimaced. "It is a cruel way to die."

"Do not forget, Smenkhkare, that it is the death he intended for you. He causes suffering wherever he goes so do not feel sorry for him."

I nodded. "If he dies we have lost his possible testimony."

"If he dies then we would never have got it anyway. He cannot live for he has seen both of us. Look on it as justice."

"That is what I am doing," I said.

I heard screaming. "The snake is out of the basket!"

"Stop screaming and shout when you are ready to talk," yelled Coreb.

The screaming stopped and all went silent again. I looked at Coreb and he shrugged. The minutes passed by and then we heard from Metos again. "I am ready to talk!" he screamed.

Coreb nodded to his guards and they withdrew their swords and quickly entered the hut. It was too late, the fangs had done their deadly work and the venom was in his blood. A swift cut from a sharp blade dispatched the snake, but Metos was already incoherent.

"The fool called out too late," sighed Coreb. He put his ear to the mouth of Metos but it was a waste of time for the man was already in his death throes. "He is lucky for death is coming to him quicker than is usual after a bite from a cobra."

"So not as bad a death as you described," I commented.

"The cobra is deadly but I exaggerated. Now we must decide what to do next."

"Coreb, what has occurred here has shaken me badly. I need to get back to the palace and have time to consider."

"Your brother will soon be pharaoh. He might have lost Metos but that is hardly going to stop him. He is almost certainly responsible for the death of Thutmose and probably responsible for the snake under your bed. Did you see how Metos reacted to the basket? We cannot dally on this. We have had some years of peace and made allies of the Mitanni and Nubians, but the Hittites are pressing gradually south and there will come a time soon when they must be stopped and I will have to leave Egypt. If you want to bid for power then my army is behind you but we must act now. If you want to avenge the death of your brother then Akhenamun must be stopped and he must pay for his foul deed."

"I know, but Akhenamun is not pharaoh yet and will not be for two weeks. I will consider my options and return to you in a few days with a decision. You must realise that I will be going against my entire family and that does not rest easy upon me."

He nodded understanding. "In a few days then, Smenkhkare. Farewell your majesty," he said.

Murat came over to join me and we walked towards the great river in silence. Murat must have been curious but he asked no questions about what had occurred at the army camp. I was grateful for his silence for my mind was in turmoil.

Chapter 9

By the time we returned to Malkata it was early evening and Nebetah was waiting for me in my dressing room. "Brother, there you are at last, where have you been?"

"I have been taking part in exercises at the army camp," I informed her.

"Mother has been trying to hold another family meeting but both you and Akhenamun had disappeared."

"Where is Akhenamun?" I asked.

"He was last seen leaving Malkata with some of the palace guard. I suppose they have gone to search for Metos in the city."

"Why would they be searching for Metos?" I tried to look puzzled.

"He has disappeared too," she replied shaking her head. "It is all very strange."

"So Akhenamun has mislaid his henchman on one of their midnight forays," I retorted.

"Smenkhkare, you must stop attacking Akhenamun in this way," she advised.

"Why, sister?" I asked.

"He is wild but he is a good man and he will look after all the family when he is pharaoh."

"That is your opinion, Nebetah," I responded.

"Mother is with Sitamun, we must go and collect Iset and join them."

I nodded. "Then let us go."

We knocked at the door of her chambers and Iset emerged from the apartment grinning. "I see, sister, that you have managed to find one of the men."

Nebetah smiled back. "I thought we should see if mother wants to go ahead with the meeting now, as Smenkhkare has returned."

Iset looked at me. "What have you been up to, little brother? The palace has become so much more fun since you grew up."

"Just some army training," I replied and Nebetah gave her grinning sister a dirty look.

The three of us trooped into our mother's apartment and entered her private audience chamber where Tiye, Sitamun and Ay were waiting for us. "Smenkhkare has returned, mother, but there is still no sign of Akhenamun," Nebetah informed her mother.

Tiye sighed. "We will go ahead without him and I will speak with him later privately. I wished to speak about our visit to the valley of the dead when we pay our respects to your father and celebrate the final journey of Thutmose to the afterlife and the sealing of his chamber in the tomb. First I want to reprimand Smenkhkare for his recent behaviour and as it is about Akhenamun it is probably better that he is not here." All my sisters looked at me and I groaned inwardly.

My mother continued: "Smenkhkare, you have been under a great strain recently and I understand that. I know how much you loved your brother, Thutmose, as we all did but you must pull yourself together and stop making wild accusations. Akhenamun has been deeply offended by what you have been saying to your sisters in and about the palace and it has to stop."

Sitamun then began to speak: "Brother, Smenkhkare, I know you are hurting. I have in the past shared, at times, your dislike for Akhenamun. His morals in the past have been in question but when he becomes pharaoh he has promised to mend his ways and serve his country. We must give him the opportunity to do so for he is now the legitimate heir."

I was amazed at this sustained attack from my mother and eldest sister. "You are right that I am hurting. My brother has been murdered and there has been an attempt on my life."

There was a collective gasp from my sisters and mother. "There has been no murder and perhaps this attempt on your life is another of your fantasies," my mother rebuked me.

I had had enough. "There are witnesses to the attempt on my life. However, mother, I will only discuss these matters in front of my family."

"We are all family here," she replied.

"Only in front of my immediate family, "I said and looked at Ay. Everyone looked shocked except for Iset who was grinning.

"Ay is chief vizier and a member of the royal family," my mother reminded me.

"Either he goes or I go," I retorted.

Ay puffed out his cheeks as if he were about to protest but then he thought better of it. "I will leave you to discipline your foolish boy." He glared at me as he left the audience room and I glared back. I did not know where my bravery was coming from.

"What has got into you?" my mother reprimanded me again. "What witnesses are you talking about?"

"You may question Murat and my servants if you wish, mother, but there is a witness standing next to me. A cobra was strategically placed in my inner chamber. I was meant to suffer a horrible death from the grotesque fangs of the king of snakes; first Thutmose and then me. Nebetah was there and helped to save my life."

They all looked at Nebetah. "Tell us exactly what happened and what you saw, daughter."

Nebetah took a deep breath. "It was evening and I wanted to play a game of senet before I went to bed. I always play senet with Smenkhkare. I went to his apartment and was directed to the outer chamber by his servant, Murat. Smenkhkare was in the bedchamber presumably asleep even though the hour was early. I was pondering on whether to disturb him or not when I heard a commotion from within his chamber. I was worried and I got Murat to go and investigate. I followed Murat into the chamber. Inside a cobra was raising itself up and ready to strike Smenkhkare who had his back to the wall. Murat, who fortunately had his sword, struck off the head of the snake before it could strike. Thankfully Smenkhkare was saved but I fully believe that the snake must have found its way into his apartment from the garden. Nobody could possibly have wanted to hurt Smenkhkare."

I sighed. "It emerged from a basket which had been placed under my bed. Am I to believe that it came in from the garden, climbed the staircase and made its way along the corridor unseen? It then opened my door and made its way into my outer chamber and then opened another door and made its way into my inner chamber. Then it climbed into a wicker basket that had not previously been there or perhaps it brought the basket with it."

They all stared at me in disbelief. I did not know whether it was my story or my audacity that had dumbfounded them all. Iset shattered the silence with laughter. "It was a very talented snake to have achieved all that."

Nebetah looked crestfallen and Tiye and Sitamun were rendered speechless.

At last my mother spoke. "I need to absorb what has been said. We will not talk about the funeral now for we can do that later with Akhenamun. It is obvious that someone tried to kill you Smenkhkare, but it does not mean that Thutmose was murdered. It was probably a servant with a grudge. We need to find out who that might have been but I now understand fully why you have not been yourself of late. I withdraw my criticism of you for you have had a terrible time recently and a very bad experience and to come so near to an awful death at such a young age excuses your behaviour."

Now I was rendered speechless. They still did not get it.

"You are all dismissed," my mother added.

The three of us filed out of my mother's apartment leaving my mother with Sitamun. Nebetah looked close to tears and wandered away. I started to go after her but Iset took my arm. "Let her go for she must learn what you have learnt."

"Which is?" I asked.

"That there is a big bad, dangerous world outside the cosy confines of our family."

"And within," I said.

"And within," she conceded. "And you, my little brother, have certainly shaken it up today. I will take my leave of you, too, and digest what you have said."

I started back towards my own apartment when I passed Ramose, Ay's assistant. "I was seeking you out," he said blocking my way down the corridor.

"I am suddenly popular," I replied.

"I do not know what this is about but Ay has instructed me to pass a warning on to you. Stop stirring things up and for your own safety you should go back to the anonymity you enjoyed before."

"And if I do not?" I asked.

"I do not know, but I will give you some advice of my own. A man or boy who crosses Ay is asking for trouble."

"Thank you, Ramose; I will keep your advice in mind."

Murat was waiting for me when I returned to my apartment. "I hope all is well," he offered.

"Try and keep me protected at all times," I replied.

"I will," he promised and I retired to my inner chamber.

The next morning I received another shock. I had a visitor and that visitor was my wife Taduheppa. "I was about to go for my morning walk in the gardens," I informed her.

"Then if I may, I will go with you." She smiled that stunning smile that always captivated me.

"Of course you may. How about we take a boat out on the lake," I suggested.

"Wait here and I shall go and tell Turet to gather up some refreshing fruit for us to take with us. It will be hot out on the lake where there is no shade."

Off she went and I was left feeling more than a little bemused. It was the first time she had ever taken the initiative in suggesting we do something together. A few minutes later she returned clutching a basket of fruit. The watermelon looked particularly appealing. We made our way slowly down to the lakeside and I noticed that a few guards were keeping me under surveillance. It did not worry me for I recognised them as being comrades to Murat and I presumed he was keeping his promise that I would be protected at all times. The royal barque, though now completed, was too large for the two us and so I took a rowing boat out on the lake. I rowed and Taduheppa sat opposite me, her delicate hands holding on to the side of the boat as she looked down into the cool waters of the lake. She was relaxed in my presence in a way that I had never seen before. I continued to feel bemused.

She opened the conversation after a period of silent reflection in the morning sunshine. "I heard about the meeting and that the cobra was placed in your room in a basket proving it to be an attempt on your life."

"It *was* an attempt on my life." I searched her beautiful face.

"Surely you do not think I had anything to do with it?" She was annoyed but was curbing her anger.

"I never said that. In truth I do not know what to think." I was not yet ready to divulge to her my suspicions about Akhenamun for she had recently been enjoying intimacies with him.

"If they tried once then they may try again," she warned. "You will have to be careful, Smenkhkare."

"I believe the same person who was responsible for the murder of Thutmose tried to have me murdered."

"You are no doubt right," she conceded. She did not try to suggest that the death of Thutmose had been accidental.

"How do you know about the cobra being planted in a basket?" I asked. "When it first happened I went to your apartment to tell you but you were not there. You were otherwise engaged."

She looked guilty. "Last night I went to see Nebetah for some female company because I no longer enjoy the friendship of Nefertiti. It was obvious that something was wrong with your sister. You had had another family meeting to which I was not invited this time. It was clear that the meeting had upset her but she was distressed and would not disclose all the details except that a cobra was placed in your room in a basket."

"My poor sister," I sighed.

"I did not press her but instead went to see Iset and I think she told me all that was said. She was amazed at the way you had stood up to your mother and that insufferable man, Ay. I was impressed when she told me about it."

"So who do you think murdered Thutmose and tried to murder me?" I asked.

"I firmly believe it was Akhenamun. He is the only one I can think of who would gain from the death of Thutmose, but why he should wish to murder you I do not know."

"You shared his bed just days ago and now you accuse him of murder," I sneered. "I believe I was making things uncomfortable for him and I was starting to pose a threat."

"How could you pose a threat?" She ignored my condemnation.

I avoided her question for I did not want to give too much away. I had realised that with the death of Metos I was involved in dangerous plotting. "Where do you stand in all this?" I asked.

"I stand with you," she responded.

"That is convenient now that Akhenamun has rejected you."

"Yes, I hate him." She was getting more animated. "I know I have been foolish but I am a Mitanni princess and he has humiliated me. Not even the next pharaoh of Egypt can treat me this way. He promised that I would be his chief wife but it was just a ruse to get me into his bed. He always intended that his chief wife would be Nefertiti. Having got what he wanted he told me to go back to the ugly youth who was my husband and he laughed in my face. That was when I struck him and that was when he hit me back, knocking me to the floor. I want him on that same floor at my feet begging for his life." She sat back in the boat and stared at me and I stopped rowing and let it drift into the middle of the lake. "That is what I want, Smenkhkare." There was hostility in her dark eyes but it was not aimed at me.

"Do you also see me as an ugly youth?" I asked.

"You are a boy, but you are growing fast and you are not so ugly," she smiled.

"Am I your husband?" I asked.

"Not completely but you will be when you are a man. Let us now relax and enjoy the beauty of your father's lake."

The promise was enticing. I smiled and closed my eyes and dipped my hands in the water.

"Is it safe to do that?" she asked.

I opened my eyes. "There are no crocodiles in the lake. The gardeners make sure that none wander this way."

"I hope they do a good job," she mused. "I will dangle my feet in the water." She kicked off her sandals and pulled up her dress and lifted her legs over the side of the boat.

"Be careful or you will capsize the boat," I warned.

"I do not want to do that for I cannot swim but you would rescue me, wouldn't you?" she laughed.

"I might," I grinned, and I watched as she splashed her feet in the lake. I carefully moved across the boat to distribute our weight more evenly and make the small boat steadier. I looked at her bare legs and remembered her nudity when she had emerged from her bath. I loved her and wanted her so badly. If only she regarded me as a man.

She looked at me as she pulled her legs back into the boat and I knew that she knew how much I desired her. She pulled me from my reverie with a question. "Where were you yesterday, Smenkhkare? I came to see you but you were not in Malkata."

"I was at the army camp across the river, Taduheppa."

"Why were you there?"

"Just some training," I answered.

"Who did you see?"

"Coreb, the general," I replied.

"I have never spoken with this Coreb but I have seen him at the palace. Does he command the entire army?"

"He does. He is our general but he was also a good friend of Thutmose."

"Who is he loyal to, Smenkhkare?"

"To Egypt," I replied.

"Is he your friend too?"

"He is my friend too," I replied. "Where is this leading, Taduheppa?"

"I am just curious. Would he be loyal to Akhenamun if he were pharaoh?"

"Not if Akhenamun murdered his friend."

"As the general of the army he must wield much power."

"That is true." I was intrigued.

"You must tell him that you believe Akhenamun had Thutmose murdered."

"I do believe Akhenamun had Thutmose murdered."

"Even better, Smenkhkare, but if only we could prove it to him."

"And then what?" I asked.

She took my hand. "And then with Coreb and the army at your disposal you could become pharaoh. The army could cross the Nile and take Malkata."

"But what of Akhenamun and the palace guard?" I asked.

"The palace guard could not oppose the army and Akhenamun would be at my feet begging for his life."

I offered her back her sandals. "The great pharaoh, my powerful brother, prostrate at the dainty feet of the Mitanni princess," I said and smiled at the vision.

"He is not yet pharaoh and he is certainly not great," she smiled back. "Think about it, Smenkhkare – the throne and Egypt would be yours."

"And what of you, Taduheppa?" I inquired.

"When you become pharaoh, you become a man and I become a true wife, your chief wife. Akhenamun would pay for his crimes and I would have Nefertiti as a servant girl."

"You are talking treason," I pointed out.

"You have not contradicted me," she said.

"Do you not think that I have not thought of these things myself?"

She ran her still bare foot up my calf. I felt the pangs of almost uncontrollable desire and reached out for her leg. She withdrew her pretty limb. "You are not yet pharaoh," she pointed out.

"I am your husband."

"Not yet but soon; go and see Coreb again," she urged. "Put these proposals to him. Convince him that Akhenamun murdered Thutmose. Do not wait too long. Try to be a man and meanwhile I will think how we can best place the blame on Akhenamun for the death of Thutmose."

"He almost certainly did kill Thutmose," I pointed out.

"Whether he did or not, it is essential Coreb believes he did."

"See what you can come up with," I said. "It is the funeral in a few days but I will go and see Coreb at the military camp before then."

I could see the excitement in her stunning black eyes and it was contagious. "Let us go back to the palace and start our plans. You must get a message to Coreb that you will go tomorrow."

"And we must not speak of these matters with anyone," I said.

"Of course not," she replied.

I rowed the boat back to the lakeshore and we returned hastily towards the palace.

A figure stepped from behind a bush and blocked our passage. "Are the little husband and the pretty wife getting on at last?" he asked.

"What do you want, Akhenamun?" I replied.

"My most valued servant, Metos, has vanished. I wondered if you had seen him or have any idea where he might have vanished to." He was obviously in a dark mood and so I decided not to antagonise him further.

However, that did not stop my wife. "It is very careless to mislay your servants, Akhenamun," she mocked.

He turned to me. "Tell your wife to watch her tongue, brother, or I might have it cut out."

"My father would not take kindly to that," she retorted.

"I do not care in the least about your father. He is king of a petty state while I am the lord of Egypt."

"The Mitanni kingdom is not a petty state," I pointed out. "I cannot help you with regard to Metos. I am sorry you have lost him for I know he was a loyal servant to you."

He calmed down a little at my soothing words and shook his head. "It is most strange," he muttered and walked away.

"It is strange that Metos should have vanished," said Taduheppa.

"It is strange indeed," I replied, and we walked back to the palace.

****

On return to my apartment Murat was waiting for me. "I felt I was being watched," I said.

"Those men in the gardens are working for me. They have strict instructions to keep you safe," he assured me.

"Good, I hope they continue to do so. I want you to go to the army camp again and tell Coreb that if it is convenient I will come myself early tomorrow morning, and on your way stop at my wife's apartment and tell Rana to inform her mistress that I leave tomorrow morning."

He looked at me quizzically.

"It is safe to say that, but say no more than that. I will make an early start in the morning as I did last time and I want you to accompany me again."

"Of course, your majesty. I will return at nightfall," he said and promptly left my presence.

Once again I had a period of waiting for my tortured mind to deal with.

Murat was later than I expected and I had retired to my inner chamber. He entered and bowed. "I am sorry, your majesty, but I was delayed on the way back. The boat I was on sank because the boatmen had packed too many people into it. It was all very chaotic at the riverside."

"These things happen. Why do you always call me 'your majesty'?" I asked.

"That is what you are," he replied.

"It has become common to call members of my family 'your majesty' but it is not strictly correct. It is a title that should be reserved for the pharaoh. You have saved my life and you should simply call me Smenkhkare."

"Then I will, but perhaps one day soon I might revert back to 'your majesty', Smenkhkare."

I smiled. "You know what is going on, Murat."

"Even servants have eyes and ears," he observed.

"Now what did the general have to say?" I asked.

"I told him that you would come in the morning if it were convenient. He said it was very convenient and advised that we leave at an early hour."

110

"To avoid prying eyes. My general is as diligent as ever. We shall leave early in the morning, Murat, and now you are dismissed."

"In the morning, Smenkhkare," he said and left, and soon Taduheppa was once again in my dreams.

****

It was early when we left the palace and entered the glorious gardens that were part of the splendour of Malkata. I smiled at the thought that what Taduheppa had urged from me had already been suggested by Coreb, the man she would have me persuade. "It is a fine morning," I said to Murat with feeling for I felt surprisingly optimistic about the day ahead.

"Smenkhkare, wait." It was the unexpected voice of my wife. She came over and took my arm and drew me away from the hearing of Murat.

"You are up early, Taduheppa," I said smiling at this unexpected pleasure.

"I spoke with Nefertiti yesterday," she grinned. "As we shared a drink she entrusted me with a great confidence."

"What was that?" I asked.

"She told me that Akhenamun had murdered Thutmose."

"Did she?" I gasped.

"No, of course not, but that is what you will tell Coreb. Tell him that your wife and Nefertiti are great friends and that she confided in your wife."

"You are very cunning," I said with both a degree of admiration and surprise.

"I do my best but it is up to you to sound convincing, Smenkhkare."

"I will do my best too, Taduheppa."

"Remember, Smenkhkare, that total power is within your grasp. Seize it with both hands. If the army is yours then Egypt is yours."

"I will remember. Tell me, Taduheppa, when Akhenamun begs you for mercy will you grant it?"

"No, I will not. Besides it would jeopardise our future if he were to remain alive."

Her words were frightening but part of me knew she was right and that Coreb would agree with her. Sometimes my resolve was strong and at other times it faltered. I rejoined Murat and we walked towards the

111

palace gates. I looked back and saw Taduheppa waving. My wife was determined that I should become pharaoh and that she should become chief wife.

Chapter 10

We covered our faces with our hoods and made our way down to the pier and Murat hired a boat for our journey across the great river. We thought it better that we travel anonymously, just the two of us, and so he took the helm and steered the boat towards the east bank. We were alone under the emerging rays of the dawn sun. "Do you know of the decision that I have to make, a decision that haunts me?" I asked.

"I think I do," he replied.

"What do you think it is, Murat?"

"I think you must decide whether you will use the army to displace your brother as pharaoh, Smenkhkare."

"It may be the only way I will be able to stay alive," I mused.

"And the only way I will get to call you 'your majesty' again," he smiled sympathetically.

"What do you think I should do, Murat?"

"I think you should make sure that you stay alive."

"And depose my brother who is the legitimate heir?"

"If I may speak freely, you will make a much better pharaoh than your brother. A man who brutalises his own servants is not a man who will rule for the good of the people of Egypt."

"Does he really do that?" I asked.

"He does and worse. The servants all fear him. You know from our visit to the Magisa district how violent he can be."

"Tiye and Sitamun say that he will change when he becomes pharaoh."

He shook his head. "That is unlikely. It is rare for a man's character to undergo such a change. He is who he is."

I nodded and remembered the words of the pretty prostitute, Lana. "I am sure you are right, Murat."

"There has already been one attempt on your life, Smenkhkare. If Akhenamun becomes pharaoh then I am sure that it will not be the last. He will eliminate any possible rivals – and already you are proving a rival."

"Thank you for your opinion, Murat."

We pulled into the pier on the east bank and made our way to Coreb's army headquarters. Coreb was there to greet us as always. He bowed. "It is good to see you again, your majesty."

"Thutmose told you to call him by his name as you were his friend. I tell you to call me Smenkhkare as I hope I am also your friend."

He smiled. "You are indeed. Let us go inside, Smenkhkare." We entered his base and sat ourselves on two plain wooden chairs. He looked at me expectantly.

"You wish to know if I have arrived at a decision" I said.

He nodded. "A decision is needed urgently."

"I am convinced that Akhenamun had Thutmose murdered. My wife is also convinced that Akhenamun had Thutmose murdered. We are also both convinced that he was responsible for the attempt on my life."

"I hope you did not tell your wife of our plans," he gasped. "It is better that as few people as possible know of such matters."

"Taduheppa can be trusted, of that I have no doubt. The only way that I can guarantee my safety is to become pharaoh."

"And you will also be saving Egypt from a tyrant," he offered.

"What are your plans for making me pharaoh?" I asked.

"It is simple. I will cross the Nile with a large section of the army and we will take Malkata and declare you pharaoh. The only question is when to act. I feel that it must be very soon before Akhenamun is declared pharaoh."

"I want there to be as little bloodshed as possible."

"Your brother must be executed plus any who might prove close supporters."

"No other member of my family must be harmed," I said.

"No member of your family will be, apart perhaps from Ay. It will depend on what Ay does and says during the coup for he is the chief vizier and is in charge of the palace guard."

"I do not want a battle with the palace guard," I said.

"I will ask them to lay down their arms and support the new pharaoh, but I cannot guarantee they will obey though they will quickly realise their cause is lost in the face of such superior numbers."

"It will depend on Ay," I replied. "I will talk to him when the situation for the palace guard is hopeless and try to get his support. I will remind him that if he does not concede to my demands then his guard will be decimated and he will forfeit his life." I could not stand the man so I knew that would be a very easy course of action for me to take.

"When do you suggest we act?" he asked.

"Thutmose will make his final journey in three days' time. It would be possible to occupy the palace when the family is at the funeral but the idea of doing it then does not weigh easily on me."

"Also Akhenamun and Ay will not be at the palace and that would make their escape easier. If Akhenamun escapes then you will never feel secure," he replied.

"Then the day after the funeral," I suggested. "You can make the final arrangements undetected while we are all at the funeral. Cross the Nile early the next day and the palace will still be sleeping after the exertions of the previous day. Malkata will be in your hands before most are even awake. The guard should then surrender without a fight."

"The day after the funeral it is," responded Coreb. "That gives me time to plan and it will be before Akhenamun is declared pharaoh."

"When Malkata is in your hands, Coreb, what will you do?"

"Akhenamun and Ay will be made prisoners. Ay's fate will depend on him. You will be declared pharaoh immediately."

"What will be your position?" I asked.

"I will be your loyal general and advisor. I was always totally loyal to your brother, Thutmose. I have transferred that loyalty to you. I will always remain loyal to the Pharaoh, Smenkhkare, of that you can be certain. I will remain a powerful man in Egypt but I will always be your subordinate and on that you have my word."

He had realised what I was asking and I believed his reply completely. He was not of royal blood and was loyal and content to be general and of that I was certain. "You will be needed to secure my realm in the face of the Hittite threat," I said.

"I will do my duty and serve you well," he replied. "You are a good man, Smenkhkare, and unlike your brother, Akhenamun, you will be good for Egypt. Now we must not meet again until the day for if we meet too often it might arouse suspicions."

I smiled. "You are right for I can say we are friends meeting for military exercises once too often. The morning after the funeral I will be waiting for you outside the palace and I will be ready to join you as we make a triumphant entry into Malkata, and I will position myself alongside you at the head of the army."

"So be it, Malkata and Egypt will be yours and Thutmose will, at last, be avenged," he said smiling. "I will move some men across the river on the day of the funeral, downstream of Malkata and it will look like training manoeuvres. The rest will cross during the night while Malkata sleeps." We clasped hands in a token of unity. "It will be a momentous day."

"We shall next meet outside Malkata just to the south," I confirmed again.

The excitement was coursing through my veins as we climbed aboard the boat for the return trip across the Nile.

"Did it go well, Smenkhkare?" Murat asked as he steered our small vessel towards the west bank.

"It went very well," I replied, but I did not divulge any of the details. The less anybody knew the better.

He smiled. "Coreb is a good man and like me, though a general, he is a loyal servant," he assured me.

"You are right and I am lucky to have you both," I responded enthusiastically.

****

I hoped that I had not been seen and I returned stealthily to my apartment. When I opened the door I expected to see my wife waiting for me and keen to hear my news but to my surprise it was my sister, Nebetah, instead. "Where have you been, Smenkhkare?" she asked.

"To see my friend, Coreb, and to indulge in a little more army training," I replied.

"You left very early," she said.

"I like to make an early start, sister. What is this about?" I sensed her tension.

"You go too often to the army camp and Akhenamun does not like it."

"Why would he not like it?" I inquired feigning surprise.

"There is so much going on at the moment and he gets suspicious about what you are doing. I assure him that you and Coreb have become close friends and there is nothing for him to be concerned about, but this does not satisfy him."

"I do not really care if it does not satisfy him," I responded sharply.

A tear rolled down her face. "I know that both my brothers are good men. Please, Smenkhkare, do not return to the army camp until after Akhenamun becomes pharaoh."

I put my arm around her and gave her a hug. "Do not worry, I have always had a strained relationship with Akhenamun. I do not like to see you so upset, Nebetah. Is that all that is worrying you?"

"I have been sick with worry since I realised that the cobra could not have been an accident. I just do not know what to think about anything anymore. I fear that one of the servants might try to murder you again."

"You know it was one of the servants?" I said.

"It must have been, Smenkhkare. Please let me tell Akhenamun that you will not return to the army camp until after Akhenamun is made pharaoh."

"I have no plans to return to the army camp in the foreseeable future," I assured her.

She sighed with relief. "I will go and tell him for he has been concerned about you."

I nodded and watched her depart my apartment leaving the door open as she left. I hated being economical with the truth with regard to Nebetah but there was no other way. It also upset me to see her in such a distressed state. I wondered if she would ever forgive me for what I was about to do.

"What did she want?" Taduheppa was standing in the open door way.

"She wanted to know where I had been."

"Why did she want to know?" she asked suspiciously.

"She is concerned about me and I am concerned about her. You must remember, Taduheppa, that she and Thutmose have been the two people most close to me since the day I was born. I no longer have Thutmose so Nebetah remains my one dearest friend."

"That may be, but she makes me nervous for she is always sniffing around."

"It is her nature. She has a curious mind and she loves Malkata."

"By the way, your mother had another meeting today regarding the funeral and I was asked to stand in for you as you had disappeared once again. I told her you had got so enthusiastic about your military training that it was taking up a lot of your time."

"Was anything important discussed?" I asked.

"No, it was all very boring and I will fill you in on the details you need to know before the funeral." Taduheppa closed the door. "Now tell me all that happened with Coreb at the army camp."

"Plans have been made," I said somewhat secretly.

"Please expand on that, Smenkhkare," she responded irritably.

"Perhaps it is better if you do not know … for your own safety," I suggested.

"We are in this together. I need to know the details so that I can be of help to you. It was me who encouraged you in this course of action in the first place."

"True," I said, but it was not strictly true and still I hesitated for I knew Coreb would not approve of me telling anyone, not even my wife.

"If I am soon to be a true wife to you then you must share with me."

The connotations in her words were not lost on me, for more than anything else I desired her to be a true wife in every sense of the word. "I talked with Coreb and he has placed the army behind me. We will take Malkata."

"You convinced him then of the guilt of Akhenamun. Did you tell him of your wife's conversation with Nefertiti?"

"Yes and that helped to convince him."

"When will you take Malkata and make yourself pharaoh?" she asked. I could detect the excitement in her voice.

"The day after the funeral," I replied. The palace will be relaxed and in a state of slumber after the anxieties of the previous day. I hope to be able to accomplish the takeover without loss of blood."

"Except for the blood of Akhenamun," she sniffed.

I nodded. "Regrettably yes. I will meet Coreb and some of the army outside the palace and we will ride into Malkata together."

"Can Coreb be totally trusted?" she asked.

"I am absolutely positive he can."

"Then for the next couple of days before the funeral and during the funeral we must continue as normal so that we do not arouse suspicions. I will tell Nefertiti that you have accepted that an unidentified servant must have planted the cobra in your room and then it will get back to Akhenamun."

"Are you on good terms with Nefertiti again?"

"Now that she believes she is destined to be chief wife she has been very magnanimous and has suggested we become friends again for she genuinely loves me as a sister – or so she says. Akhenamun will feel that all is well."

"Then he is in for a surprise," I suggested.

"We must not appear to have become too friendly either. Let everything in Malkata appear to be unchanged," she grinned. "I will go and speak with my dear friend Nefertiti." The irony in her tone was unmistakable.

"Keep your ears open and appear to take Nefertiti back as a friend for you never know what she might divulge, but do not openly question her."

"I am very subtle, husband."

She left my apartment and left me with my thoughts and my recriminations. Being the leader of a palace revolution did not rest easy on my shoulders particularly as it was a revolt against my own family. However, if I was to avenge Thutmose and ensure my own survival I had no choice. The die was cast.

The next few days passed quietly and I was sure that nothing was suspected regarding the plot. With the exception of my wife all of my family members kept out of my way and it was a state of affairs that pleased me for I could not help feeling large doses of guilt. Taduheppa visited each day and she seemed equally confident that our plan was unsuspected and would be successful. She told me what I needed to know about the funeral and encouraged me in the coming enterprise with enticing promises and persuading assurances. I went to bed the night before the funeral with my mind once again in turmoil. It was extraordinary that, so recently before the death of Thutmose, I had no worries and no ambitions. How things could change in such a short space of time.

****

The next day the royal family with many servants and guards left the palace of Malkata at mid-morning on a rare cloudy day. I wondered if the clouds were an omen for what was to come. All of the royal family including my wife and Ay and Nefertiti and five servants travelled on the new royal barque down the Nile to the valley of the dead. The royal barque could comfortably seat 14 passengers with the servants acting as rowers. The barque was very grand and was a fitting vessel to begin this sombre and momentous day – a day when one pharaoh would begin the process of preparation for his time in the afterlife and his son would undertake the final journey to that same afterlife.

We were all dressed in fine clothes to match the occasion and this seemed to all of us like the end of one era and the beginning of another. The journey was in the most part undertaken in silence for frivolous conversation seemed inappropriate in the circumstances. The royal barque docked at the pier for the valley of the dead and joined a host of small boats and some large ones which had gathered for the occasion. The notables of Upper and Lower Egypt particularly those from the great city of Thebes had assembled for the occasion.

My family took its place at the head of the procession and the rest of the mourners filed in behind us for the walk to the tomb. There we would see my father's corpse before it was prepared for the great journey, and we would see Thutmose off as he began the journey on which my father would soon follow. It was quite a unique occasion for rarely had a pharaoh and his eldest son both died in such a short space of time. The procession then started a slow walk from the great river to the valley of the dead.

Following the royal family was a group of many priests led by the head priest. Behind the head priest was a sledge pulled by oxen and led by three of his more illustrious colleagues. These priests poured donkey's milk over the firm, desert sands to help the sledge move more smoothly. I could not help being disrespectful as I remembered Taduheppa emerging naked from her bath of donkey's milk. My wife was at my side and she grinned at me as if she read my thoughts. My mother joined us. "It is good to see you both getting on well at last," she said.

"Yes, mother," I replied.

She continued. "It is also good to hear that you have dropped these absurd accusations against Akhenamun and that you have resorted back to your former self."

"Things have been difficult of late," I responded.

"I know you took the death of your brother badly and then there was the awful incident with the cobra. After the funeral I will make it my business to find out which servant was responsible for such an action. Ay is wonderful on palace security and he has an idea on who it might have been."

"Who?" I asked.

"I should not tell you but I will put you on alert. Ay believes that your servant Murat cannot be trusted."

"Really, mother." I gasped at the audacity of Ay.

Tiye walked back to the other members of the family and said something to Ay. Taduheppa whispered in my ear. "They think you are being a good little boy again. How little do they know."

The sledge was moving smoothly, and on the sledge was the substitute for my father – a priest wrapped in linen. The preservation process had already started on my father who was at rest and protected in his open tomb. I glanced at the crouching figure that represented my father and smiled. I could not help feeling that some of the rituals that the priests insisted upon were strange and obviously Taduheppa found them bewildering. "A strange lot you Egyptians are," she commented quietly.

Musicians walked among the procession playing their instruments and priests leaped about wearing their animal masks. The presence of Anubis was particularly prevalent as many priests wore the head of a jackal. Behind the priests followed notables who had been able to make the journey to Thebes for such a prestigious occasion. At the rear of the procession came the servants and slaves who carried items that would be buried in the tomb for use in the afterlife. The array of furniture, clothes, jewellery and even weapons was quite staggering. My father would be very well off in the afterlife as he had been in his mortal life.

We slowly made our way through the valley to the accompaniment of religious music. Iset came to talk with me, followed closely by my other sister Nebetah. "I hear that you accepted the official line," she said. Nebetah scolded her. "Do not provoke him, sister."

It seemed strange to me that Iset, to whom I had never been close, believed in my concerns while Nebetah, with whom I had shared so much over the years, was sceptical. It saddened me a little. "It seemed the sensible thing to do," I explained.

"You have become a disappointment," said Iset and walked away.

"Take no notice of her," said Nebetah. "You are doing the right thing to accept what is undoubtedly the truth."

Ay then came over to join us. "I think I heard Iset say that you have accepted the official line. If you achieve manhood then you may realise that is the only line possible for a member of your family." There was a degree of scorn in his words.

"I intend to live for a long time yet, Ay."

Ay put his arm around Nebetah. "Come, I think Akhenamun wants to speak with you," he said and they left us.

"Can we execute him too, please," said Taduheppa.

I was not sure if she was joking. "I am tempted," I replied. I looked at Akhenamun, Ay and Nebetah talking. They were pointing at the tekenu who was still reclining on the sledge. "They are talking about the coming ceremony," I added. I noted that Akhenamun had not said a single word to me since we left Malkata. He had clearly not forgiven me but then I had not forgiven him either.

We had arrived at the tomb. The first chamber was the tomb temple where my father was at rest, and deeper into the tomb was the chamber in which the body of Thutmose would be sealed. I would be able to tell him that I was keeping my promise. Each member of my family went in to have few private words with my father, Amenhotep, before the embalming process began. I kissed him on the forehead in greeting but I could not bring myself to speak to him. I had rarely spoken to him when he lived so there was equally little to say now that he was dead. The priestess of Isis entered as I was looking at my father and wailed at the passing of a great pharaoh, burned some incense and left. I shook my head at him and thought how astonished he would be if he knew that his successor would be his idiot son, Smenkhkare, the son he was so ashamed of. I kissed his forehead again. "I am not the idiot now, father."

This was mainly Thutmose's day and the family and chief priests gathered in his tomb for the opening-of-the-mouth ceremony. This was the most important ceremony and would set Thutmose off on his great journey to the afterlife. Everything was ready; his mummy was prepared and his needed possessions had been assembled. The sky boat was ready to take him on his final journey. The head priest placed the palm of his hands on the sarcophagus and started his prayers. He then touched the mouth, eyes, ears and nose to awaken the senses. Thutmose could breathe again and when he reached the afterlife he would be able to speak and use his body and his limbs. More prayers were said by the priest and now he could eat, drink and function again. My brother was transformed into a divine being and could take his place at the side of

Osiris in the realm of the Gods. The priestess burned more incense and we each took one more look at Thutmose before the coffin lid was put in place. You will be avenged was the thought that I sent to him as I took my last look at my much-loved brother. I knew he understood, and that would make his journey to the afterlife even more serene.

We exited his tomb chamber, past the empty tomb intended for my father and through the tomb temple, in a solemn group but now it was time for celebrations. We would now have a feast to celebrate the start of Thutmose's glorious journey to the afterlife and when the feast came to an end the tomb chamber of Thutmose would be sealed. We were all happy for Thutmose was, in theory, no longer dead. The problem was that I knew he was still dead despite the promises and acclamations of the priests.

It was a huge banquet for the pharaoh's eldest son. Dancers performed the sacred dances and musicians played the sacred tunes. Taduheppa danced with the man she despised but this time she also danced with me. Wine and beer flowed in copious amounts and food was consumed on a huge scale and I knew that in 60 days it would be repeated all over again for my father. We had all drunk and eaten our fill and the tomb had been sealed when we returned on the royal barque for the journey back to Malkata. I was the exception for I had been cautious, knowing I had such a big day ahead. Ay occupied the seat next to me on the boat much to my distaste. "You were not celebrating as hard as your siblings," he observed.

"It is not my way."

"It is not my way either." He smiled his mirthless smile. "I think, Smenkhkare, that our feuding has gone on long enough. Perhaps I will bring you a gift to show you the sincerity of my words."

"I am touched, Ay, but that is not necessary."

He shrugged. "A new era is about to begin and—"

"May I sit next to my husband?" Taduheppa interrupted him.

Ay moved away and Taduheppa sat next to me. "What did he want?"

"I am not sure," I replied.

Night had fallen when the royal barque docked at Malkata. We crossed the gardens and we all made our way to our separate apartments. I was sorry to be alone for I knew that sleep would not be easy, for in some ways I dreaded the coming day.

"Good luck tomorrow, husband," Taduheppa whispered in my ear as she left me to return to her own apartment. It would be a long night.

Chapter 11

It was indeed a long night or so it seemed. My sleep was intermittent and punctuated with fears of the reaction of my family to what I had done. I was confident that my plot had not been discovered because Akhenamun and Ay had attended the funeral and did not appear suspicious. I roused myself from my interrupted sleep and rose from my bed before dawn and hastily dressed in one of my finest tunics. I wanted to look my best when I entered Malkata at the head of the army.

It was still dark when I stealthily left the palace and made my way through the vast gardens towards the exit gate close to the river. It was the very early hours of the morning and the palace and the world seemed quiet and at peace. When I reached the gate I looked back at the palace which was barely visible in the poor light. I did have a final regret with regard to what I was doing, but assured myself that this action was essential if I was to be sure of surviving and avenging my brother, Thutmose. I left the palace behind me and made my way south following the course of the river Nile and being cautious to avoid any of the night dangers.

I did not travel far, for the plan was that I should meet Coreb and his troops close to the palace. I would then take my place in a chariot next to Coreb and we would make a grand entrance into Malkata. There was no sign of Coreb or the army. This puzzled me considerably for I felt there had to be some sign of the assembled troops. It would be a small army of selected troops for even a small brigade would heavily outnumber the palace guard. I waited but there was still no sign of my troops and I grew ever more concerned for even a small army should make its presence known.

The rays of the rising sun were now making a spectacular appearance above the distant horizon and I was still quite alone. I decided to make my way further down the river for it was possible they had assembled further to the south than originally planned. I walked for an hour but there was still no evidence of any army. The world was still completely at peace but I was beginning to feel a sense of panic. The call of the birds as they flew above the waters of the great river seemed to mock me and I knew now that something was seriously wrong. I decided to wait a bit longer feeling that Coreb would surely get a message to me if he had temporarily called off the coup for some reason.

I waited but no army appeared and no message arrived. Coreb had certainly aborted our plan, of that there was no doubt. Perhaps he had encountered some unforeseen complication and it was difficult to get a message to me. When the middle of the morning was reached I decided that I could not stand around waiting any longer. I had two options as I saw it. The first was to return to Malkata and behave as if nothing had happened and wait for a message from Coreb. The second was to find a boat and cross the Nile to the army encampment and seek out Coreb for an explanation.

I decided on the first option. If Coreb had a problem I did not want to wander into it and perhaps add to it by my presence which might further complicate matters. I also knew that Taduheppa would be at her wits end with worry when it became obvious that I was not going to appear at the head of a conquering army.

I trudged my way north once again staying close to the mighty river until Malkata came into sight. I was nervous with the fear that the plot had been discovered and that was why Coreb had not taken the intended action. I entered the gate that I had exited hours ago before dawn and all was still peaceful. To my relief there was no Akhenamun and the palace guard were not waiting to arrest me for treason. Malkata was bathed in sunlight and there was no sign of any human activity in the gardens. The palace was still at rest after the exertions of the previous day. However, I did not let the silence fool me completely for I knew something had gone badly wrong. As I made my way through the exotic gardens I felt growing trepidation and wondered if I should turn around and even now cross the river and seek out Coreb at the army camp.

I then saw Taduheppa rushing from the palace. She hurried towards me, her long green dress flapping around her ankles and blending in with exotic green plants of the Malkata gardens. "What has happened?" she demanded.

"Coreb and the army did not turn up," I said simply.

She grabbed my arm. "Look, the gardeners arc beginning to start work, and so let us get back to your apartment where we can talk secretly without interruption."

"They are late in starting work," I commented.

She looked at me with a degree of scorn. "Come," she said. I followed her into the palace and along the empty corridors towards my apartment.

We dived inside and closed the door behind us. "Well, what happened, Smenkhkare?"

"I told you, Coreb and his army did not turn up. I waited and I waited but they did not show, so I returned to the palace."

"You are a fool. Everyone thinks you are an idiot and I should have listened to them. I should have known not to trust you with such an undertaking. We have probably been discovered."

Once again I felt a degree of panic and hit back. "I should not have trusted you, Taduheppa. You were the only one who knew of our plans. Did you sell them to Akhenamun for the price of being his chief wife?"

She slapped me hard across the face and stormed out of my apartment. My face tingled and reddened from the force of the blow and I was at a loss at what to do next. I called for Murat, but instead a female servant answered my call. "Where is Murat?" I demanded.

"I do not know," the nervous servant replied.

I dismissed her with a wave of my hand. It seemed that Coreb and Murat had both disappeared and I was left with my treacherous wife. I had to think and form some sort of plan in case the plot had been discovered as I feared. I had to think what to say in my defence – or should I simply flee the palace.

Murat then hurried into my apartment, his face full of concern. "I heard you were back and wanted to see me," he said.

"Cross the Nile and see Coreb at the army encampment. I want a full report from Coreb on where we stand in our undertaking. Now hurry and come back as soon as possible for I need to know what the situation is."

His eyes were full of understanding at my plight. "I will go immediately and return with news," he said and quickly strode out of my apartment. I was left to continue to ponder on what could have gone wrong.

My thoughts were soon interrupted by the return of my wife. She entered my chamber arm in arm with my sister, Nebetah. My sister was smiling nervously. "Taduheppa said you wanted to speak with me, brother."

"Did I?" I replied somewhat bewildered.

What happened next took me completely by surprise. Taduheppa struck Nebetah a blow across the face so hard it knocked my sister off her feet. She was kneeling on the floor, sobbing as Taduheppa took a fistful of her hair and forced her to look at me. "Tell your brother how you have betrayed him," she demanded.

"I have done nothing," protested Nebetah.

"Have you gone mad, Taduheppa? Let my sister go," I said disbelieving the scene that I was witnessing.

She did not let her go but instead kicked Nebetah in the ribs which resulted in more sobs. "She is always sniffing around the palace and having secret talks with Akhenamun. She knew what you were up to because you had part confided in her, believing her to be your dear, innocent little sister."

I looked at Nebetah. "Is there any truth in these accusations," I asked.

"No!" she screamed.

Taduheppa then began to drag Nebetah by her hair across my apartment from the outer chamber to the inner chamber and then towards the balcony and I followed bemused. "I am going to throw you over the top if you do not tell the truth," she threatened.

I was about to intervene on my sister's behalf when Nebetah sobbed. "I did not mean any harm to come to Smenkhkare."

I was stunned by these words and I knelt down on the floor facing Nebetah while Taduheppa stood over her, still holding her hair in a tight grip like a dark avenging angel of death. "Tell me everything," I said sympathetically.

"I am so sorry, brother, but I did not think it would come to this," she wailed.

"Tell him!" Taduheppa demanded giving her hair another tug.

"Let her talk," I said to Taduheppa.

Nebetah groaned and started to speak. "Father and mother had found a husband for me. It was the King of the Kushites and he is an old man. I was desperate for I did not want to marry him and leave Malkata to live in Kush."

"Why did you not tell me?" I asked.

"What could you have done?"

"What has this to do with my present predicament?" I asked.

"When father became seriously ill I went to plead my case with Akhenamun as he would shortly be the new pharaoh. I could not bear to leave Malkata, Smenkhkare, for this is my home and I love it here. I could not be sent to some strange land and marry an old man."

"Was Akhenamun sympathetic?" I asked for I knew that he had always been kindly disposed towards his little sister, perhaps the only person he was kind to.

"Yes, he promised me that I would not have to leave Malkata."

"What was the price of his promise?" I asked starting to feel uneasy at these revelations.

"He said that he would make me his minor wife but I would not have to live in the harem with the other minor wives."

"You were happy with that arrangement to be a minor wife?" I was astounded. "You are a princess of Egypt."

She sobbed again. "He was being kind to me. He said I could then stay in Malkata and be with the man I love."

I was even more astounded. "The man you love?" I repeated.

"Ramose," she sobbed.

I could not believe my ears. My sister was in love with Ay's steward. "Did you know of my plans and did you tell Akhenamun about them?"

"I had worked them out by what you had said to me and by your numerous visits to Coreb. I feared that you were planning a revolt. Akhenamun is the rightful heir and he had made me promises."

"So you were willing to sacrifice me to be with your lover?"

"No ... yes ... but it was all right. Akhenamun promised me that you would not be harmed if you were planning anything but he did not really believe me anyway. He said you were not capable of such a plot and my imagination was running wild."

"I would not be harmed, but what about the cobra, Nebetah?"

"Yes, that worried me for a while as you know but Akhenamun assured me that he had nothing to do with the cobra and so it must have got in from the gardens."

"Have we returned to that silly explanation? Open your eyes, Nebetah. Do you really believe that Akhenamun intended me no harm? What has happened to Coreb?"

"I do not know," she cried. Taduheppa pulled at her hair and gave her another kick. "I really do not know!" she screamed.

"Let her go," I said to Taduheppa.

I thought for a moment that my wife was going to continue her assault on my sister but then she shrugged and released her grip on her hair. Nebetah rose unsteadily to her feet. "Just go," I said.

Taduheppa moved to stop her. "Are you really going to let her walk out of here after what she has done?"

"Yes, I am. Let her go, Taduheppa."

My wife took a step back and glared at Nebetah. "I suppose she is of no further use to us." Nebetah limped painfully and sadly out of my apartment and I felt that I had lost my lifelong friend. I could not believe that Nebetah had betrayed me to Akhenamun.

"Now what are we to do?" moaned Taduheppa. "You really have messed this up, Smenkhkare."

I shook my head. "I do not know. I have sent Murat to Coreb to find out what the situation is at the army encampment. Perhaps we should flee the palace, though you are not in as much danger as me. You are a Mitanni princess and I do not think that Akhenamun would harm you – but I am an Egyptian traitor."

"Perhaps then you should flee the palace to save your life and I should stay," she offered.

"But you are my wife and I am sorry I accused you of betrayal, Taduheppa."

"They could come for you at any time."

"I am still the son of the pharaoh."

"Let us walk around the palace, act as if nothing has happened and try to gauge the situation in Malkata and then see what Murat has to report when he returns. If we feel you need to flee then you can do so," she suggested.

I nodded, for it was a sort of plan.

The corridors of the palace were empty except for a few servants rushing around. It seemed that the members of the royal family were still in their apartments and that was hardly surprising after the hard work and festivities of the funeral. After we had made our way around the palace we decided to go back to the gardens and here we were rewarded. Taduheppa pointed to Nefertiti sitting on a bench near the lake and we decided to join her. As the intended great royal wife of Akhenamun and the daughter of Ay she seemed like a good person to question on the state of current palace affairs.

She looked up with surprise on her beautiful face as we approached her. "Can we sit with you?" I asked.

"It is good to see my greatest friend looking so relaxed," added Taduheppa.

"I am not relaxed, far from it," she mused.

"Is there something troubling you?" Taduheppa asked. I did not speak for Nefertiti was my wife's friend and so I left the questions to her for she might be able to learn something if Nefertiti indeed knew anything.

Nefertiti hesitated. "I was considering coming to see you."

"What did you wish to tell us?" Taduheppa probed.

"I know we have had our differences, Taduheppa, but we have been friends ever since you arrived in Thebes and I would not wish to see harm come to you." She looked at me. "To either of you, you are my cousin, Smenkhkare and I know you did what you did because you felt your life was threatened."

"I did feel that," I said with feeling.

"I do not think Taduheppa is in real danger, but you, Smenkhkare, I fear for you. I was coming to see you to warn you to leave Thebes and disappear into the desert. You must go soon for I do not think there is much time and you must not go to the army encampment."

"Why do you fear for me and why must I not go the army camp?" I sought for an answer.

"Thebes, the palace and the army camp are no longer safe for you. You should leave immediately but I cannot tell you any more details." She rose from the bench and hurried off before another word could be said.

I turned to my wife. "She is right and she was good enough to warn us. I will leave Malkata and Thebes immediately. Are you coming with me, Taduheppa?"

"No, Smenkhkare, I am safe at the palace for they would not dare harm a Mitanni princess and there is no proof that I was involved in your scheming. I will look after your interests in Malkata."

"As you wish," I replied. I was disappointed but I sensed there was little time to argue and why should I inflict hardships on my wife. "Let us hurry back to my apartment for if I am to leave I need money to survive and I have a good sum back in my chambers."

She nodded and we made our way quickly back to my apartment. I gathered up a bag of coins and a robe for the cold nights that sometimes occur in the desert but I felt I had no time to pack anything else. I wanted to take Taduheppa in my arms and tell her how much I adored her, but reading my thoughts she took a step backwards to deter me. "Smenkhkare, find Coreb and see what has happened. You have no time to wait for Murat to return. Be careful and do not enter the army camp without first observing it. Your chief royal wife will expect to see you back in Thebes at the head of an army when you will take your place as pharaoh. Now go." She had also sensed the urgency of the situation.

"May I kiss you first, Taduheppa" I asked.

She nodded and planted a kiss on my lips which made my whole body tingle with pleasure. I returned the kiss and we lingered for a moment and then she broke away. "Now go, Smenkhkare."

I reluctantly left her and opened the door to exit my apartment but my way was blocked by the royal guard.

"What is the meaning of this?" I blurted out as I retreated back into my room to find myself once again alongside Taduheppa. Four well-armed members of the palace guard entered closely followed by Ay. He was smiling that mocking, mirthless smile. "Are you going somewhere, Smenkhkare?"

"Is that any of your business, Ay?" I was trying to sound bold.

"I have had a little chat with your sister, Nebetah, and it was most interesting."

"I will kill her," said Taduheppa.

"Do not be hard on her for she meant you no harm. She was worried about you and where your pathetic plotting might lead. Her brother, Akhenamun, would not listen to her concerns and so she came to me. I also pretended not to listen but I sensed there was an element of truth in her fears. You are a stupid boy, Smenkhkare. Did you really think that you could outwit the chief vizier? I have years of political intrigue and experience to call upon and you are nothing but a child."

"What is it to do with you? This is between me and my brother."

"How wrong you are. Let me tell you something, Smenkhkare. I had served your father, Amenhotep, for many years but your headstrong brother, Thutmose, wanted to dispense with my services. I was not going to allow that to happen."

"You had Thutmose killed?" I gasped.

He smirked and this hideous smirk answered my question. "Akhenamun will make a better pharaoh and he will listen to his most valued advisor."

"You were working for Akhenamun when you had Thutmose murdered?"

"Indirectly. He was a bit reluctant to agree to the death of a brother, but now the deed is done he is suitably grateful."

I wanted to throw myself at this vile man and tear off his head but Taduheppa put a restraining grip on my arm. I forced myself to calm down as he studied me with a knowing smile that showed his arrogance and disdain. She was right, for he was flanked by well-armed guards and any hopeless attempt to take revenge would have resulted in my injury. I could not trust myself to speak and instead stared at him with eyes full of hate.

"I want to introduce you to someone," he said. He clapped his hands and a large but young military man entered my chamber. I recognised the man, for I had seen him a number of times at the army camp.

"He is one of Coreb's officers," I said.

"You are wrong, Smenkhkare. May I introduce you to Horemheb? He is the new general of our illustrious army. He is now in complete control of our armed forces."

I stared at Horemheb. "Is this true?" I asked him.

"It is very true," Horemheb replied.

I saw the coldness in his eyes and I sensed the extreme danger I was in and so did Taduheppa. "How dare you bring this man uninvited into the apartment of Smenkhkare, the son of Amenhotep and the brother of Akhenamun," she blustered.

"I thought your husband might like to meet our new general," Ay replied with a measure of contempt as he uttered the word husband.

"Where is Coreb?" I asked.

"I thought you might ask that question, and so very shortly I will be giving you an eloquent answer. Please be patient for a very short time for I will not keep you waiting long."

"Akhenamun is not stupid. He will not tolerate your wickedness and your ambition."

"I have no ambition except to remain chief vizier, the next most powerful man in Egypt after the pharaoh but the man who really runs Egypt. Akhenamun knows this and he knows he owes his position to me. Without me he had no hope of becoming pharaoh and he would have ended up a priest, a position for which he had no desire. You are right that Akhenamun is not stupid and for that reason he will do as I advise."

"Thutmose saw through you and therefore you had him murdered." My words were spat out with hatred.

"Yes, Thutmose was stupid but Akhenamun is not." He turned to Taduheppa. "You also have been very foolish to support this boy, but I will overlook that. You are a Mitanni princess and it would not be diplomatic if any harm was to come to you. As the second most powerful man in Egypt I may, at some point, take you for my wife for I am not immune to your great beauty."

His words staggered me and enraged Taduheppa. "You are a vile and ugly man and I will never be your wife. You cannot even believe that such a gross thing will come about. I am a Mitanni princess."

He smiled at her tirade. "We shall see but that is something for the future. Now return to your room for what will soon entail is not for your delicate eyes."

His words sent fear coursing through my body. Was he going to order the palace guards to kill me right now in my own apartment? Surely not for I was still the son of the last pharaoh and his wife Tiye, who now currently ruled, and the brother of the new pharaoh-to-be. He would not dare.

"I will stay," said a shocked Taduheppa.

Ay must have read my fear and laughed. "You will die, Smenkhkare, but not yet. I always do things properly. I will ask your mother to sign your death warrant but I rather regret that she will refuse despite my persuasive tongue and so when Akhenamun becomes pharaoh I will try again. Unfortunately for you I have no doubt that he can be convinced that this would be his only sensible course of action." He looked round as Ramose entered the room carrying a wicker basket. "This is what I have been waiting for, Smenkhkare. I promised you a gift when we spoke on the royal barque, and an eloquent answer to your question."

I stared with horror at the basket for it was identical to the one that had contained the cobra. The basket rekindled all my fears regarding the deadly snake which had almost taken my life. I felt Taduheppa gripping my hand as she also gaped with trepidation at the innocent-looking basket. "You placed the snake under my bed," I said with revulsion.

Ay smiled. "What snake was that?"

I looked at Ramose. "Did you place it in my apartment?"

He grinned, which for me was ample confirmation. "My sister loves you," I uttered.

"I am fond of her," he replied.

"Fond," I gasped. "She loves you and she was willing to become a minor wife of the new pharaoh just to be able to stay in Thebes with you."

He shrugged and pushed the basket towards me with his foot.

"Your sister was useful," said Ay. "Now, Smenkhkare, it is time for you to take the lid off the basket and see what is inside."

I looked again at the basket. "And have a second confrontation with a cobra, I think not Ay."

"Foolish boy, do you think I would be standing this close to the basket if it contained a cobra," said Ay with disdain.

He had a point. If the basket contained a snake he was as close to it as I was and would be in equal danger for the snake could strike in any direction.

"Shall I remove the lid?" offered Ramose.

"No, let the honour go to Smenkhkare," replied Ay.

Ay, Ramose, Horemheb, flanked by the palace guards, stepped back and looked at me with expectant and amused eyes and indicated for me to proceed. Taduheppa still gripped my hand and almost restrained me, fearing another deadly cobra.

I released her hand and moved her behind me and I took one pace forward so I was standing over the innocent yet dangerous wicker basket. Slowly I bent down and removed the lid. Inside was a large object covered in a cloth and I breathed a sigh of relief that it did not appear to be a snake. Then I saw there was a bloodstain on the cloth and I was filled with apprehension. In one sweeping movement I pulled the cloth aside and retched. I was filled with a whole series of emotions – from horror to sadness to revulsion. The unseeing eyes of my friend and general looked lifelessly up at me from the bloodstained sockets within his severed head. I shuddered with grief and misery.

"You asked me where Coreb was and now you have your answer," said Ay coldly. I threw myself at Ay but the guards blocked my path. "Coreb was a traitor and paid for it with his life as you will, in due course, Smenkhkare."

"You are the traitor, Ay!" I shouted with frustration. "You murdered the rightful pharaoh, Thutmose, and you tried to murder me with that vile snake."

"Akhenamun will be pharaoh and I will be his chief vizier. It is done and so are you, Smenkhkare."

"You are despicable and reprehensible. Even Akhenamun will not let you get away with this."

"Yes he will," he smiled. "Now, what to do with you in the meantime?" he mused.

"My mother will hear of this," I stormed.

"Your mother will hear how you plotted to overthrow your older brother. She will have little sympathy and she trusts me implicitly as did your father."

Taduheppa gripped my hand again and looked into my eyes. "Ay and Akhenamun have won and Egypt belongs to them. They are the victors and we must accept that." Her eyes belied her words and I knew my wife did not mean a word that she had just said.

"At least one of you speaks sense and you should listen to the good counsel of your wife," said Ay. "Taduheppa, you will return to your apartment. You will have the freedom of the palace and the gardens but do not attempt to leave Malkata. If you tried you would quickly be found and punished. As for you, Smenkhkare, you will be confined to your apartment and guards will be placed outside. You will continue to be attended by servants except for the servant Murat wherever he may be."

"I am a prisoner in my own chambers," I retorted.

"You conspired against the pharaoh and so you are under house arrest for treason until it is decided what to do with you." He grinned and added: "And your death warrant is signed."

"My wife will stay with me," I said.

"She will not," he retorted. "Do you think I would leave you two together to do more plotting? She will not be visiting you."

He addressed Taduheppa. "Now leave, and if you behave things will not change for you." Taduheppa glanced at me and obediently hurried from my apartment.

"As for you, Smenkhkare, you also will be treated well until a decision is made on your punishment for we will not forget your royal status and so think yourself lucky."

"I am so lucky," I sneered.

"If you need anything then a guard will take a message to Ramose and he will decide on your request. Be realistic though, for we will ignore any inappropriate demands. Your confinement will not be uncomfortable if you are sensible." There was an obvious threat in his final words as he left my apartment followed by Horemheb.

"How could you treat Nebetah so badly?" I asked Ramose as he replaced the lid on the basket and picked it up. "She loves you."

"I told you I am fond of her and she was useful. She has a lovely little body and I have enjoyed it."

I knew he was provoking me, so I did not rise to the bait. "Am I allowed visitors?" I asked.

"You may not make requests but if anyone asks to visit you then their request will be considered."

"I see," I said, hopeful that I might get to speak with my mother and other members of my family. I still had my case to put to them.

Ramose must have read my thoughts. "Suitable visitors only," he added.

"You would prevent me seeing my family?"

"It depends. Ay will have the final say, but I would prevent it if it were up to me."

He turned and exited my apartment followed by the palace guards.

Chapter 12

In the ensuing days, after my incarceration in my chambers, I took to spending time on my balcony overlooking the exotic gardens of Malkata. I was rewarded on numerous occasions with the pleasure of seeing Taduheppa. She would wave and I would wave back but we could not talk for we would have had to shout and she was closely followed by a guard and our words would have got back to Ay. I also saw Akhenamun and Nefertiti as well as Sitamun but I was ignored by all except by Nefertiti who gave me a pitying look. Three days passed and I had not had any visitors, not even members of my family. I was desperate to see my mother and put my case to her but she never came and I guessed she was under the sinister influence of Ay. Then on the fourth day I had three visitors.

The first was my sister Iset. I welcomed her enthusiastically for except for servants I had spoken to no-one for the past three days.

"Welcome sister," I enthused. I never thought I would ever be so glad to see Iset but I knew that I would get a reliable update on my situation from her.

"Greetings, brother, you really have got yourself into a mess."

"Tell me what is happening in the palace. I have not spoken to anyone for days. It seems as if my entire family has deserted me and are not willing to hear my case."

She sat down and sighed. "It seems Ay discovered your conspiracy and engineered a successful mutiny in the army."

I sat opposite her. "I know that, but why am I not being allowed to put my case."

"Because you have committed treason against your brother, or at least that is the way the family sees it and the way that Ay has presented it."

"If I had not done so then I would have been murdered. It was the only way I could survive."

She leaned closer. "I believe you, Smenkhkare, but I am the only one who does. Ay has seen to that."

"Even mother," I said sadly.

"Particularly mother," she sighed. "She relies heavily on Ay and believes everything he tells her. She believes you have betrayed Akhenamun. Ay advises her not to see you as she may feel pity and she has agreed to his wishes, but she still refuses to sign your death warrant despite his urging."

"Ay had the snake put in my room. Ramose placed it under my bed. Ay admitted it to me but it is my word against his and who would believe me?"

"I do, but that is of no value to you."

"Could you not plead my case, Iset," I begged.

She shook her head. "If I were to do that then I might also end up a prisoner in my apartment, such is Ay's power at present. He brooks no opposition. I am sorry, brother, but for my own preservation I will keep quiet. However, I will try to discreetly persuade others to see you though I cannot be seen to be supporting you."

"Thank you, Iset. I suppose that is as much as I could ask for."

"It is a tragedy, brother, for you will never get the chance to prove that you are not a fool. You are still very young and you could have made a good pharaoh. Akhenamun will probably be a tyrant who relies too heavily on the chief vizier."

"You think that I am doomed."

She nodded her head. "Ay will do things properly but he will get that warrant signed sooner or later. I wish I could have helped you, Smenkhkare. I would have made you a good chief royal wife but it is not to be," she smiled sweetly.

"What of Taduheppa?" I smiled back.

"I would have had her disposed of, for after all she is hardly a wife to you."

"She is the only one supporting me at the moment while my own family has abandoned me."

"She may appear to be, Smenkhkare, but I am not sure that she is trustworthy. She was quick to jump into Akhenamun's bed."

"And she regrets it," I replied.

She shrugged. "That is what she now says. I would not trust her, Smenkhkare. She may only now be backing you because she has lost out to Nefertiti."

Now I shrugged. "It seems the world is against me and it is only a matter of time before Ay gets his warrant signed."

"It looks that way, but do not get too despondent for things can change quickly and unexpectedly in Malkata. I will suggest to your mother, brother and sisters that they should see you because you genuinely accept your wrongdoing. Then if I am successful the rest is up to you. That is the best I can do and now I must go." She stood up and I followed suit. She kissed me on both cheeks. "Farewell, brother. If I am successful then I will deserve a reward."

"Farewell, sister," I responded.

She turned and left my apartment. Iset had given me some hope but I knew she was only looking after her own interests but, as she said, things could change swiftly in Malkata. I could not blame her for that.

My next visitor a few hours later was a surprise. My servant showed in Turet, one of Taduheppa's handmaidens, into my apartment.

"Greetings, your majesty," she said, smiling at my surprise.

"How is your mistress?" I inquired, eager for information.

"She is well, but can we talk in private?" she asked, glancing at my hovering servants.

Her words intrigued me for, unlike Rana and Taduheppa's other servants, Turet seemed to hold a privileged position. I dismissed my servants with a wave of my hand. "Come into my inner chamber, Turet, where we can have complete privacy." I walked into my bed chamber and she followed and I closed the door behind her. I beckoned her to sit down and then I sat next to her, eagerly looking into her dark Mitanni eyes that resembled those of her mistress.

"I have much to say on behalf of my mistress," she smiled.

"Is there no written message from Taduheppa?" I asked, feeling the first pangs of anxiety beginning to cancel out my eagerness. How did I know that she was still serving Taduheppa and that she had not been got at by Ay? I would have to be cautious in what I say for I did not want to give more weapons to Ay in his bid to have me executed.

"No, she feared that anything in writing might fall into the hands of your enemy. She has fully authorised me to speak on her behalf."

I realised that I would have to trust this pretty Mitanni servant. "How were you able to get permission to see me, Turet?"

"I did not get permission but I am able to come and go as a servant. The guards recognised me as a servant and as such they do not prevent my entrance." She smiled. "It also helps when I flutter my eyelashes at them and engage them in conversation."

This Mitanni girl had some of the fire of her mistress. "Please tell me everything that has been happening these past few days."

"My mistress has been talking to all the members of the royal family. Your mother and Sitamun are furious with you and have washed their hands of you though your mother refuses to sign Ay's death warrant. Iset sympathises with you but will not help you in any way."

"I know for she came to see me," I interrupted.

"My mistress has also spoken to Akhenamun who seems to be in torment but will not help for he insists that you deserve everything you get. The one who is most sympathetic is your cousin, Nefertiti, who has promised to do her best to save you. She is Ay's daughter and he does listen to her, and she will soon be chief royal wife and queen when she marries Akhenamun."

"Why does she wish to help me?" I wondered out loud.

"She is the only one, apart perhaps from Akhenamun, who believes that Ay tried to murder you with the cobra. She knows how ruthless her father can be when his position is threatened. My mistress now believes that Akhenamun knew nothing of the assassination of Thutmose or the attempt on your life. However, he will not help for he is a brutal man who is happy to benefit from the crimes of Ay even if he did not sanction them."

"How can Nefertiti help me?" I asked.

"She is a great friend to my mistress and my mistress is working on her. She seeks to persuade Nefertiti to influence her father into offering you a pardon in return for you taking an oath to behave and proffering loyalty to your brother. My mistress then believes that once you have your liberty you can continue with your plans."

"My wife never gives up. Has it not occurred to her that, if in the unlikely event I am offered a pardon, I might rather take the safe course and give up my ambition?"

"You would never be safe." I stared at Turet for it could almost have been Taduheppa speaking these words, such was the vehemence in which they were spoken.

"Ay will not agree to me being pardoned," I replied with certainty in my voice.

"My mistress tends to agree with you and that is why she believes you must have an alternative plan – an escape plan."

"How am I to escape for there are guards outside my door all day and all night? I am not at liberty to even leave my apartment."

"My mistress is working on that. Akhenamun will be crowned as the new pharaoh a week today even before your father makes his final journey and so she realises how urgent your escape will become. She fears that Akhenamun intends to sign your death warrant as soon as he becomes pharaoh. Ay will certainly try to persuade him to do so."

I sighed with misery. "So I may only have a week."

"Do not despair, your majesty, my mistress works tirelessly on your behalf and she can be very persuasive and resourceful."

I smiled. "I know. Will you be able to keep me informed?"

"I will visit you daily as a servant so as not to arouse suspicion," she replied.

"How could I escape?" I mused.

"All things are possible," she assured me. "Now I must return to my mistress."

"One more thing, Turet, do you know what happened to my loyal servant Murat? I have not seen him since I began my confinement."

"I do not know. I do not think he has been seen at the palace since you were made a prisoner. Now I must go, your majesty."

I nodded and sighed as she hurried from my apartment. I was very pleased to have the support of my inventive wife but I was aware that she did what she did out of ambition to become the chief royal wife of Egypt and out of hatred for my brother, Akhenamun, who had scorned her.

I did not have time to dwell further on the words of Turet for she was promptly followed by another visitor. My sister cautiously entered my apartment, unsure what type of reception she would receive. I stared at her with a certain degree of contempt but then reminded myself that this was my sweet sister who had been such a good friend to me virtually all my life.

"Greetings, Nebetah," I said formally.

"Greetings, Smenkhkare. Iset said that you wanted to see me. I wondered if we could play senet like we used to do."

I removed the senet board from a drawer and placed it on the table and indicated that she should sit and she did so. I sat opposite her and stared at her nervous face. "We will play senet while the death sentence hangs over my head. Excuse me if I do not play as well as usual."

Tears started to run down her pretty face. "I have been to see Akhenamun to plead with him to spare you. I have told him that you were under great strain and did not know what you were doing and that perhaps Coreb persuaded you towards insurrection."

"Is that what you think, Nebetah?"

"Yes, that is what I think. Akhenamun had nothing to do with the death of Thutmose or the snake in your bed chamber."

"I forgot, the snake entered from the garden and made its way through the palace," I said sarcastically.

"No, that was stupid of me, I realise that now. It is as mother said, a servant tried to kill you for an unknown reason."

I shook my head with disbelief. "My name was and still is on a death list and that list was compiled by Ay and will soon have the consent of Akhenamun."

"No, you are wrong brother. Ramose has told me that Ay had nothing to do with it."

"Your lover, Ramose," I said contemptuously.

"Ramose is a good man and he loves me," she whimpered.

"Ramose is the servant who placed the cobra in my room on the instructions of Ay."

Nebetah was shaking violently and stood up. "I must go," she said.

I gripped her arm and forced her to sit down. "You have forgotten our game of senet, sister."

"I cannot listen to your accusations."

"Ramose admitted it to me. He is using you, sister, as are Ay and Akhenamun."

"I do not believe it. Ramose loves me and I love him. Akhenamun has been kind to me and he will let me stay at Malkata with Ramose."

"It is true that Ramose put the cobra under my bed, and it is true that he does not love you and is using you. I know you did not mean to sister, but you have brought about the death of the loyal Coreb who loved Thutmose, and you have brought my death closer." She broke down in floods of tears with her whole body shaking and out of control. My words had been too cruel and I got up and took her in my arms. "Sister, I love you as did Thutmose, and I know you did not mean any harm to us. You were beguiled by an unscrupulous man and did not know what you were doing."

"It cannot be true," she sobbed.

"Beware of Ramose for he will only tell you more lies, and Ay is totally evil and unscrupulous. Work on Akhenamun for me. He is my brother and though he can be a violent man he does love you, sister. I have seen it with my own eyes. Persuade him to spare his brother and promise him that I will never try to take his throne again. He will listen to you, Nebetah. Do this for your little brother and for all the enjoyable times we have had together."

"I cannot play senet," she said.

"Neither can I," I replied sadly. "Will you do this for me?"

"I do not know what to think, I do not know what to believe." She was crying again.

I had to convince her for she might be my one hope of survival. In a week's time Akhenamun would be pharaoh and Ay would be pestering him with his persuasive tongue and my death warrant.

"When I asked Ramose if he loved you he shook his head arrogantly but said he enjoyed your body." I was being cruel again but I had to be. She began to sob violently again. She could not cope with her conflicting emotions.

"Did he really tell you that?" Her voice was barely audible.

"I would never lie to you, sister. I love you too much."

She brushed the fresh tears away from her tear-stained face. "I believe that you tell me what you believe to be true."

"In that case please do your best to persuade Akhenamun to spare me and not to listen to Ay. Be persistent on my behalf and Akhenamun may just listen to you. You could be my only hope, Nebetah." I kissed her on the forehead. "Let us have many games of senet in the future even if we cannot play today."

She smiled wanly. "I will do my best."

"May I ask one last thing, sister? Do not tell Ramose or Ay of our conversation for they will try to convince you to ignore my words."

"But I do love Ramose."

I sighed. "Please do not tell him but just speak to Akhenamun on my behalf."

She nodded. "I will only speak to Akhenamun."

"Thank you, my dearest sister." I hugged her and then watched as she left my apartment. It had been a very trying conversation for her and I realised just how fragile she was at the moment. I hoped she had the strength to do as I had asked. I felt more hopeful for I now had Nebetah working on Akhenamun and I had Taduheppa working on Nefertiti and if all else failed there was the possibility that my resourceful wife might come up with an escape plan. I did not have much faith in escaping but I still believed that there was a good chance that members of my family could save me from the clutches of the hated vizier.

****

The next day, true to her word, Turet returned to my apartment but she had little more to report though I told her of my conversation with Nebetah and the optimism I derived from it. For the next few days, apart from Turet who still had no further news, I had no other visitors. Neither Nebetah nor Iset came to see me again and I began to wonder if Nebetah was doing as I had pleaded. The tedium of my confinement was making me irritable with the servants and I took to spending most of my time alone on my balcony reflecting on how I had come to be in such dire straits.

Then with Akhenamun's investiture growing ever closer Turet at last visited me with something to report.

"Greetings, your majesty, I have some news for you," she smiled.

I indicated that she sit as usual to tell me. "Now, Turet, please go ahead."

"First I must report that your family are showing no interest in seeing you or coming to your aid. My mistress has spoken to all of them. Your mother, Sitamun and Iset seem to have washed their hands of you. Your mother and Sitamun have disowned you for plotting against your older brother but your mother has refused to authorise your execution. Nebetah seems to have once again fallen under the spell of Ramose and my mistress has despaired of getting help from your 'stupid sister' as she puts it."

I shook my head. "My poor sister is infatuated with the man."

145

Turet continued: "My mistress has spoken with Akhenamun and Nefertiti but although Nefertiti shows signs of being receptive to her pleas Akhenamun does not. She despises Akhenamun and finds it even difficult just to speak with him."

"This does not sound good," I commented.

"It is not all bad news; Murat has made contact with my mistress."

"He is still alive." I was relieved.

"He is on the run, but stays close to the palace. I have spoken with him down by the river and he is willing to give us what help he can."

"What help can he give?" I asked.

"He can help you escape and find somewhere in the poorer part of Thebes for you to hide."

"How can he do that?" I was getting interested at the prospect of a possible escape.

"My mistress believes that escape is your only option. You are not going to get help from your family and when Akhenamun is made pharaoh in a few days your fate will be sealed."

"How do I escape?" I asked.

"My mistress has a plan. In three days' time Akhenamun will be crowned at the great temple in Thebes even though he has made it clear that he has little time for the old gods. All of the family and most of the palace guard will, of course, attend the coronation as she will have to do."

"They will still have me well guarded," I commented. "I will not be able to overcome the guards that are left to look after me."

"You will not have to. I have made myself very friendly and very popular with the men who guard your apartment. I often flirt with them and make them promises and bring them refreshments. On the day of the coronation I will drug them."

"You can do that?" I gasped.

"We Mitanni women are good at many things," she smiled. "Once I have done this Murat will enter the palace with some recruits and free you. He will then take you to the hiding place in the city. You will remain there until your next move is decided upon."

"I will probably have to flee Egypt," I said sadly.

She nodded. "You may have to in order to be safe."

"Will Taduheppa come with me?"

146

"My mistress will not. A dangerous life on the run is not what she seeks. She will look after your interests in Malkata and she will see you next when you return to Malkata with a conquering army to reclaim her and Egypt."

"Will I not see her before the escape?"

"No, your majesty, for she is prevented from seeing you now, and on the day you escape she will have to be at the coronation," she replied. "She will see you when you return to Malkata."

I knew I would have to trust my wife even though I knew how ambitious she was. It seemed she was keeping her options open though hopefully her feelings were strong enough for me to want me to live and help me escape. "Then that is how it will be, Turet," I conceded reluctantly.

"I will continue to see you each day and keep you informed for the guards now expect to see me as I have set a routine. I gave them wine today but I will prepare a slightly different drink for them in three days' time." She smiled confidently as she looked to reassure me of success.

"Turet, I cannot thank you enough and I will not forget your help."

"I serve my mistress and we both wish to preserve your life. Of course, as I will see you each day I will keep you informed of any further developments. Your rescue will be put into effect at about midday in three days' time." She stood up to leave.

I took her arm. "Tell your mistress that I love her very much."

She smiled. "She knows that. Now I must go."

Once on my own I felt the excitement rush through my body and take my breath away. I would soon make a bid for freedom aided by my loyal servant, Murat. I did not know whether I would ever return to Thebes at the head of a conquering army, but I would make an attempt to be reunited with Taduheppa some day in the future.

Turet returned each day but she had nothing to really add to what she had already told me. The plan was in place and I was told that Murat had his recruits and had found a suitable hiding place. It simply remained for me to wait for the day of my escape.

I woke up early on the morning of the coronation and watched the early departure of the royal family from Malkata, flanked by many of the palace guard. They did not give me a glance, as I stood on my balcony, for it seemed that I was now considered unworthy of any sort of recognition. The exceptions were Taduheppa who gave me a smile and Nebetah who looked at me sadly. I smiled at them both and watched as they exited through the palace gates. I was now just hours away from my planned escape.

Chapter 13

The hours passed slowly. I was brought food and drink by my few remaining servants and I spent much time on the balcony overlooking the gardens. I saw some activity at the gate leading from the royal gardens but the grove of fig trees obscured a clear view. At last with the sun high in the midday sky my door burst open and I felt a pang of fear. Murat and Turet entered my room and I felt a sense of overwhelming relief for I had feared for a second that I might be about to succumb to an assassin's knife.

"It is good to see you both." I grasped their hands.

"We must not delay," said Murat. He offered me an inferior robe with a torn hood. "For your journey into the city, Smenkhkare," he smiled.

"What of the guards?" I asked.

"Turet has made sure that neither the guards outside your room nor those that were stationed at the gate will hinder our progress."

I turned to Turet. "You are a wonder."

"Good luck, your majesty. I will see you when you return to the palace," she said with a smile.

"Are you not coming with us? You cannot stay here for they will soon work out who drugged the guards."

She smiled. "I will take my chances here with my mistress. They will not harm a Mitanni princess and she will place me under her protection. We will come to no harm."

I was far from sure that she was right. "Do not take that chance Turet. They will not harm your mistress but I am not so sure that they will not harm you."

"My place is with my mistress. Now you must go for Murat is getting impatient."

"She is right. We must leave for we have a journey to undertake and the sooner it is achieved the safer we will be," urged Murat.

I nodded and followed him out of my apartment. I saw the sleeping guards outside my rooms and marvelled at the work of Turet. I watched as she hurried down the corridor towards Taduheppa's apartment and then I followed Murat out of the palace. We emerged into the sunlit gardens and we were joined by several men that I did not recognise. "These are my recruits in case we encountered any opposition," Murat explained. "However, your entire family are at the temple for the ceremony."

We made our way through the exotic gardens towards the gate and my heart was beating fast. Some gardeners looked up and watched as we approached the fig trees but they did not attempt to stop us for it was not their business. When we reached the gate I saw more sleeping guards. "What an amazing job Turet has done," I commented.

"The Mitanni people are very resourceful and she is one of the most resourceful of them," Murat replied.

We passed through the gate and approached the great river. I could not believe we had managed to escape from Malkata without any incident. Horses were waiting for us and once again I was impressed how meticulous Murat and Turet had been with their planning. However, I knew that many dangers still lay ahead before we were safe. Once again I was heading south alongside the mighty river and we quickly reached the spot where I had walked to a week earlier and where I had waited to be joined by the army of Coreb. We were now about half way to the newer and wealthy part of Thebes on the west bank of the river.

The great city of Thebes, the capital of mighty Egypt, was a further short journey to the south where it had spilled on to both banks of the river Nile. It seemed we were bound for the newer part of Thebes.

Murat must have read my thoughts. "New Thebes will not be safe, so we must cross the river to old Thebes."

I nodded agreement for I accepted his judgement.

"I have a secure hiding place in old Thebes," he reassured me.

"You have done well, Murat." I praised his endeavours on my behalf.

We continued our progress into the heart of new Thebes. We continued along the same route as we had taken on the night we followed Akhenamun and Metos on their clandestine excursion. I knew that this part of Thebes could be travelled through in comparative safety but once we crossed the river it was another matter. I remembered the incompetent thief who had tried to stab and rob me.

Once again we made our way past the large villas of the wealthy and I remembered that this part of the city was home to nobles, priests and merchants. Last time I had passed through it had been at night and very dark but now I could appreciate the wide streets and exotic gardens in the afternoon sun. At last we reached the pier shaded by sycamore trees and there was a boat waiting for us.

"You have thought of everything, Murat," I commented.

"I organised this side of the operation but your wife organised the palace side and financed the whole thing."

"You are right, Murat. Mitanni women are very resourceful. She has fooled Ay and that takes some doing."

"We are not safe yet," he warned. "Let us board the boat quickly for I will feel happier and safer once we are on the other side of the river."

We clambered aboard the boat and I sat next to Murat while his recruits rowed the boat across the Nile. I watched in awe as crocodiles swam alongside the boat. They were vicious creatures but not as vicious as some humans.

We crossed without incident for we looked like hard-up travellers returning to our home in the slums of the western part of the city. When we reached the pier on the east bank Murat jumped from the boat and helped me ashore. He then turned to his recruits. "You may go," he said and handed them each a fistful of coins.

"Taduheppa's money," he said to me smiling.

"Do we no longer need them?" I asked.

"It is better that they do not see our final destination for then they cannot be bribed or persuaded to divulge the information. We only needed them in case we encountered some opposition at the palace. As it happens they have made some easy money."

I nodded as I watched them disappear from sight. I looked back at the great river; the river which supplied the bountiful harvests which made Egypt so prosperous. Boats of all sizes plied back and forth in large numbers seeming to emphasise the greatness of Egypt. I could not help wondering if I would one day rule this great empire.

"Pull up your hood, Smenkhkare," advised Murat snapping me out of my reverie. "Be wary in the city for though it does not pose the dangers during the day that it did when we travelled the streets, at night we must still be vigilant." He too remembered the thief who had attacked us. "These old robes will help to protect us for we are obviously not worth robbing."

We now headed swiftly towards the old and poorest part of the city passing through the labyrinth of alleys and narrow streets. The city was a mass of people going about their business. "Pickpockets abound," warned Murat as we passed close to the great market. The stalls were a scene of great activity as people dashed to and fro like angry bees buzzing around a precious hive. I marvelled at the huge number of traders and artisans and the hovels in which they worked. This was all such a far cry from the great palace at Malkata.

"We are now in the most notorious part of the city and not far from our hiding place," smiled Murat.

"We may be safe from Ay here, but are we safe from danger?" I mused.

"As safe as we can be," he replied. We arrived at a metal works situated a short distance from the market. "I have hired rooms behind the metal works. It may smell a little when they are working but the rooms can hardly be seen and are an excellent place to lie low until the hunt for you dies down, and it will give us time to think about our next move."

"Can the man you hired them from be trusted?" I inquired warily.

"In this part of Thebes they take the money, mind their own business and don't ask questions," he replied. "The owner of the rooms, who is known to me personally, runs the metal works and is trustworthy. Wait here while I tell him we have arrived for I do not wish him to even see you."

I nodded agreement and I looked around at the neighbouring buildings and alleys. This was a heavily populated and poverty-stricken district with many unfortunates begging for bread or coins. Fortunately, in my poor robes I blended in quite nicely. Murat was only gone for a few minutes and he returned looking pleased. "Everything is good; you have your own room and you will be looked after by the metal worker's daughter. She will be your only contact. Do you have money to pay her for her father is a poor man?"

"I brought funds with me," I replied.

"Good, then between us we have ample money for your wife was most generous but I may need these finances to fund our future plans."

"Why are you doing this for me, Murat?" I asked.

"I have been your servant since you were a small boy. That is my position and you and your brother, Thutmose, if I may say so, were always the most worthy of your family."

"Thank you, Murat," I smiled.

"Now I must show you your new accommodation." I followed him to the rooms at the rear of the metal works. He pushed a door open and entered and I followed him in.

"It is not quite Malkata," he said.

He was right. It was small and dark and dingy but I could see that efforts had been made to clean it up and make it more comfortable. "It is fine," I replied. I walked over to the bed and sat on it. It was not as hard as I imagined it might be.

"It will not be for too long," he assured me. "My room is next door but I will not be there much of the time for I will be trying to find out what is happening in Malkata, and I will continue to keep in contact with Turet. I will also be making plans for the future as we cannot remain here for long because you will be the subject of a man-hunt. I will probably have to try to secure our departure from Egypt."

"Where would we go?" I asked.

"Perhaps to Kush," he replied. "I have not had time to look that far ahead. The first thing was to get you out of immediate danger. I will leave you now to get used to your new abode. The metal worker's daughter will bring you dinner. It is best if you do not leave the room for there are dangers in the streets particularly at night." He then left me to my own devices and I rested on my bed in my new but temporary home. I felt safer but still vulnerable.

A few hours later there was a knock on my door and I opened it tentatively. I looked out at a young woman with a tray of food. I opened the door wide and beckoned her inside. She placed the tray containing bread, cheese and fruit with a flagon of beer on my small table. "I am Lia," she said smiling nervously.

"Do you know who I am?" I asked.

She nodded. "You are the brother of the pharaoh."

Her words reminded me that Akhenamun must now be pharaoh. "So you realise the dangers of providing me with refuge."

She nodded again. "Murat explained it to me and my father."

"And you were still willing to hide me?" I said.

"Murat pays us well and is our friend," she replied.

"I am grateful to you and your father."

She smiled. "I am in the room next door so if there is anything you need just knock and ask."

"I thought that was Murat's room."

She looked slightly embarrassed. "It is our room."

"I see. Murat never told me."

"He works at the palace most of the time but he sees me when he can."

"I hope he has not been followed on these visits." The sudden prospect of my servant being followed was worrying to say the least.

"He has not been followed for he has been most careful. It would be impossible to follow Murat in the Theban ghetto for he knows the area so well and takes all precautions."

"That is good to hear, Lia. If you need any further money then let me know."

"I will do that, your majesty."

"I am hardly 'your majesty'," I laughed, looking around me. "I am most grateful for the accommodation but it is not a palace, so please address me by my name which is Smenkhkare."

She grinned. "I will do that willingly, Smenkhkare, but now I have to help father at the forge."

I watched as she left my room and then my eyes fell on the food. I had not eaten a meal since I left Malkata and I realised just how famished I was. I devoured the food with relish even though it was not as grand a meal as I was used to.

****

The days passed slowly and tediously and turned into weeks. I had now been a fugitive for two weeks. I stayed most of the time in my room and only stepped out occasionally for fresh air though I never strayed far from my mediocre accommodation. The only person I saw regularly or spoke to was Lia who had little information to tell me about events at Malkata. I rarely saw her father who kept to himself and seemed to spend all his waking hours toiling at the metal works. I did see Murat a few times during my first week and he informed me that Akhenamun was now pharaoh and all had gone well at his coronation until they had returned and found that I had escaped. An extensive man-hunt was under way but it seemed I had vanished into thin air. His words were reassuring

154

for I lived in fear of the palace guards suddenly turning up at my hiding place to put me under arrest.

However, Murat had not returned at all during the second week of my concealment and the doubts that he had allayed returned even stronger with his non-appearance. I could tell from her worried demeanour that Lia was equally concerned. She became less and less inclined to converse with me and I was sure that it was not only the disappearance of Murat but also my presence in her home that was concerning her. I knew that next time she delivered my food I would have to speak with her on the subject. She brought me my evening meal as usual and turned to leave without conversation. I stood at the door and barred her exit. "We must speak, Lia."

She sighed and nodded. "I know."

"Sit down," I invited.

She obeyed with an air of resignation. "Yes, Smenkhkare," she said.

"It is now eight days since Murat returned. It is not like him and I fear that something may have happened to him. What do you think, Lia?"

She sighed again. "I am very worried. I have been speaking with my father and we are now very concerned about him and about the fact that we continue to harbour a rival to the pharaoh."

"Were you going to ask me to leave?"

"We were considering it for I fear that your presence places us all in danger."

"Do you think that Murat has been captured?"

The tears rolled down her cheeks. "I fear it," she admitted. "We are very close and he would not stay away for as long as this without getting word to me." She was most distressed.

"You love him, don't you, Lia?"

"Yes, Smenkhkare, I do. I cannot bear to think of him in the hands of his enemies." I realised that if Murat had fallen into Ay's hands then we were in extreme danger. Lia read my mind. "He would never talk. He would never betray you."

"I know, Lia," I said, but I also knew that Ay and his minions were expert at extracting the truth.

She sobbed and I knew that she knew it too. "You must leave. I know a boatman who will take you down the Nile away from Thebes but that is all I can do for you now. If you can give me some money I will arrange it

155

tomorrow and then if Murat does not return within two days you must go. We cannot wait any longer than that."

I nodded agreement and handed her some coins. "That should be enough. Tell the boatman I will leave as soon as possible. I cannot continue to place you and your father in danger any longer for I fear the net is closing in on me. I am sorry, Lia, for I know that you love Murat and I hope that he returns to you safely, but I must be on my way."

She wiped away the tears. "Night is falling but I shall arrange it first thing in the morning. I pray you will be safe until then."

She departed leaving me deep in thought. If Murat had been captured by Ay then he would not easily talk, of that I was sure, and that would buy me time. I could not bear to think of my faithful servant being tortured in order to divulge my whereabouts. I also wondered if Lia and her father would be safe even after I had left. I shuddered for these possibilities were not things I wished to think about. I knew that Lia would leave at daylight and probably return with news by midday. I would have to be patient once again until she returned. I did not sleep easy that night for life on the run was a hard and dangerous life and one that I had never envisaged.

The next morning I gathered my few belongings together and waited for Lia to return. I had been right, for she returned just after midday with news that a boat would take me down river that very afternoon.

"I have hired a boat, Smenkhkare," she informed me. "He is ready to leave and so we must go to the pier right away. I have paid him well and so there is no need for you to offer him any further money."

"Did you have enough money?" I asked knowing that she and her father were poor and underprivileged.

"Murat also gave me funds to look after for he did not wish to carry it with him." She offered me a pouch containing a large number of coins.

"I do have some money but I will keep some of this for I do not know what lies ahead for me." I took about half of the coins from the pouch and handed them back to her. I thought she was going to refuse to take them but in the end she accepted them. "Thank you, Smenkhkare," she said gratefully. "Now we must go."

I nodded. "Thank you, Lia, for helping me despite the dangers you place yourself in."

We left the metal works and hurried through the poverty-stricken area of old Thebes towards the river. The unpleasant smells of waste and refuse and the pleasant fragrance of food and herbs invaded my senses like a cocktail of everything that was good and bad in the old city. We did not go to the pier that I had been to with Murat but one a little further downstream which was not so large and less frequented. "Does the boatman know who I am?" I asked as we approached a small felucca.

"No, he has been paid well and does not ask questions."

"Where am I going?" I asked remembering rather foolishly that in the rush to leave I had not asked.

"He is taking you to Edfu. It is far enough from Thebes for you to feel safer but you will still have to be very vigilant."

We had arrived at the boat and I kissed Lia on both cheeks. "I will not forget what you have done. I will pray to the gods that Murat is safe. However, Lia, you and your father must remain alert and be ready to also leave in a hurry for Ay has spies everywhere. You have funds to start up again if necessary."

"I will be brought news if soldiers are entering our part of Thebes for it would be a rare event. We will be safe and now you must go. Farewell, your majesty," she whispered out of hearing of the boatman.

I climbed aboard the small vessel and the wizened, suntanned man nodded to me and I nodded back. No words were spoken for this was strictly a business venture. We gradually pulled away from the shaky pier and moved slowly towards the centre of the great river. We were now just one of many vessels heading back and forth under the late afternoon sun. It was a long trip to Edfu and I knew that we would not arrive until the next morning. However, we were still too near to Thebes and Malkata for me to feel comfortable. I relaxed in the boat as the boatman took the helm. So much had happened in the last month that I could hardly believe the situation I found myself in.

The small craft continued the journey to a destination I had never visited before. I would have to explore the town and find discreet lodgings when I arrived until I could make more definite plans on what to do next. After several hours the sun began to set and darkness fell rapidly over the great river. The boatman lit a lamp and I noticed that other boats on the river were doing the same. He spoke at last. "There is nothing to fear on the river at night for I have done the journey many times during the hours of darkness."

"I do not doubt your skill," I answered and drew some threadbare blankets around me for the temperature was falling rapidly. I closed my eyes and tried to sleep.

The next morning we pulled into the docks at Edfu. It was mid-morning and the temperature was already exceedingly high. It seemed that the further south you travelled down the great river then the hotter it became. I took off my robe in the heat and revealed my tunic. It was the worst tunic I had been able to find in my wardrobe at Malkata but it still gave me the appearance of a fairly affluent citizen. I would have to buy some less eye-catching clothes when I arrived at Edfu.

On arrival at the pier at Edfu I stepped off the boat and thanked the boatman. I put my robe back on despite the heat for I did not want to draw attention to myself as I walked into town. The pier at Edfu was fairly crowded but the activity did not compare with the bustle at Thebes. I looked around in wonder for I had never before left Thebes and its environs.

I began the short walk into the centre of town, staring about me at this strange city. Edfu was the old capital of Upper Egypt and an ancient place. As I approached the outskirts of the town I passed by a huge granary which was situated next to a temple to the god Horus, where there was also a large cemetery. I felt people were looking at me though I might have imagined it, so I pulled my hood further over my head, seeking obscurity. I passed a number of tenement buildings until I came to the town market. It was not as big as the one in Thebes but it was large enough and seemed to sell every possible item for use in everyday life and most particularly food and clothes. I decided my first priority was to find lodgings and then head back to the market for supplies. My situation was daunting for it was the first time in my young life that I had ever felt truly alone.

A short distance from the heaving market, down a side alley, I found what I was looking for. I extracted a coin from my pouch and looked at the premises which seemed neither too impoverished nor too affluent. A young boy outside assured me that there were excellent, vacant rooms within. I knocked at the door of the two-storied building and waited for a response. After just a few seconds the door was opened by a sturdily built man with a scarred left cheek. His politeness belied his appearance. "Can I help you?" he inquired.

"I am seeking a room," I blurted out.

"We have two rooms on the upper floor. You can even choose which one you want if you have sufficient funds to pay the rent."

"I do and I would probably only wish to stay for a couple of weeks at most." I knew that Edfu was too close to Thebes for me to feel entirely safe and I would soon have to move on. I probably needed to leave Upper Egypt which meant pushing on to Kush or Nubia. It was a prospect that did not appeal to me but I knew it would soon have to be faced. Two weeks would give me time to consider and make plans.

He nodded his large head. "Follow me and take a look."

I followed him up the rickety staircase on to the second floor landing. He opened two of the four doors and I looked inside at the two rooms on offer. I chose the slightly larger of the two rooms but in truth there was little difference between them. "This one will be fine," I said.

"I need one week in advance and then if you stay two weeks then I will also need the second week in advance."

I handed him the necessary coinage and he nodded appreciably. "You look like a fine young man but I must inform you that I will not put up with any trouble. I am discreet and I expect you to be discreet. I ask no questions and you ask no questions."

"I understand," I replied.

"You have a bed and furniture. Everything else you need you get yourself. Make yourself at home but remember you have neighbours and the walls are thin. So no noise and no trouble and we will get on fine."

"You will find that I will give you no cause for worry," I assured him.

He grinned and slapped me gently on the back. "Excellent, I am sure you will make an ideal tenant and so I will leave you to settle in."

I could not believe how simple it had been to obtain lodgings. I placed my few belongings under the bed and decided to go to the market to buy some clothes and some food.

Once again I went out into the bustling city of Edfu with my robe on and with my hood up. I did not spend long at the market and quickly returned with what I needed.

Now I could at last relax, though I still did not feel completely safe. I lay on the bed and made the decision that I would stay no longer than one week in Edfu but I was not sure of my next destination.

Chapter 14

That evening I lay in bed going over the options in my mind and I could only think of one viable proposition. I decided that Kush was out of the question as I knew that Egyptian relations with Kush had been strained of late, bringing the two nations close to war. The proposed marriage of my sister, Nebetah, to the king of Kush was obviously aimed at decreasing tensions but that seemed to have failed with Nebetah remaining in Malkata. It would therefore be dangerous and perhaps foolish to throw myself on the mercy of the king.

The viable proposition was further to the south in Nubia or Wawat as it was sometimes called, and the more I thought about this option the more I liked the idea. To us Egyptians, Kush and Wawat were all part of the vast area known as Nubia but in recent times it had become two kingdoms with Kush in the north and Wawat in the south. Egypt was on very friendly terms with the southern kingdom due partly to the marriage of my sister, Henuttaneb to the Nubian king. The only problem was that to get to Wawat I would have to pass through Kush.

I had not seen Henuttaneb for over two years and my sister was nearly four years my senior. She had always been most friendly with Iset who was close to her in age and she had had little time for her retiring small brother. I knew that messages passed frequently between Iset and Henuttaneb and so she might well be aware of all that had happened recently in Malkata. She was my sister and I would hope she could be relied upon to persuade her husband to give me refuge in their capital, Napata. Napata was a very long way from Thebes and therefore well out of the reach or influence of Ay. I was still the pharaoh's brother and could hope for a hospitable reception.

The fact that Napata was such a vast distance from Thebes down the great river was a problem particularly because the long journey would entail travelling through Kush. I was aware that camel trains with large numbers of traders made the journey regularly all the way from Thebes to Napata and on the way passed through Edfu. I would have to find out when the next camel train was due and try to join it. It would probably be months before I reached Napata and sought out my sister but once there I hoped I would be safe and I could start to make plans for the future.

I found out by asking around at the market the next day that the next train was due in Edfu in nine days' time. It would then be a question of seeking to join the train when it arrived and buying what was needed for the long journey down the Nile and across the desert. I informed my landlord that I intended to stay in my lodgings for about another ten days and I gave him the extra money he required. I was told that the traders seldom lingered in Edfu for more than a day or two before continuing the journey south. It was now just a question of being patient and waiting for the camel train to arrive. The long journey brought with it a feeling of great excitement for I was about to see more of this vast and mysterious world.

My excitement was brought to an abrupt halt just two days before the camel train was due to arrive. There was a knock on my door as I was eating and I got up to see who it was. I nervously opened the door and saw my landlord staring at me, looking equally nervous. The big man seemed agitated but subdued. "There are people to see you," he croaked and stood aside.

A small, middle-aged man dressed in fine clothes entered my room closely followed by four armed guards. He looked me up and down. "Who are you?" he asked in an authoritative voice.

"My name is Metos," I replied, giving the first name that came into my head.

"I have information that you might go by another name," he said. He turned to one of the guards. "Fetch the witness." He then turned back to me. "I am Tolu, the governor of Edfu."

"And who do you think I am?" I asked warily.

"The pharaoh's young brother is on the run after plotting treason. He is about your age."

I felt fear lodge in my brain and course through my body. How had he found me? I thought about rushing out of the tenement in a bold bid for freedom but I knew it was hopeless. The armed guards barred my exit. "What has this to do with me?" I asked shakily.

"We will soon find out," he said.

"I have done nothing wrong and I must insist you leave." I tried to sound bold.

"If that is true we will not keep you. Here he is. I found this man who is from Thebes. He said he would recognise the young royal, Smenkhkare, the man we seek." The guard had brought a young man not much older than me into the room. I stared at him and though I did not know who he was I feared that I saw recognition in his eyes.

"I have never seen this man before," I blurted out.

"But I have seen you in the gardens at Malkata when I made a delivery," he said. "You are Smenkhkare."

"Are you sure?" asked the governor.

"I have definitely seen him in the Malkata gardens," he confirmed. "I have a good memory for faces."

Then the governor turned to me. "It seems you are probably the pharaoh's young brother and so you are under arrest."

"This is nonsense," I said. "Do I look like the pharaoh's young brother?"

"Smenkhkare would not wish to look like Smenkhkare," he smiled. "Now you will come with me. Guards take him."

Two guards closed in on me and took an arm each. "You have made a mistake," I pleaded and protested my innocence.

"If you are telling the truth I will soon know. I will find more men who will hopefully recognise you before I send you back to Thebes. It would not be wise to send Ay the wrong man, though I am quite sure that we have the right one."

Ay, I thought to myself. It was always Ay. My hatred for Ay welled up as they escorted me from my room.

I was led through the town like a common criminal, flanked on either side by the two guards who did not lessen their grip on my arms. We soon arrived at an impressive building that proved to be the governor's residence. The building was large and stood out against the nearby smaller tenement buildings. I was led through the entrance into an impressive hall.

"This is where I conduct local law cases," the governor explained in a surprisingly friendly fashion. He then led me into an office off the main hall. "Take a seat, Smenkhkare," he offered.

I sat down. "Why are you calling me Smenkhkare?" I asked.

"Because that is your name, as my name is Tolu, and I am governor of Edfu so please do not insult my intelligence."

I shrugged. "What do you want from me?"

"You could start by admitting who you are. We both know that you are the pharaoh's brother Smenkhkare."

I could see no point in denying it any longer for he obviously knew who I was. "I am Smenkhkare."

"I have nothing against you personally, Smenkhkare, but as you have probably found out it is best not to antagonise Ay."

"Ay is pure evil," I said.

"That may be the case, but he holds power in the land and cannot be ignored. I received a communication from him some days ago to stay alert for the young pretender to the throne who may turn up in Edfu, and lo and behold you did."

"How did he know?" I gasped.

"He seems to know everything. Your mistake, Smenkhkare, was taking off your robe when you disembarked from the felucca. You were seen, though it took us a little time to find you."

"It was hot," I said simply with an air of resignation.

He smiled. "And you have been burned."

"What will you do with me, Tolu?"

"I will return you to Thebes and Malkata tomorrow. I do not wish to have you in Edfu any longer than I have to. You will soon be back in Ay's custody."

I sighed. "He will have me murdered."

"Why did you try to overthrow your brother?"

"I did so to survive. I was seen as a threat to the throne," I replied.

"You must have done something to be seen as a threat," he offered.

"I was there when Thutmose was murdered by Ay. I knew that Ay had had my brother murdered in order to secure the throne for the more pliable Akhenamun. What I knew and my hatred made me a threat. The only way to survive was to secure the crown for myself before Ay also had me murdered."

"I see," said Tolu. "I do not know whether it is true or not but, if it is, I see."

"It is true," I assured him.

"Even if it is, I cannot let that influence what I do. Ay wants you back at Malkata and I serve Ay and owe my position to him. I cannot go against him, Smenkhkare."

"Nobody dares go against Ay," I shrugged. "It seems that evil conquers all, even the son of a pharaoh."

"You are under house arrest. You will have a good meal and a comfortable last night in Edfu. I am afraid that is all that I can offer you, just good hospitality for one night. You will be well guarded so please do not do anything stupid. I really do not wish to harm you, Smenkhkare."

"In sending me back to Ay you are harming me."

He shrugged. "As governor of Edfu it is what I have to do."

****

I was taken by the guards to a room on the upper floor. Tolu was true to his word and the room was most comfortable, certainly far preferable to my previous accommodation in Edfu. I was also served with an excellent meal and a supply of wine. My treatment, however, did not alter the fact that I was a prisoner for I was well aware that guards had been placed outside my door. When I looked out of my small window there were also guards on duty in the courtyard below. Tolu certainly did not mean me to escape.

My bed was comfortable and my appetite was satisfied. I could now only contemplate another journey up the Nile back to Thebes and almost certain death. Did I have any allies left at all? I was back to thinking that my only hope was my family once again and that was a very slim chance indeed. How I managed to sleep I do not know but I did.

I was served an early breakfast and then I was escorted from the governor's residence and back to the great river where a large vessel was waiting for me. My guards accompanied me on board and it was obvious that they were going to escort me all the way back to Malkata and hand me over to Ay and the palace guard. They watched me very carefully all the time and gave me no chance of possible escape. When the boat had drawn away from the pier and moved towards the middle of the river I thought about jumping overboard. It was a silly idea. I was not a strong swimmer and the river was full of crocodiles. Perhaps a crocodile would be preferable to Ay, I contemplated, but failed to convince myself. I accepted there was no escape and with that conviction I was able to relax. It would be nightfall by the time we reached Malkata and with the advent of darkness perhaps an opportunity for escape would be presented to me. Once again I failed to convince myself.

It was close to midnight as I was marched through the exotic gardens of Malkata. I felt a sense of doom overwhelming me though I was excited at the prospect of seeing Taduheppa once again. A messenger had been sent on ahead to warn Ay that we would soon be at the palace. No escape opportunity had offered itself to me and I was still flanked by Tolu's vigilant guard. The moon shone brightly down and illuminated the beautiful gardens of which I was so fond, but I was far from happy to have returned.

Ay, Ramose and the palace guard were at the palace entrance to welcome us. Ay was smiling that mirthless smile as we approached, and I felt revulsion. The Edfu guard handed me over to Ay, their task successfully completed. "Welcome home, Smenkhkare, it is good to see you again," he said.

"It is not good to see you, Ay," I replied

"The hour is very late and so I will speak with you properly in the morning. Follow me," Ay retorted giving me a look of contempt. I was led to my own apartment and pushed inside. "I have bad news for you, Smenkhkare, but it can wait until the morning. Sleep well, though I doubt that you will."

"The guard will be at your door," Ramose added. "Escape is impossible."

"I demand to see my mother and Akhenamun," I replied.

"You can demand all you want," Ay replied and closed my door behind him leaving me alone in my apartment.

I waited a few minutes and pushed the door open gently. There were several guards posted outside and it seemed Ramose was right and escape was impossible. Ay was also right for I did not sleep well as my fears invaded my mind for I knew that my execution was probably imminent.

Early the next morning Ay and Ramose returned. They sat down uninvited and looked me up and down. "You really are a foolish boy," Ay observed. "Did you seriously believe that I would not find you? You have caused me considerable trouble, but in a way you have played into my hands and the feelings of your family have hardened against you. Akhenamun has agreed to authorise your execution and so your short time in the world is close to termination. However, I have some other news for you."

I scowled at my tormentor. "You will pay for your crimes, Ay, if not in this world then the next."

"In just over a week your sister, Nebetah, will marry my son, Ramose, and I am going to allow you to attend before you are executed."

"Your son, Ramose," I gasped.

"My wife only gave me a daughter, Nefertiti, before she then died in childbirth. It is such a long time ago now. However, I had an illegitimate son with a woman from the harem and that son is Ramose."

"You kept this hidden all this time," I said.

"Your father would not have approved, and my position was not as secure as it is now. Your father was religious and believed in the sanctity of the family. I gave Ramose a prominent position in my household and he has proved a great asset to me. While you were on the run I acknowledged him as my true son and your family have accepted it."

"Is that how you see him as an asset," I asked.

"On the contrary, he is much more than an asset. Ramose and Nefertiti are the only two people in this world I love. I have total power and two wonderful children. What more could a man want?" he grinned at me.

"A life," I said.

"You have forfeited that," said Ramose. "You will die after I marry Nebetah, and I shall watch you die."

"My poor sister, to have to marry such a vile individual as you," I said with feeling.

Ramose went to strike me but Ay pulled him back. "It will be a great torment for him to witness your marriage to his dear and stupid little sister, and so there is no need for violence, Ramose."

I flinched at the intended attack and then thought about retaliating by attacking Ramose or Ay. I thought better of it for the armed guards were at their side. "She is not so stupid that she will not see you for what you are," I said to Ramose.

"That is not the only news I have for you, Smenkhkare," said Ay. "There will be a second marriage, but unfortunately you will not be able to attend this one for I need you dead to make it happen."

I gasped with horror as realisation at what his words meant filtered into my beleaguered brain.

He continued. "Very soon after your execution I will marry Taduheppa. She will be a good match for me as Nebetah will be for my

167

son." He smiled with satisfaction. "I have always admired her spirit and her great beauty."

"She will never marry you, Ay," I sneered.

"She has already consented to do so. She is a pragmatist and she is ambitious. She knows that I am the power in the land."

"You are an old man," I said with disgust.

"Not so old that I cannot enjoy the body of a beautiful young woman." He laughed at my distress.

I was stunned. Could Taduheppa really have consented to this travesty of a marriage? She was a Mitanni princess and of too high a rank for a mere vizier.

"I am a member of your family," Ay reminded me as if reading my mind.

"A distant one," I reminded him.

He shrugged. "It is all settled. First Ramose will be married, then you will die and then I will be married. There is much to look forward to in Malkata. You will remain in your apartment under arrest until Ramose is married in ten days' time. It will be as before; your servants will attend to your needs with the exception of Murat and Turet. You will be well guarded and you will not be allowed any visitors."

"Where are Murat and Turet?" I demanded.

He ignored my question. "I will return later today for I have not finished with you yet." They turned and exited my apartment.

I was left to mull over his words and wallow in my immense sorrow. Worst of all for my tormented mind was the knowledge that Ay would soon marry my wife Taduheppa. I could not bear to think of that terrible prospect.

A few hours later Ay returned once again flanked by the usual guards. "It is a hot day outside," he observed.

"I demand to see my family," I said. "You cannot stop me seeing them."

"I think you will find I can. Now here is Ramose."

Ramose entered clutching a wicker basket. I stared at the basket in absolute horror, remembering the contents of the previous two. Ramose placed the basket on the floor and gave me an inviting look. Ay was grinning and appeared expectant. I did not wait for any words; I strode over to the basket and threw the lid at Ramose who ducked and grinned even wider. Once again and almost in a trance I removed the blood-stained cloth that covered the contents. This time it was the pale, lifeless face of Murat staring up at me. I retched and convulsions passed through my body as I felt as if I was going to choke. First it had been Coreb and now it was Murat.

"This is what happens to traitors," Ay warned me.

"Then it will happen to you," I replied coldly and full of hate.

"I rather doubt that," he replied.

"I will kill you," I said.

"I doubt that too. You may wish to, but you never will. In fact I have a third basket reserved for your head and then I will have a set. Your execution is imminent and will take place the day after my son's marriage."

I scowled. "My family will save me." Unfortunately these words sounded hollow because I did not really believe them myself.

Ay shook his head. "They will not."

"Send my wife to me. I wish to see her," I demanded.

"My wife-to-be," he smiled. "I have told you that you will have no visitors."

"Not even my mother," I sighed.

"No, you will not see your mother and you will not see me for a few days, but you will continue to be well guarded. Do not try to speak with anyone from your balcony. There will be guards posted in the gardens as well as outside your door. I will return just before the marriage of Ramose and Nebetah. I want you to witness it, but you will be well guarded at the ceremony and you will not be allowed to speak with anyone there.

"I wish to see my brother, Akhenamun. He is pharaoh and so you cannot stop me seeing him."

"Akhenamun is not in Thebes. He has gone north to find a site for his new capital. He intends to call it Amarna."

"A new capital?" I gasped in disbelief.

"He wants a break with the past and a new capital will provide that. You must know he does not believe in the old gods and wishes to make Aten the one, new supreme god. A vast new temple will be built to Aten in Amarna."

"He cannot unravel hundreds of years of Egyptian history," I offered.

"He is pharaoh and so he can, and I will support him for it will make my position even stronger and it will make him even more dependent on me. This need not concern you, Smenkhkare, for you will never see it happen."

I watched Ramose replace the lid on the basket and pick it up. I stared, once again in shock at the basket. "How did Murat die?" I asked.

"He died because he helped you. He died when I plunged my sword into his body," Ramose boasted.

I looked at Ramose open-mouthed. My dear sister, Nebetah, was soon to marry this creature.

"Now we must go," Ay said. "The servants who will attend you are all in my pay so do not bother to try to persuade them to come to your aid. They fear me far too much to listen to your words or bribes. You will see nobody else but them until I return. Ay swept up his robe and exited my apartment followed closely by his obnoxious son, Ramose.

I collapsed on my bed. Murat, like Coreb, had paid the ultimate price for supporting me. I was wracked with grief and guilt. I thought of poor Lia, the daughter of the metal-worker who had loved Murat. I hated Ay and Ramose with all my being, but I was helpless and could do nothing. Soon I would be dead like my dear friends and it was probable that there would be no tomb for me in the valley of the dead and no afterlife for me. At least Thutmose was allowed that rite of passage.

****

It was now a question of waiting for Ay to return which would then signal how close my execution would be. I had not even asked him how I was to die. One death would be as good as another as long as it was relatively painless. I fervently hoped I would not have to suffer too much pain.

The days passed until I calculated it was three days before the coming marriage, and then early in the morning I surprisingly had some unexpected but welcome visitors. The new chief royal wife, Nefertiti, accompanied by my Mitanni wife, Taduheppa, entered my rooms and I looked at them with astonishment and with pleasure.

"It is so good to see you again," I gasped as I looked at my beautiful wife. I had almost forgotten just how good she looked.

She smiled at my obvious pleasure. "We are leaving," she said.

I stared at her in astonishment. "How can we be leaving?"

170

Nefertiti answered my question. "I have arranged for transport for you to go to the Mitanni capital, Washukanni. You must leave immediately for my father and Ramose return tomorrow and then it could be a little awkward." I stared in equal astonishment at Ay's beautiful daughter. Was I dreaming this or had two goddesses come to rescue me? "Gather all that you need for the journey and do it quickly," Nefertiti commanded. She had already acquired the demeanour of a queen.

"But the guards will stop us," I offered.

"They will obey me. I am Nefertiti, Queen of Egypt. In the absence of my husband, who is at the new proposed capital, Amarna, I am in charge at Malkata. You will be allowed to leave." Taduheppa nodded agreement with her friend's words.

"What of Ay?" I said.

"He is at Amarna with Akhenamun."

"When he returns he will send the guard or the army after me and I will not get far," I put to her.

"He will not do that, for my husband is the pharaoh and he will order Ay not to pursue you. Your journey to Washukanni will be unhindered."

"He will not take any notice of my brother." I was sure in my conviction.

"My husband will make sure he does and I will be at Akhenamun's side supporting him. We both know that Ay's power must be curbed if Akhenamun is to rule Egypt as pharaoh. This is just the beginning."

Her words brought me joy but I was still unconvinced. "I wish you luck, but why would Akhenamun help me to escape? He wants me dead."

"You have been mistaken about Akhenamun all along, Smenkhkare. He did not know that my father had plans to murder Thutmose or you. Akhenamun was ambitious and he had no wish to become a priest, but he would never have agreed to such measures."

"He was happy enough to accept what Ay had done," I reminded her.

"That is not true. He was happy enough to take power but he will never forgive Ay for the murder of Thutmose. He may never have had much time for you, Smenkhkare, but you are his brother and he does not intend to let you die at Ay's hands."

"There is trouble ahead between your husband and your father, Nefertiti."

171

She nodded her head. "But my husband is pharaoh, not my father, Smenkhkare."

"Why are you doing this for me, Nefertiti?" I asked.

"I support my husband in this and not my father. Your wife has become a great friend to me and I will not leave her to her fate. I have always had a fondness for you, Smenkhkare, for I watched you grow up. Like Akhenamun, I am not prepared to let you die. I too have to exert my authority alongside my husband as Queen of Egypt."

"You will be a great Queen, Nefertiti, and I will always be in your debt."

"Now stop talking, Smenkhkare, and gather up your belongings," said Taduheppa. "We must leave quickly."

"You are coming with me?" I could not believe how suddenly I was so fortunate. My glorious wife was coming with me.

"Of course, I am," she said.

"You want to be with me?" I felt another glow of pleasure.

She laughed. "Do not get ahead of yourself, Smenkhkare. I do not wish to be forced into marriage with Ay. I also wish to return to Washukanni to see my father and family once again."

I felt a tinge of disappointment. "Will I be welcome at Washukanni?"

"Yes you will because you are my husband and a member of the Egyptian royal family. You will be useful to my father, but we can talk about all these things on the long journey ahead of us. Now you must quickly gather up the belongings you wish to take."

I rushed to get what I needed and then I followed the two women out of my room. The guards were still placed at my door and they looked fearfully at me as I left. Ay had obviously ordered them to stop me leaving and Nefertiti had countermanded those orders. They were confused and frightened for their lives but they made no attempt to stop me.

I entered the blinding sunlight of the exotic Malkata gardens and my transport awaited me as did, I hoped, a new life with Taduheppa. There were two wagons that hardly matched the caravans with which Taduheppa had entered Malkata, an event that seemed such a long time ago now.

"One wagon is for me and Turet and the other for Rana and the rest of my servants." Turet waved to me from her mistress's wagon and I grinned and waved back. It was a relief to me to know that Turet still lived.

"What about me?" I asked.

"There are horses and camels and we also have tents and supplies," she replied.

"I have also placed several of the palace guards under your command, Smenkhkare," said Nefertiti. "They will provide protection for your small group in case of attack from bandits."

"You have thought of everything," I thanked her, and then my heart missed a beat for I could see consternation suddenly appearing on the beautiful face of the Egyptian queen. I looked up and striding towards us was the general Horemheb with a number of soldiers following swiftly behind him.

"What is he doing in Malkata?" I asked Nefertiti.

"I have no idea," she replied cautiously.

"What is going on here?" asked Horemheb, but there was no hostility in his words.

"Why are you not at the army camp?" I answered a question with a question.

He smiled. "Are you leaving Malkata, Smenkhkare?"

"I am," I said with bravado.

"Does Ay know about this?" The huge man was still smiling.

Nefertiti answered him. "My father and husband are in Amarna and I am in charge at Malkata. They have my leave to depart."

Horemheb stroked his chin. "Does your husband know about this, my queen?"

"He does," she replied firmly.

"That is very interesting, very interesting indeed," he said knowingly. "I will of course obey my queen and not obstruct the departure of the prisoner, Smenkhkare, and his Mitanni wife. In answer to the question as to why I am not at the army camp I bring grave news. I have reports that Kushite forces are on the move far to the south."

He turned to Nefertiti. "As you are in charge here my report is therefore for you. Please convey it to the pharaoh on his return and I will go back to the army camp to put us on a war footing. It may be nothing but it is best to be prepared, your majesty."

"Indeed and thank you, general Horemheb," Nefertiti replied.

Horemheb turned to me for a final few words before he left. "I wish you good fortune, Smenkhkare, and I advise you to be on your guard for bandits, Kushite scouts and anyone else who might pursue you." I nodded but I could not forgive him for what had happened to Coreb. I watched as the general walked away. I had no idea whether I should fear him or not.

"Now you must be gone, Smenkhkare," said Nefertiti. I watched as she hugged my wife and then Taduheppa climbed into her wagon with a little help from a servant. I kissed Nefertiti on the cheeks. "Thank you cousin and thank my brother, too, and tell him that his little brother is sorry that he suspected him of complicity in the murder of Thutmose."

"I will," she smiled. "May the gods ride with you and with Taduheppa."

I mounted a horse which was brought for me. It seemed that I was not to ride in the wagon with Taduheppa and Turet but I was not prepared to argue about it. I just felt so happy that my execution had been postponed and I hoped it had been postponed indefinitely.

We rode out of Malkata heading towards the desert to the east. Once again I was striding into the unknown but this time I had my wife at my side.

Part 2 – The Desert

Chapter 15

Our plan was to head due east across the desert until we reached the vast stretch of water known as the Red Sea. We would then head north along the shore of the great inland water, stopping at some of the settlements along the banks. Then we would cross the huge desert known as the Sinai until we reached the vassal state of Canaan. The rulers of the small land of Canaan were in the main loyal to the Egyptian throne though there were always troublemakers to be subdued. From Canaan we would enter the land of the Mitanni and proceed to the Mitanni capital at Washukanni. All of the lands we would pass through paid homage to Egypt and the pharaoh and so we hoped there would be no enemies to be faced. However, it was a hazardous journey through lands that,though friendly, could suddenly become hostile, and there was always the possibility of encountering bandits.

Taduheppa and her loyal Mitanni servants had made the journey from Washukanni to Thebes and so for them it was merely a question of retracing their steps. Their journey to Thebes had been one with no incidents and so they were confident that the return journey would be equally without difficulty. The small number of palace guards took their orders from me and the Mitanni took their orders from Taduheppa and so the great journey began with much optimism. I felt elated that, for the moment at least, I no longer felt the terror of imminent execution, and Taduheppa was obviously delighted to have escaped the clutches of Ay and to be returning to her homeland.

The eastern desert, unlike its western counterpart, was not vast and we made steady progress towards the Red Sea, named because of the many red blooms that flowered seasonally near the water's surface. I slept in a tent that was put up each night, while Taduheppa slept in her wagon. Our discourse was friendly but never intimate though I longed for her love and the feel of her perfect body next to mine. It seemed I was still a boy despite everything I had been through, or perhaps she just did not like me in that way. The situation caused me distress but I did not dwell too much on it for I still enjoyed the glowing sensation of being free and relatively safe. I would bide my time with Taduheppa for that was the advice my brother, Thutmose, had once given me.

As we drew ever closer to the great inland sea our situation changed dramatically. I cursed at our bad luck and the new extreme danger that now confronted us. Our small wagon and camel train had driven straight into the large Kushite army that Horemheb had warned Nefertiti about. They had obviously sought to march north from Kush close to the shores of the sea in an outflanking manoeuvre which they hoped would not be detected by the Egyptian army. I assumed they then intended to attack Thebes from the north while the Egyptian army sought to locate them to the south of Thebes. We had simply wandered straight into them, and though their main army was distant it was visible and we were surrounded by Kushite scouts. We had been seen and there was no hope of escape.

A group of about 30 horseman started riding slowly towards us. I knew that resistance was hopeless as we were heavily outnumbered and we were watched by further more numerous horsemen at a distance. They obviously did not see us as a threat and unfortunately they were right in their assumption. I waved and made gestures of peace but I was acutely aware that some of us were Egyptian and Egypt was their enemy. I dismounted from my camel and was promptly joined by Taduheppa who had emerged from her wagon.

"Tell them we are Mitanni," she suggested.

"The problem is that only half of us look like Mitanni and the other half, including the palace guard, look Egyptian." I was rapidly trying to think of any credible lie that might explain the reason for such an unusual contingent in the eastern desert. I could hardly admit that I was an Egyptian prince. If I did that I was sure that I would not be treated with the respect my position deserved but instead I might be murdered or held as a hostage.

The leader of the Kushites approached me. "Peace to you and your soldiers," I said meekly.

He looked about him at the two wagons. "Who are you and what business do you have in the land of Kush?" he asked brusquely.

I could hardly point out that he was mistaken and this was Egyptian territory. "We are traders travelling to the Red Sea and beyond," I replied.

He looked about him again. "You do not look like traders, especially them." He gestured towards the palace guard.

"They are here for our protection. There are many bandits in these lands and we are most fortunate that it is you and not bandits who have found us."

He dismounted and ambled over to one of the wagons and peered in at the Mitanni servants. "They do not look like traders either," he observed. He walked back to me and Taduheppa. "You look like Egyptians but those in the wagon do not. You are a curious group."

"Traders are often a mixture of races travelling together," I offered.

"Most traders carry merchandise for sale but strangely you do not seem to have any wares, unless the women in the wagon are the merchandise."

I shrugged, not really knowing how to answer the question. "The horses are the merchandise and we keep the camels," Taduheppa helped me out.

"Then you are poor traders for you do not have that many horses. I think Prince Lisore may have some questions that he would like to ask you. You will follow me and I will escort you to our main camp. Consider yourselves prisoners until the prince decides what to do with you."

He remounted his horse and he and his soldiers led the way and we were expected to follow. We had no choice but to do so and my heart sank for once again I was a prisoner along with my wife, guardsmen and servants. I watched with dismay as the large cloud of dust that signalled the position of the main Kushite army grew ever larger. They were coming towards us as we were approaching them. Eventually the dust settled and I could see the Kushites more clearly. It was a very large army and I could not help but feel dismay for not only were my wife and I in danger but they also threatened Thebes and the whole of Egypt. There was no Thutmose or Coreb to deal with this threat and I was not sure how Akhenamun and Horemheb would cope.

"They have now made camp for the night," the Kushite leader informed me as we drew ever closer.

I nodded acknowledgement of his words while I tried to think of what I might say to the Kushite prince. My mind would not function and indeed I felt that what I said would make little difference for we were probably doomed. We entered the Kushite army camp and made our way through hundreds if not thousands of resting and eating troops. They looked exhausted for they must have marched at great speed in the hope of enjoying the element of surprise over an unsuspecting Egyptian host. They watched us with a little curiosity but were too tired to take too much interest in their surprise visitors.

At last in the heart of the encampment we reached the headquarters of the Kushite prince. It was an impressive system of luxurious tents which stood out against the background of vast numbers of ordinary soldiers sleeping and eating without shelter. The leader that we had followed once again turned to me. "You are young but you seem to be the leader of this motley band. Is that correct?"

"That is so," I answered.

He then went over to the wagon and looked again at the Mitanni servant girls. He selected one and gestured to her to follow him. "Why do you require her?" I asked when he came back to me.

"She looks very frightened which is why I selected her. If you refuse to answer questions truthfully then I am sure she will. Now I want both of you to wait here while I seek out the prince and see if he wishes to speak with you." He entered one of the large tents and disappeared from view.

I looked at the young Mitanni servant. I did not even know her name. "Do not be frightened. Leave the talking to me and you will be fine." Taduheppa joined us and softly gave further words of encouragement to her servant. "I will come with you both. It will be difficult to talk our way out of this." A brief nervous smile crossed her face.

I nodded but could not return the smile for I felt the situation was hopeless. They were not going to let us go and they might even murder us. "He will see you now." The Kushite had returned. "You will come with me, but not you." He gestured that Taduheppa should return to her wagon and she did so reluctantly. I followed him with the Mitanni servant at my side into the largest and most luxurious of the Kushite tents. I never imagined that the leader of an army on the march might enjoy such extravagance.

Then I saw him. He was lounging on an opulent chair, dressed in a rich array of multicoloured robes which not only covered his body but also the top of his head. He looked to be in his mid-20s and I was sure that under those flowing robes he was muscular and powerful. There were also several powerful-looking guards watching us closely.

"I am Prince Lisore, son of Ka, King of Kush and general of the formidable and invincible army that you have just observed."

I bowed. "I am Metos, a humble trader.

He smiled. "You are no humble trader. You are a man or boy of some consequence. Do not insult my intelligence any further. You are also obviously Egyptian and so please reveal your true identity."

"I am Metos, a prosperous trader of some consequence," I answered.

The smile disappeared. "I cannot be bothered with a long drawn-out process of extracting the truth from you which is why she is here. She will quickly tell me who you are, so save her the pain and give me the truth."

I looked at the servant and she was shaking with fear. "I will tell you if you would send the poor girl back to her mistress."

"Her mistress, is it?" He nodded and a guard escorted her back to Taduheppa. "Now tell me who you are and who her mistress is."

"I am Smenkhkare, prince of Egypt, and her mistress is my wife."

He grinned. "You are the brother of Akhenamun, pharaoh of Egypt and she is Taduheppa, daughter of Shatuarra, king of the Mitanni. I have stumbled across a rare treasure trove. Both of you would no doubt provide me with a huge ransom if that is what I required."

"I doubt that you would get a ransom for me," I said.

"Why were you wandering across the eastern desert?"

"We were heading for Washukanni to start a new life together in the Mitanni capital."

"I know you Egyptians are a strange lot, but even with you the wife lives in her husband's land and not the reverse. Why have you left Thebes?"

"I was accused of plotting against my brother and we were fleeing from Thebes."

"Were you plotting against your brother?" he inquired.

"Yes, but only in order to survive. I was perceived as a threat and so I became one."

"It seems, at the moment, we are almost equals, but you are also my prisoner. If circumstances were to change would you become my vassal, Smenkhkare?"

I wondered where he was going with this. "That would seem unlikely, Lisore."

He smiled. "I am going to conquer Egypt and decimate your army. The present regime in Thebes will fall. I envisage a situation where I might need to put a vassal king on the throne of Egypt who would be acceptable to the common people; a person who would owe his good fortune to me and be loyal to me. It seems that I might just have found such a person. You must hate your brother for putting you to flight."

"I do hate the present regime in Thebes and I do find your words interesting." I needed to go along with the Kushite prince in order to secure the safety and comfort of my small group of Egyptian guards and Mitanni servants and indeed the safety of my wife and myself."

"So, Smenkhkare, you do not find my suggestion abhorrent?"

"I do not find your suggestion abhorrent," I agreed.

"There would be no need to go into exile in Washukanni. You could return to Thebes, a man of power."

"And a Kushite servant," I said.

He laughed. "You would be a servant who rules his own land in another's name; that is better than a life of exile."

"You assume you will defeat my brother's army," I reminded him. "You do not have a good record in such matters where Egypt is concerned."

"We will achieve victory for we will take them by surprise and my army is large and well trained. We shall win, Smenkhkare. Of course surprise is important and so you realise we cannot let you and your people go."

"I realise that."

"You will be spending the coming campaign with me and my troops. You are a prisoner but you will be treated very well for I hope you will soon be a partner. Think about what I have said for there is plenty of time for you to reach a decision."

"I think you mean vassal rather than partner, but I will think about it most definitely for it is a very attractive offer."

"And I will get to know you, Smenkhkare, for I do need to feel able to trust you if you are to be a powerful subordinate. I also need to think about it myself for the idea simply jumped into my head when you revealed your identity. You and your people will march with my army and you will now be heading west instead of east."

I nodded. "We will travel with you and your army and I will hope for a bright future." I had secured our immediate safety and had also secured time to think, even if we were heading in the wrong direction.

"Now, Prince Smenkhkare, you are dismissed and I will contemplate the good fortune that we might both derive from this unexpected meeting."

I bowed. "Thank you, Prince Lisore, I almost think this meeting was pre-ordained." I left the audience with the Kushite prince with much to tell Taduheppa but I was not sure how she would react.

I went immediately to Taduheppa's wagon where I found her sitting on a couch and laughing with Turet. Her mood changed rapidly when she saw me. "What did the Kushite priest have to say?" she asked anxiously.

"I am glad you are both able to laugh," I said smiling at the two Mitanni women. I looked at Turet expectantly.

"You can talk in front of Turet. Surely you have learnt to trust her, Smenkhkare."

"I trust her implicitly," I replied and then relayed in full the conversation I had just had with Prince Lisore.

"I am not sure that it was a good idea to reveal our identities," Taduheppa commented after listening intently.

"I do not think I had a choice. He would soon have found out."

"I think I would rather be heading for Washukanni than going back to Thebes," she replied thoughtfully.

"So would I, but that was not an option."

"Do you think he is genuine in his offer to make you a puppet pharaoh?"

I contemplated the question. "I am not sure, but I think he might be. Anyway we are prisoners and he can do with us as he likes. If we are to stay alive then we go with him and agree to what he suggests. If he is genuine it is a possible way back to power in Thebes and a way to end the domination of Ay."

"And your brother, Akhenamun, and my friend Nefertiti," she reminded me.

I nodded. "I have no wish to betray my brother and dispose of him. He did let us leave Thebes whilst Ay sought to have me executed and I certainly wish no harm to Nefertiti."

She smiled. "But we would become rulers in Thebes and who knows after that."

I knew my ambitious wife. "You mean we use Lisore to depose Akhenamun and then sometime in the future shake off the Kushite yoke."

She nodded agreement. "Yes, but it is not that simple. Lisore has to defeat the Egyptian army first."

"He is confident and his army is numerous."

"But your Egyptian army is well trained."

"Horemheb is a young and untried general," I reminded her.

"Lisore is also young," she countered.

"I would feel more confident of an Egyptian victory if Thutmose and Coreb were in charge," I offered.

"But if it is an Egyptian victory what happens to us," she asked.

"I do not know," I admitted.

"Then perhaps we should try to persuade this prince of Kush to let us continue unobstructed to Washukanni. I am a Mitanni princess and I am sure he would not wish to make an enemy of my father."

"He strikes me as being a confident and arrogant prince. I do not think he would much care about your father."

She sighed and turned to Turet who had not said a word during the conversation. "What do you think, Turet?"

"I think that Smenkhkare is right. With this army at his back this arrogant Kushite prince is not going to care about the reputation of your father who is a vast distance away. I do not think you have a choice either, your majesty, and so you must play along with him and his ambitions. Tell him how you will both help to bring Egypt under his control and how you will willingly accept the role he offers you. Tell him how you wish for revenge on Ay, which will sound convincing because it is true. He will understand the need for revenge and he will believe you. Indulge his ego and reap the benefits. Seek safety for now by allying yourselves to his cause and then the future may bring new chances and new developments."

Taduheppa turned to me. "My Turet is a clever girl."

"I knew that already," I agreed.

"I will have Prince Lisore eating out of my hand," Taduheppa exclaimed smiling.

"I am not sure that I want you to go that far," I responded. "But Turet is right, we pander to his self-importance and we bide our time. That way we continue to survive and hopefully become both valuable and comfortable prisoners."

Taduheppa clapped her hands. "It is decided then."

****

The next morning the army swiftly abandoned the overnight camp and marched in a northern direction across the eastern desert. Prince Lisore insisted that I ride alongside him for he liked the idea of two princes together in co-operation as long as it was clear that he was very much the senior partner. "Speed is of the essence," he remarked as we made our way across the barren, lifeless desert.

"If you are to take your enemies by surprise," I agreed. "How far north do you intend to go?"

"Further north than Thebes and then we will turn west. It will be an outflanking movement for they will never expect us to descend on them from the north. We will take them by surprise and win a great victory."

I wiped the sweat from my brow for the desert sun was hot. "You have planned the campaign very well," I congratulated him.

"Indeed I have, and have you considered the proposal that I made to you?"

"If you depose my brother and set me up in Thebes you will enjoy the support of the people of Egypt. I can win them over, for Akhenamun and his chief vizier, Ay, are not popular with the populace and I am a prince of Egypt. I will rule in your name and Egypt will be yours, but I would make one demand in return."

"You are in no position to make demands," he laughed.

"I want Ay, and I want to do with him as I please."

"Request granted," he said. "This Ay is yours."

"I have talked it over with my wife and with that proviso I agree to your proposal," I smiled.

"Excellent, Smenkhkare, and now that you have agreed I will consider whether to accept your agreement."

"I hope you will find it to your liking." I tried to sound a little subservient in order to further massage his ego.

"I will offer you some advice, Smenkhkare. Never seek the concurrence of your wife – even if she is a Mitanni princess." He smiled. "Wives should be told and not asked. You are young and she is older than you and perhaps her age and rank makes that difficult for you, but heed my words and you will be much happier."

"Thank you for your advice, Prince Lisore."

"Now, Smenkhkare, I must consult with some of my generals."

With that he turned his mount, almost full circle, and rode off. I was alone close to the front of the army and I looked ahead as the gleaming sand of the vast desert spread out before me. The sun seemed to dance on the golden surface as it beat down with searing heat on the land below. I looked behind me at the vast host that Prince Lisore intended to use to bring Egypt to its knees. Then I heard shouting and realised that orders were being barked out. The army was turning in a new direction and I realised that we would now be heading west towards the great city of Thebes.

****

The days passed as we moved relentlessly towards our destination at a speed that surprised me considering the size of our large army. Lisore seemed to like our chats but also enjoyed indulging himself in the small harem that accompanied him on his grand conquest. He believed that he would take Egypt for his father, Ka, but that he himself was destined to rule the world. I realised though, that despite the high opinion he had of himself, the army was well organised with several efficient generals who would give Lisore excellent advice. Egypt was indeed under great threat.

While I rode with the army Taduheppa, Turet, Rana and the other servants stayed in their wagons nominally still protected by the small contingent of Malkata guard. Much to my relief she made no attempt to have Lisore eating out of her hand, and the prince was too occupied to give any thought to my wife. She was happy to leave it to me to persuade Lisore of the good sense of a partnership between us though I was still slightly apprehensive for I felt she was holding her own wiles in reserve if I failed. However, failure for this prospective partnership was unlikely because Lisore favoured it as it had originally been his own idea. This was confirmed one evening as the sun was going down.

I was joined by the prince as I rode with one of the palace guard who discreetly rode away when he saw the Kushite prince approaching. "I have considered," he said.

"What have you decided?" I inquired.

"That you will rule in Thebes as the instrument of my power," he said regally and smiled waiting for my gratitude.

"I will rule in Thebes in your name," I confirmed.

He slapped me on the back and then rode away shouting, "And you will have the head of this Ay."

Ay was going to have me executed and so to have Ay executed after all the crimes he had committed appealed to me greatly. The problem was that it meant a betrayal of my country – and that did not rest easy on me. Taduheppa had no problem with it but she was not an Egyptian. Could I really assist Lisore in the conquest and pacification of Egypt? I had all this on my mind plus the knowledge that the ceremony for the final journey of my father to the afterlife must be taking place about this time back in Thebes and I would not be attending. He never had much time for me and so in a way it was fitting I would not be attending the ceremony. It did, nevertheless, prey on my mind but not as much as the betrayal of my country.

Chapter 16

The next day my dilemma became increasingly focused on my mind for the powerful Egyptian army had appeared and faced us across the desert wasteland. The time had come for the outcome to be settled. I had been resting in the wagon after a hard day in the saddle when I heard the unmistakable noise of one army suddenly seeing an opposing army. I rushed out of the wagon only to be met by Taduheppa who was returning with Turet after drinking from the water supply at the large Kushite water caravan. "The Egyptian army is here," she gasped as dusk began to settle over the eastern desert.

"I heard the noise of everyone talking about it and it woke me from my slumber," I responded.

"I suppose we can now only await the outcome," she said excitedly.

"Go back to your wagon, Taduheppa." I was concerned for her safety. "I fear that there will be a great battle and it could be soon."

"What are you going to do?" she asked.

"I will seek out Lisore." I kissed her on the cheek and went to get my horse which was tied to the wagon and she followed me.

"Do not get involved in the battle," she warned. "It is not your fight, Smenkhkare."

"I will not," I assured her. "But I wish to find out what Lisore intends to do."

"He will fight," she said. "He has come all this way, so he must fight."

"You are right but I am interested in his battle plans and who leads the Egyptian Army."

"When you have found that out then return to the wagon for it is safer here at the rear of the army and I do not want you killed on the battlefield. We have gone through much together, Smenkhkare, and I do not wish it to end here."

Her concern touched me. "Neither do I," I smiled.

"If Lisore wins we go ahead as planned. If the Egyptians win then we will throw ourselves on their mercy."

"They will show mercy to you, Taduheppa, but I doubt that they will to me."

"Then we must hope Lisore wins," she smiled.

I kissed her again gently and tenderly on the lips and she kissed me back. "Now go and do what you have to, Smenkhkare, and then return to the wagon." It seemed that with these dangerous times there was an improvement in our relationship. It was almost worth the extreme danger.

I smiled and mounted my horse and rode away to find the Kushite prince. I was quickly joined by two Kushite guards who rode a short distance behind me. They had no intention of allowing me to try and join up with the Egyptian forces but what they did not know was that I had no intention of trying. The Egyptian camp was probably a more dangerous place for me than the Kushite camp. I saw Prince Lisore in conversation with some of his officers and I dismounted my horse and joined him.

He turned when he saw me approaching. "Smenkhkare, I was just about to send for you."

"Then I have saved you the trouble," I commented.

"They have anticipated our movements and so the benefit of the element of surprise I was hoping for has almost disappeared. I have been discussing the Egyptian army with some of my confidants. It seems they are of similar strength to us with neither of us holding any significant numerical advantage."

"Then it should be a close-fought battle," I offered. I looked across the desert at the large Egyptian force.

"I plan to seize the initiative and launch an attack. They have many chariots and we have few, but their chariots will be less effective if we attack first and do not allow them space to operate."

"That would seem like a sensible course of action," I agreed, though I had no experience of battle tactics.

"My scouts report that the Egyptians are led by a giant of a man so I will not offer single combat," he grinned. "Do you know of this man?"

"I know who he is, his name is Horemheb."

"Is he an experienced general, Smenkhkare?"

"No, he is not, Prince Lisore. He is new to leading the army having recently replaced the experienced general Coreb in a coup." The reminder of Coreb and his fate rekindled my anger.

"You sound bitter. Was Coreb supporting you, and are we talking about the same coup as the one you were involved in?"

"We are," I confirmed.

"Good, so he is not experienced and big men often have a little brain," he grinned again.

"I do not think that is so in the case of Horemheb. I have only met him twice and he seemed an intelligent man to me. I think he might prove a good general."

"That is what I wanted your opinion about. I will not then underestimate this Horemheb."

I saw a large dust cloud on the horizon beginning to move. "It looks like they may intend to attack us first," I offered.

"You are right, Smenkhkare, but we will still strike first and quickly. He started giving orders to the officers that were standing around us and they began to dash into action. "We will pre-empt their attack. Now go back to your wagons at the rear where you will be comparatively safe, Prince Smenkhkare. You are young and you and your wife are still valuable hostages. Stay there until the outcome is settled, and if you are genuine in giving me your allegiance then you can pray to your gods that Kush wins the day."

"How many men will fight this battle?" I asked, looking once again at the vast Egyptian army across the hard-packed desert sands.

"Both sides have several thousand. Now leave us." He mounted his horse and called out fresh orders to his generals and rode away. The Kushites were quickly preparing to launch an attack and meet the Egyptian forces in the expanse of wasteland between the two armies. I mounted my horse and made my way to the wagons and baggage at the rear of the army followed by my two ever-present guards. There was about to be a huge loss of life and I was glad that I did not have to fight.

Taduheppa was waiting for me. "I was worried that you might get involved in the fighting," she said.

"I am to wait here for the outcome," I mused.

"Good, then let them kill one another and hope that whoever wins will not prove to be our enemy," she shrugged.

She was a Mitanni princess and she did not much care for either Egyptians or Kushites, but I was an Egyptian and could not help feeling sad that many Egyptians would die this day. "I am going to climb that dune over there where I can get a better view of the battle."

"Be careful of any stray arrows," she advised.

"We are out of range," I laughed. "But it is good to know you care."

"You staying alive helps me to stay alive. I will come with you."

"Stay here. A battle is not for the eyes of a Mitanni princess,"

"You are frailer than me," she answered decisively.

"Let us go then," I said and I walked towards the dune. Taduheppa followed and so did the two guards.

When I reached the sand dune I took off my sandals and Taduheppa followed suit. We scampered to the top followed by the two guardsmen though they kept their distance affording us some degree of privacy. We were out of breath when we reached the top for it was not easy climbing the large dune. We surveyed the scene that met our eyes. We had a good view of the desert but the armies, particularly the Egyptian forces, were at a good distance so it was difficult to see exactly what was going on. One thing that was clear was that both armies were advancing and the area separating them was diminishing. I gasped as I realised that both armies were charging, with the Egyptian chariots bearing down on the Kushite cavalry. I remembered training in a chariot with my brother Thutmose for just such a day as this. I was pleased that I was not in a chariot now for the dead and dying were about to litter the desert floor.

"They will clash very soon," said Taduheppa, and then a flurry of Egyptian arrows darkened the sky followed by a similar flurry of Kushite arrows. Men were dying on both sides and I saw Egyptians falling from their chariots. The space between the two opposing forces had disappeared and the first vicious clashes were starting. The battle had begun in earnest.

We both strained our eyes to see what was happening on the desert battlefield. The fury of the killing held us spellbound. The Egyptian chariots cut a swathe through the Kushite cavalry and then flooded into the front ranks of the infantry. Kushite spears were swept aside by the speed and power of the chariots. I could see that the Kushites were targeting the charioteers and their passengers but they kept low down in their chariots to avoid heavy losses. Prince Lisore's cavalry then turned to come to the aid of their infantry but could not engage the Egyptian chariots because they had now wheeled towards the flanks of the Kushite forces in a spectacular motion that caused havoc in the ranks of the Kushite infantry.

In the mayhem that followed the Kushite cavalry could not engage the chariots and were running into their own infantry. The Egyptian chariots wheeled again, attacking the rear of the Kushite army, and I feared for our wagons but they turned again towards their own infantry ranks that were now pushing relentlessly towards the Kushite infantry. The chariots were going through the manoeuvres and routines that had been practised so frequently at the command of Thutmose and Coreb on the fields outside Thebes. It was now all being put into good effect by Horemheb. Prince Lisore had wished to deny the Egyptian chariots space to work their havoc but had failed completely and it was the Kushite cavalry that was being denied the space to operate.

There was a mighty roar as the two lines of infantry met, with the Kushite cavalry stuck between the lines with no space to work. Egyptian spears were unseating the cavalrymen and then meeting the spears of the Kushite infantry. Prince Lisore's cavalry had been decimated and now the sides and flanks of their infantry were being attacked by the chariots while they tried to engage with the Egyptian infantry. Horemheb had proved himself to be a very capable general.

"The Egyptians are going to win," said Taduheppa.

The battle had been short but I felt Taduheppa was right for already the Kushites looked beaten. "I think you are right," I replied.

The Kushite infantry battled on for longer than I expected but they had suffered very heavy losses and it seemed only a matter of time before Horemheb claimed an overwhelming victory. Then I saw Prince Lisore and some of his lieutenants fleeing the battlefield and riding south at speed away from the disaster.

I pointed them out to Taduheppa. "The Prince is fleeing."

"The coward is abandoning his men," she replied.

Word of the flight of their leader must have reached the infantry for now their lines were beginning to break up alarmingly. There was one massive shout of triumph from the Egyptian host as they realised that victory was now theirs for the taking. The men of Kush were fleeing the battlefield and they were being pursued and hunted down by Egyptian infantry and charioteers.

"We must return to the wagons," I said to Taduheppa.

"I wish to see what happens and watch as the Egyptians achieve final victory." She resisted my plea.

I took her arm and pulled her down the dune. I noticed the two Kushite guards had deserted us to flee for their lives. "The battle is over and the massacre begins and all that remains is slaughter and a bloodbath," I said. "It is not something you would wish to witness, nor I for that matter."

She nodded, and for once my headstrong wife heeded my wishes. The Kushites were abandoning the baggage train without a thought for their prisoners in their rush to escape. My palace guardsmen had also disappeared, probably seeking to join up with the Egyptian host. The only people still in the vicinity of the wagons were the Mitanni servants.

"I will protect you," Taduheppa shouted to her servants and they, led by Rana, scampered into one of the wagons. I was not sure that Taduheppa could fulfil her promise but I said nothing. I entered the other wagon with Taduheppa and Turet. The noise outside was deafening but we did not want to enter the chaos for fear of being slaughtered. The comparative luxury of the two Mitanni wagons might show us to be of note and not Kushite and I was at least in Egyptian dress and so obviously not one of the enemies. The wagons therefore seemed to be the safest place to wait until we were inevitably discovered. I did contemplate trying to run with the Mitanni women but that would be hopeless and we would not get very far.

"Do you think they will kill us?" asked Turet.

"They will not kill us if they give us a chance to tell them who we are," I reassured her.

"But they will make you a prisoner once again and they will return me to Malkata to marry Ay," Taduheppa commented bitterly.

"At least we are still alive and that is more than can be said for all those who have died on the battlefield this day," I said ruefully.

Taduheppa sighed. "Then we wait."

I pulled back the cover of the wagon slightly so that I could see outside. There was noise, screams and dust but as yet no sign of any Egyptian soldiers. "What can you see?" asked Taduheppa.

"Not much, except for sand and dust," I replied.

"The screams of the dying are awful," said Turet putting her hands over her ears.

"I know," I remarked sadly.

"What is taking them so long?" said Taduheppa.

"I think it is the slaughter," I replied sadly. Then I saw some soldiers riding towards us, slowly taking in the scene and being careful in case they faced an ambush. They were Egyptians and I could make out a very large man at their head.

"What is that noise?" asked Taduheppa.

"They are coming," I replied simply and the three of us became very tense. The waiting was over.

Taduheppa then came over to my side to peer out of the gap in the canvas with me. "It is Horemheb," she said.

I nodded. "It is the general."

"Is that Ramose at his side?" she observed nervously.

She was right and I gasped in horror. "It is Ramose."

I saw the revulsion in her face. "Ay's awful son."

"Let us show our dignity and not hide away in the wagon. Let us go out and meet them," I suggested.

"We will do that," she agreed. Together we climbed out of the wagon and strode out to meet them closely followed by Turet. Horemheb and Ramose showed signs of recognition as they surveyed us.

Horemheb dismounted and Ramose followed suit and now they were coming to meet us. As we drew close Horemheb bowed his bulky but muscled frame. "I thought I recognised those wagons. Welcome, your majesty, to what is now the Egyptian encampment," he smiled.

"He is not 'your majesty'," said Ramose with distaste.

"Is he not a member of our most immediate royal family and the brother of the pharaoh? That I believe makes him 'your majesty'," corrected Horemheb.

"That may be so, but he is also my prisoner as is his wife," stated Ramose firmly.

"You have no authority over me and so we are not your prisoners," I said.

He called to some of the palace guard that accompanied him. "Arrest them and put a stop to this absurd conversation."

"Halt," said Horemheb. "Smenkhkare makes a good point. He was released by Nefertiti, Queen of Egypt." The guardsmen stopped at the bellowing command of Horemheb.

"Nefertiti had no authority to release them," stuttered Ramose indignantly. "They were prisoners of the chief vizier."

"Does not the queen outrank the chief vizier and did she not have the support of her husband, the pharaoh?"

"No, she did not, and she is Ay's daughter and should not have gone against her father."

I stood with some amazement listening to the conversation. "It seems you have no authority here, Ramose."

He looked at me with considerable hatred. "My father runs Egypt and I am his representative and you are my prisoner."

Horemheb raised his eyebrows. "I will settle this disagreement. Smenkhkare and his wife are my prisoners until I decide what to do with them."

"I order you to take them back to Malkata," blustered Ramose.

"I might, but then I might not," Horemheb smiled.

Ramose once again addressed his guardsmen. "Arrest them." He turned to Horemheb. "That is why I accompanied you here, and I have authority over you."

"Stop," Horemheb reiterated. "You have 50 men and I have nearly 5000 men. I think that gives me the authority, Ramose."

The guardsmen hesitated and Ramose stormed off in disgust. "Now you can return to your wagons until I reach a decision on what to do with you," said Horemheb.

"Thank you, Horemheb," I said.

"Do not thank me for I might yet return you to Malkata as Ramose wishes, but I just do not like to be told what to do by that upstart who owes his position to his devious father."

"I see." The words of Horemheb surprised me. It seems that all is not well at Malkata.

"Now you will send your servant Turet to me later for I wish to speak with her."

"No, we will not," stated an outraged Taduheppa.

"You misconstrue my intentions," Horemheb laughed. "She is extremely pretty and I would not be adverse to a little fun after the exertions of battle but I only wish to speak with her."

Taduheppa was not sure how to now view his request. "Why do you wish to speak with her?"

"She will no doubt tell you, when she returns, after we have spoken. Send her to me for it is not in your interests to refuse."

I looked at Taduheppa wondering how she would react and she looked at me. "We hesitate for Turet is more than just a servant – she is a friend," I said.

"Then she will be treated by me as a friend. I know that she is extremely inventive and was instrumental in one of your escapes from Malkata. She may help me to decide what to do with you. We will spend about a week here before returning to Thebes so I have time to ponder over the decision."

"We will send her to you in the morning if it is her wish," said Taduheppa.

"I will go to see what the general has to say," said Turet.

"Good, now I must be on my way for there is still much work to be done. Part of my army is pursuing the remnants of the Kushite forces. We must ensure that it will be a long time before Kush dares to attack Egypt again."

"Is there any news of Prince Lisore?" I asked.

"None as yet. By the way, today is also the day of your father's passing to the afterlife and so it is a very significant day in Egyptian history," replied Horemheb.

"I knew it must be about this time. It is fitting that Amenhotep joins Osiris on the day of a great Egyptian victory."

Horemheb nodded and remounted his horse and rode away leaving us to contemplate the new situation that we found ourselves in.

We returned to the wagon in thoughtful mood. "All is obviously not well in Malkata. Do I detect there is jealousy and animosity?" Taduheppa seemed pleased at such a prospect.

"I expect Ay is proving insufferable. If Horemheb is disillusioned with the situation in Malkata then that may be to our advantage," I observed.

"I wonder what he wants with Turet," asked Taduheppa.

"I will find out tomorrow morning," said Turet.

"Be careful with this general," I warned.

"I know how to handle men," she smiled.

"Just like your mistress," I laughed.

"On that note you must go to the other wagon. This one is for us, Smenkhkare."

"This is absurd. You are my wife," I moaned while Turet smiled. "Can I not at least sleep here?"

"I think not. You would not be able to control yourself and you are still too much of a boy to be my husband. We are mature Mitanni women. I will assess the situation when we reach Washukanni."

"You take liberties with the heir to the Egyptian throne. Beware that you are not discarded."

She smiled knowing that my threat was hollow.

"And we might never reach Washukanni," I added. I shook my head for I was tired and I knew further protests would fall on deaf Mitanni ears.

She saw my fatigue. "I am also tired," said Taduheppa. "It has been a long and very frightening day. I thought you would understand that, Smenkhkare."

Now she was trying to make me feel bad and succeeding. She had seen things today that no woman should have to see. "Why is it the Mitanni lands produce such beautiful and tempting but frustrating women?" That was my last riposte before I left.

As I climbed down from the wagon Taduheppa called out. "We will be up early in the morning, Smenkhkare."

"Until then," I called back.

I had made a small private section for myself in the other wagon which was cordoned off by a curtain from the sleeping quarters of the few Mitanni servants who slept within. The others tended to sleep under the stars. I could have turned them all out and had the wagon to myself but had decided against it. The night was full of sounds and sleep did not come easily.

****

I awoke to the sound of Taduheppa calling my name. I peered out from the wagon bleary-eyed at Taduheppa and Turet. "Wake up," reprimanded Taduheppa. "Turet is about to go and see Horemheb. He has sent a guard to escort her."

"I had a disturbed night." My excuse sounded hollow. I looked at Turet. "Be careful with Horemheb, I am not sure how trustworthy he is," I advised, though I knew in truth there was little any of us could do in our present predicament but concur to Horemheb's wishes.

"I will," she smiled and left the wagon with her escort.

"I fear for her," said Taduheppa resignedly.

"I know that she is not just a servant but also a good friend," I sympathised.

She shrugged and I sensed I was missing something. "Let us get some food and drink and wait for her to return." We did not have to wait for too long for late morning Turet returned. I could see the relief on Taduheppa's face when her favourite servant was walking back towards us seemingly cheerful and unharmed. We gathered around her to hear news of what Horemheb had wanted with her.

Turet sat down next to her mistress. "I pressed him but he would not tell me what fate he had in store for you," she said. "I think it is promising though."

"Why did he wish to see you?" asked Taduheppa.

"He likes me." She reddened slightly.

"Did he do anything?" said Taduheppa alarmed.

"Oh no, he merely asked me to return to Malkata with him. He sees me as a possible wife."

"So you return to Malkata as his wife and we return as his prisoners," I said.

"He would not say," she replied to me.

"What did you say to his offer?" asked Taduheppa.

"I told him that I was your servant and wished to remain your servant and any decision on my future would be yours."

"Then we will see what our fate is before deciding on yours," said Taduheppa ruefully. "Why did you say our fate is promising?"

She withdrew a short-bladed dagger from her clothing and handed it to Taduheppa. "Horemheb gave me this. He said it was for Smenkhkare." She looked at me. "He said you should keep it close to you at all times. He also said that you should not use it to try and escape, and you should not use it on any of his men for if you did he would show you no mercy."

Taduheppa stroked the deadly sharp blade. "He thinks Smenkhkare is in danger?"

"He simply said it was for his protection," replied Turet.

Taduheppa handed the dagger to me. "You had better do as he says."

I took the blade from her delicate hand thoughtfully and felt some alarm. "I will keep it close."

"Sleep in our wagon tonight for it is not wise for you to sleep alone," Taduheppa recommended. "We can put up a curtain for privacy. The three of us will face any danger together for six eyes and ears are better than two."

"I am pleased that we face this ordeal together but I do not wish you to face danger."

"Nonsense, "replied Taduheppa. "It is for the best."

"It will be good to share a wagon with my wife," I smiled.

She ignored my obvious suggestion. "It is best if one of us stays awake at all times and we should also remain alert during the day as well," she suggested.

Her obvious concern alarmed me. Would an assassin really make an attempt on my life in Horemheb's encampment? "I agree."

My fears receded somewhat as the days passed. We were ignored by Horemheb and his men and left to our own devices though it was obvious we were being well guarded and could not stray far from the vicinity of the wagons. It was also plain that preparations were now under way for leaving the camp and returning to Malkata. We had been there for five days and as dusk settled we climbed into the wagon and I began to ponder our imminent fate.

"Turet, could you get some food and water," Taduheppa asked her servant. Turet climbed down from the wagon and I was left alone with my wife.

"We are leaving here soon," I observed.

"Yes, that much is obvious, Smenkhkare. We need to speak with Horemheb."

"And find out his plans for us," I agreed. There was a rustle in the canvas and I looked up fearfully.

Ramose was looking at us with hatred in his eyes and a sword in his hand. I knew instantly that he intended to murder me. I grabbed Taduheppa by the hand and jumped out of the back of the wagon. To my horror I realised there was no escape for we were surrounded by Ramose's palace guard. Ramose then climbed carefully down from the wagon still clutching his threatening sword. I felt for the dagger that was hidden under my robes and gripped the handle. My one advantage was that Ramose did not know I was armed, but even so a dagger was no match for the long-bladed sword that Ramose was holding and even if I killed Ramose his guard would, no doubt, overwhelm me.

"There is no escape, Smenkhkare," Ramose gloated.

"I am a prisoner of Horemheb. He will not take kindly to you murdering me." My words smacked of desperation.

"My father is ruler of Egypt and Horemheb is a subordinate. He will do nothing and Ay wants your head and I am more than happy to give my father what he wants." He pointed to a basket on the ground by one of his guards.

I looked at the basket in terror for it was identical to the other three baskets. Taduheppa followed my gaze and gasped in anguish. "I am the brother of the pharaoh," I protested.

Ramose looked at Taduheppa. "Do not worry. Your life is not in danger for I am to take you back to Malkata as bride for my father." He turned back to me. "Your head will complete the set: Coreb, Murat and Smenkhkare – three traitors to Egypt." He moved slowly towards me brandishing his sword.

Taduheppa to my surprise stepped between us. Her words were smooth and matter-of-fact. "Ramose, I will willingly marry your father, for Smenkhkare is just a foolish boy. I now realise my mistake in leaving with him, for your father is the true ruler of Egypt. Surely you would not waste your time killing a mere boy?" She edged towards him slowly.

Ramose grinned in satisfaction. "A Mitanni princess will make a good wife for my father, but the boy must die."

Taduheppa was even closer and dived at his legs trying to bring him down. "Now, Smenkhkare," she shouted.

I withdrew my dagger and lunged forward but Ramose was too quick. He kicked Taduheppa in the face and sent her reeling and recovered in time to parry my attempted dagger strike. He was now grinning as he circled me. "That dagger looks puny against my sword," he boasted. The next moment he struck with his sword, and though I parried with the dagger the force of his blow knocked the weapon from my hand. I was now doomed and I knew it for he would cut me down without mercy.

Turet had returned unseen as the guardsmen were all focusing on Ramose, Taduheppa and myself and they had obviously been told not to intervene unless Ramose was in danger. Turet jumped on to the back of Ramose scratching at his eyes and neck. Ramose threw her to the ground and stabbed her and then turned back to me with Turet's blood running down his sword. She had bought me a few moments to act, and I bent down and picked up my dagger and as Ramose bore down on me I threw it. I watched as the dagger embedded itself in Ramose's stomach. He stared at me and dropped his sword and crumbled to the ground. Taduheppa ran to the stricken figure of her faithful servant and took the girl in her arms. "She is dead," she screamed in pain and disbelief.

The guardsmen hesitated, not knowing what to do. "Kill Smenkhkare," Ramose shouted while trying to stop the flow of blood from his wound.

"Wait, do not move." It was the commanding voice of Horemheb, backed by many soldiers, which boomed over the bloody scene. The guardsmen stopped for they feared Horemheb, particularly as they did not know whether their leader, Ramose, would live or die.

"Go," shouted Horemheb and his voice sounded even more commanding. The guardsmen dispersed and faded out of sight. Taduheppa dashed to the stricken figure of Ramose and picked up his sword. Ramose looked up at her in fear and dread as she plunged the sword into his body and then continued to stab him repeatedly. I realised just how much she had loved her servant, for Turet was much more than a servant to Taduheppa, she was also a very dear friend and companion. Horemheb had taken Turet in his arms and I wondered at the extreme sorrow etched into the big man's face. He really did love Turet. I rushed to drag Taduheppa away from the now dead Ramose and she then joined Horemheb beside the dead servant. Taduheppa was weeping and I saw a tear run down Horemheb's face and I wiped away a tear from my own face.

"We will bury her with full honours," said Horemheb.

"She deserves nothing less," agreed Taduheppa. "She was the most faithful and trustworthy friend I have ever had." She stood up and shuddered at the events that had just unfolded.

Horemheb rose too. "What to do with Ramose's body, for he is the chief vizier's son?" he said.

"His body will be left on the desert floor to provide a feast for the birds of the sky," I said as I picked up his sword which was stained with his own blood and the blood of Turet. "Look away, Taduheppa," I advised.

She ignored my advice even though her eyes showed that she knew my intention and probably approved of it. With one downward sweep of the sharp-bladed weapon I half struck off his head and one more blow to the neck removed it entirely from his body. Horemheb made no move to stop me. I held up Ramose's head by his dark hair and let the blood drain on to the desert floor until an area was stained red. I walked over to the basket and deposited his head into the waiting container.

"What are you going to do with that?" asked Horemheb.

"I will write a note to Ay and place it with the head, and then with your approval I will send it to Ay. I would not want to deprive him of the head of his precious son."

"I will arrange for his guardsmen to go on ahead and take the basket to Ay," he said.

"You will do that for me?" I was a little surprised.

"I will do that for you, but most of all I will do it for Turet. The son was acting for the father and Turet was killed as a consequence of their vile actions and by the son's blade. I will have the body of Turet buried. Take her back to the main camp," he commanded two of his soldiers. "Follow in a couple of hours once you have recovered from the traumas of what has just occurred."

He walked sadly away followed by the soldiers carrying the body of Turet and the basket. I was left trying to console my weeping and distressed wife.

Chapter 17

The burial was quickly carried out. Not for Turet a place in the valley of death for she was, of course, a Mitanni and a servant. However, Horemheb did her proud, gifting her all of the honours that he would have bestowed on a fallen general. The army lined up in her honour and she was buried in a style that would have befitted a brave leader of rank in the Egyptian army. She indeed had great courage which had been proven many times since she had come to Malkata with her mistress. Horemheb was shaken by her death for I think that despite her refusal he had still been determined she should return to Thebes with him and become his wife. Taduheppa had recovered her dignity during the burial ceremony but it was obvious she had been deeply affected by the death of her servant. I also had had a deep regard for Turet, but my time was spent at Taduheppa's side during the funeral doing my best to comfort her.

When it was over we all knew, despite out grief, it was time to move on quickly. Horemheb had to return promptly to Thebes and Malkata to report his great victory over the Kushites to Akhenamun and Ay. First, however, he had to decide what to do with his two prisoners and I needed to know whether he intended to take us both with him. I was given some hope by his current attitude, and if he were to set us free we needed to travel quickly to Washukanni before Ay could plan his revenge.

"I need to speak with Horemheb about his intentions," I said to Taduheppa.

"Do the best you can for us," she said sadly. "I will return to the wagon and ponder over life without my Turet."

I nodded. "I will do my best."

I watched as she walked back towards the two Mitanni wagons and then I strode over to Horemheb. "We need to speak," I said.

"Indeed we do. Come with me, Smenkhkare."

I followed him to his tent within the military headquarters. It was a simple structure and not much more luxurious than those enjoyed by an ordinary officer. "Sit down," he said. "I endure the same hardships as my men." He had seen me looking around.

"I need to know your plans," I began.

"Ramose's palace guard will return to Malkata with his head in the morning. I will follow on with the army, a day behind, once we have finished here."

"Do the guardsmen know the contents of the basket?" I asked.

"I have not told them but I should imagine that they can guess what it contains."

"Please instruct them not to tell Ay but to simply hand the basket to him."

He smiled. "Ay will think it is your head in the basket and Ramose has sent in on in advance."

"That is what I want him to think."

"He will want revenge," he warned.

I shrugged. "And so do I, for my revenge will not be complete until Ay pays for his crimes."

"What did you write on the note you placed in the basket?" he asked.

"I wrote: 'A gift from Prince Smenkhkare. I have kept the sword of Ramose which I used to cut off his head. I will need it when I part your head from your body, Ay.' Just two simple lines," I said.

"He will not like it for he seemed to genuinely care for his son."

"I know, for he once told me that the only people he cared about were his son and daughter."

"Why should I go along with this? Ay will blame me for not protecting his son," he offered. "And you are hardly a comrade for did I not plot against your friend, Coreb?"

"Why did you?" I asked.

"I am an ambitious man. I wanted power and Coreb stood in my way. I intended to send him into exile but Ramose killed him. I plotted with Ay, but I see now that Ay is a very unreliable and dangerous partner. I will firmly order the guardsmen to say nothing when they hand Ay the basket."

"So you do not trust Ay," I said.

"Malkata is a melting pot. Ay seeks total control of Egypt and believes he can dominate Akhenamun and be the real power behind the throne. Akhenamun, encouraged by Ay's own daughter, Nefertiti, is beginning to resist and the fight for power is on. I am not sure who will win and both seek my support as I control the army."

"Who do you support?" I asked.

"I support myself and only myself. I think, though, that if your brother shows signs of getting the upper hand in the power struggle I will support him. I do not trust him but I trust Ay even less. Ay is already looking for support within the army behind my back. He has played that game once before but he thinks he can do so again. He is mistaken."

"What will you do with me?"

He smiled. "I trust you more than Akhenamun and Ay despite the hostility you bear me over the death of Coreb. I will set you and Taduheppa free to continue your journey to Washukanni."

I suppressed the joy I was beginning to feel. "Why would you do that?" I asked suspiciously.

"You are a third player in the bid for supremacy in Egypt," he answered.

"My brother is pharaoh and therefore supreme," I reminded him.

"But for how long? Ay is ambitious and he has already killed your other brother when he thought his position was threatened. He would not hesitate to try and remove Akhenamun if he felt threatened again. He might also consider making himself pharaoh."

I gasped. "He is not royal enough."

"He is a member of your family if not of the royal line. My position could become precarious but as long as I have control of the army I will be difficult to replace. Another member of the family would have a claim if Akhenamun was disposed of. That would be the exiled Prince Smenkhkare who was biding his time in the Mitanni capital. You never know what will develop or whether at some time in the future you will be invited to return to Malkata and that will give Ay something to think about."

"Are you saying that you might recall me to Malkata to claim the throne?"

"I cannot claim it myself for I am a commoner, and as I said I do trust you more than the other two. Of course there is another reason."

"What is that?" I asked.

"I cannot stand Ay. Both he and his deceased son are arrogant, malicious and treacherous. The son is no more, but the father is."

"I see," I replied.

"And that is not all," he retorted and I saw the anguish in his face.

"What else?" I asked.

"He was instrumental in the death of Turet." These words were spat out with a hatred that was almost frightening.

"Ay and Ramose brought about her death between them," I offered, seeking to take advantage of his grief.

"And that I will not forget. Now make your preparations to leave as soon as possible. When Ay receives the head of his son he will seek quick and instant revenge on you. You will have a good start, so make the most of it and have a safe journey to Washukanni. Stay safe and perhaps one day you will hear from me and we will meet again."

I stood up. "I hope so."

"I will send some soldiers to accompany you for there are always bandits to consider as well."

"We will leave at daylight. I wish you well, Horemheb."

I left the general to return to my wagon as darkness was falling. We would make preparations and be ready to leave at first light. First I told Taduheppa of my conversation with the general and then we made ready for our departure the next morning.

****

I did not see Horemheb again before we left. He was busy making his own preparations to leave but I did hear from one of his men that Prince Lisore had escaped. I could not help feeling a little pleased at that news for I did not dislike my fellow prince who had promised so much but had not managed to deliver. We left at first light as planned and once again the small Mitanni caravan was on the move. This time our horses, camels and two wagons were accompanied by 50 of Horemheb's soldiers. They would be our protection in case of bandit activity.

We headed north towards the desert of Sinai and passed through that great, desert peninsula without incident. Taduheppa remained in a deep depression throughout the journey and I worried for her health. It was during this passage through the desert that I realised that Turet had been more than a servant and a friend. How naive I had been, which only confirmed that I was still a boy just as Taduheppa had always insisted. I did my best to comfort her and to raise her spirits but it was difficult for

Turet was sorely missed. I talked with her often and made sure she ate her food and kept up her strength.

It was in this melancholy state that we entered the land of Canaan. It was mostly a barren land though there were fertile parts near the many waterholes that we passed. We were approaching the city of Jerusalem and I was undecided whether to risk entering the city. The last I had heard was that the city remained loyal to the pharaoh, but the region was always volatile with many tribes vying for superiority. I was also unsure of what the reception would be for a runaway Egyptian prince. I had just decided to circuit the city and take no risk when the first danger of the journey since we left Horemheb's camp presented itself.

On the horizon I could see the tell-tale sign of a large dust cloud which signalled the presence of a large force of riders. I felt great apprehension, for having come this far it would be unthinkable not to reach Washukanni safely. There was little we could do but watch the force draw ever nearer and we could not run for we knew we could not outrun them. All we could do was wait and hope that they were not hostile. As they drew very close a small number of riders detached themselves from the main group and rode towards us. Accompanied by just two soldiers, I rode out to meet them.

To my relief they appeared to be friendly. Their leader, recognising I had authority despite my youth, addressed me: "I am Avram and I welcome our Egyptian friends to the land of Canaan. I am here on behalf of the king of Jerusalem, Abdi Heba, to escort you into the city. It is a day's ride to the east over difficult terrain."

He seemed genuine but I felt a need to be cautious. "We are Egyptian travellers heading for Washukanni." I was non-committal in my reply.

"And Mitanni too," he commented.

"Yes, Mitanni too," I agreed.

"We know who you are and we know you are heading for the Mitanni capital. You are in great danger and my desire is simply to protect you and provide you with the hospitality and safety that Jerusalem offers before you continue on your way."

"Why are we in danger?" I asked.

"The Habiru are operating in this area. We received information in Jerusalem that a small Egyptian caravan was heading this way and we were alarmed that you might fall victim to the Habiru. We left urgently in order to offer you protection and to escort you into Jerusalem. We are allies to Egypt and we are loyal to the pharaoh."

"I thank you, Avram, and I accept your kind offer." I had heard of the Habiru and I knew them to be ruthless brigands who infested the desert between Jerusalem and the coast. I rode back to Taduheppa's wagon and explained the situation to her.

"It seems we have no alternative but to visit Jerusalem." Her words were spoken in a resigned fashion that had been prevalent since the death of Turet and this was making me worry about her. Our caravan drew in behind Avram's forces and we set off for our destination.

It was a few hours later I realised just how lucky we had been when a large host of Habiru appeared on the horizon. We would have had no chance against such a large number of outlaws. I rode alongside Avram. "Will they attack us?" I asked.

"I doubt it for they do not outnumber us and they prefer easy prey."

I sighed. "And we would have been easy prey without you. I thank you once again, Avram."

"We have been trying to exterminate the Habiru in recent years but it is no easy task. I am glad we were able to offer a prince of Egypt our assistance."

This was confirmation that he did indeed know who I was but he had showed no sign of hostility and I felt reasonably safe under his protection. I nodded. "Prince Smenkhkare at your disposal," I said.

"You will be safe in Jerusalem before you continue your journey to Washukanni," he assured me.

The Habiru followed us for a couple of hours keeping their distance and then to my relief they rode away. They had obviously thought better of launching an attack and now we were free to enter Jerusalem unopposed.

Jerusalem was a modest settlement compared to Thebes. It consisted of a fortified small city with outlying villages and extensive pastoral areas. We rode through the areas of agriculture and farming and two small villages before entering the gate to the city. Inside the walls there were numerous brick buildings and mud dwellings and we were led to the grandest building in the city, the palace of the king of Jerusalem. To the best of my knowledge Jerusalem was still an Egyptian vassal city-state and so I wondered what reception a runaway prince would receive from the king. So far it had all seemed promising.

I was granted a private audience with the king and Taduheppa showed no interest in joining me such was her state of mind after the murder of her beloved servant. This was alarming because it was so unlike Taduheppa. I was led into a luxurious chamber within the palace where the king of Jerusalem obviously received notable guests. The king was a small man of middle age with a stooping back and a friendly face. He welcomed me with open arms. "I am Abdi Heba, King of the modest city of Jerusalem. I hold this place in the name of the pharaoh who enjoys my allegiance. Until recently Jerusalem was a small settlement with no walls. The walls you see have been built recently to counter the threat from the Habiru. The palace is also of recent construction and Jerusalem grows under the benign influence of the pharaoh, and therefore I have great honour in receiving his esteemed brother."

I did not interrupt his lengthy welcome. "I am Smenkhkare, Prince of Egypt. I thank you and trust that my small band of Egyptians and Mitanni will be safe during our short stay in your impressive city."

"Please sit, Smenkhkare. I must tell you that I used to exchange letters with your father, Amenhotep, and now do so with your brother Akhenamun. In fact I have just received a letter from Akhenamun warning me that you may pass through my lands and that I should offer you assistance and help you on your way, but I must tell you that you have enemies in Thebes."

"What do you mean?" I asked.

"The letter from Akhenamun countermanded a previous letter from the Chief Vizier, Ay ordering that I should have you killed."

"Ay overreaches himself and my brother must deal with his evil ambitions," I replied.

"I am pleased that I was able to save you and your followers from the Habiru. Please be my guest for a few days and rest before you continue your journey to Washukanni."

"Thank you, but how safe will I be when I continue the journey?"

"You should be quite safe and Avram will escort you for a few days just to make sure. The brigands operate west of Jerusalem and not east of the city and you will be travelling east. The desert to the east is empty with few dangers apart from natural ones and then you will enter Mitanni lands. I am on good terms with the Mitanni as I am with Egypt and so you will pass from my protection to their protection – and you do have a Mitanni princess travelling with you."

"Indeed I do. My wife Taduheppa is the daughter of Shatuarra, the Mitanni king. I must thank you, Abdi Heba, for all your help and for your excellent hospitality. I was present at the battle with the Kushites and therefore have seen enough hostilities in recent times."

He beamed at my thanks for he needed Egyptian assistance for dealing with the Habiru. "I was so pleased to hear of the Egyptian victory. Now enjoy my hospitality."

****

We stayed just three days in Jerusalem and enjoyed a much-needed rest from our travels. Abdi Heba treated us very well and we set off in good spirits and even Taduheppa seemed to have recovered slightly from her great loss though she still seemed fragile. I was there for her if she needed me but I did not force my attentions upon her. She needed time and I was willing to give it to her. I hoped that as we neared Washukanni her spirits would lift at the prospect of seeing her father and brother and her home once again. Unfortunately she did not have a mother to return to because she had died when Taduheppa was a young girl.

We now travelled east and north across the Amurru and into the Mitanni lands of Nuhashe. We were passing through friendly territory, and as we headed due north and neared Washukanni we all began to relax a little. It seemed that at last luck was now with us. After facing death for so long at Malkata I was fortunate enough to have found friends in Horemheb and Abdi Heba, and even Akhenamun was aiding us. There was obviously a considerable power struggle enveloping Malkata which I would have to watch closely from afar.

I was resting in one of the wagons when I heard a soldier shouting excitedly. I jumped down from the wagon believing our luck had ended and we were to face more trouble when I saw in the distance a great city.

"It is Washukanni," he said.

"I did not realise we were so close to our destination," I offered in surprise.

"Nor did I, your majesty," he replied.

"Is it really Washukanni?" I said in wonder.

"It really is." Taduheppa was at my side. She was smiling and her smile was like an oasis in the desert. Her beautiful face had been so devoid of happiness and so barren in recent times. In that one smile all her beauty was once again on display. Seeing her homeland had made her happy and I felt like rejoicing. Taduheppa was back.

"It is good to see you smile again," I said.

"I will see my father and my little brother. Kirta is not that much older than you, Smenkhkare and he will have grown much in my absence."

"I hope they are well," I said. "How do you think they will receive an Egyptian who is on the run?"

"You are not on the run. If Akhenamun topples Ay from his position of power you will be able to return to Thebes."

"I am looking forward to spending time in Washukanni with my wife," I said. "Thebes can wait."

She shook her head but grinned. "I have to introduce you to my father."

"How do you think he will receive me?"

"He will receive you well," she assured me.

The joint Egyptian and Mitanni caravan of two wagons and some horses and camels with a squad of Egyptian soldiers and a number of Mitanni servants drew ever closer to Washukanni. I could now see that it was a city of some proportions and though not quite of the size of Thebes it was considerably larger than Jerusalem.

"It looks grand," I said to Taduheppa.

"It is grand," she replied.

I then saw a group of riders leave the city and head in our direction to meet us. Taduheppa saw them too and I could see the excitement on her face. As they drew close a look of recognition began to form on her features. "It is my brother," she shouted with joy. She jumped on a horse and rode out to meet them and I mounted and slowly followed her.

When I caught up with her she had dismounted and was embracing her brother who had also dismounted. I remained on my horse watching the happy reunion. I felt very pleased for here was further proof that Taduheppa was herself again.

She turned to me. "This is Kirta, my little brother."

"I am much bigger than you now, sister," he replied laughing. This was so, for Kirta was much taller than his sister – or me for that matter.

"Kirta, this is my husband, Smenkhkare."

I jumped off my horse and took his hand. His grip was firm and my immediate impression was that I held the hand of an honest man.

"Let us waste no time in riding into Washukanni," Kirta said to Taduheppa. "Our father is not a well man and that is why he did not ride out to meet you himself, but he is most eager to see you again."

Taduheppa was concerned. "Is he seriously ill?" she asked.

"He has been, but he is now recovering and so all is well," smiled Kirta.

"Then what are we waiting for?" enthused Taduheppa. "Let us ride into Washukanni without delay."

I let the brother and sister ride in together and watched as they chatted excitedly, catching up on all the news they both wished to confer on the other. I rode slightly behind them, content to see Taduheppa happy again.

The streets of the capital were lined with people who wished to welcome back their princess, and I rode almost in a daze as they cheered at us. Kirta was obviously popular with the people and they were happy to have the beautiful Taduheppa return to their city. My wife was home.

Chapter 18

The palace did not compare with Malkata but it was grand enough and I felt that if this was to be my new home then I could be content. Kirta showed me to my apartment while Taduheppa, eager to see her old rooms, left me alone with her brother for the first time.

"Taduheppa has briefly told me about your troubles in Malkata and I am not surprised for we have had communications with Egypt."

"What did these communications have to say?" I asked.

"The last one which arrived by messenger just a few days ago was the important one because it was from the pharaoh himself. It asks us to look after you in a manner befitting a member of the Egyptian royal family. It advised us to persuade you not to return to Thebes because even your brother cannot guarantee your safety. He states that you should remain in Washukanni as our guest until he directs you to return."

"I will be happy to stay in Washukanni for the foreseeable future for I am tired of constantly being in danger," I said.

"It seems strange the pharaoh is unable to guarantee your safety," he offered.

"There is a power struggle going on in Thebes between my brother and the chief vizier Ay. I will remain in Washukanni until it is resolved when hopefully Akhenamun will emerge the victor."

"Taduheppa mentioned this Ay. He sounds like a man of too much ambition and a man who must be stopped."

"He is not just an ambitious man but also an evil one," I said with feeling.

"You are safe from him here. We must talk further on this subject for Egypt is our ally and we need to know the state of affairs in Thebes. The Hittites press on our northern borders and we need to know that if we require it we can rely on the pharaoh for help against the common enemy."

"The Egyptian general Horemheb has just recently inflicted an overwhelming defeat on Kush and so the Egyptian military is in a position of strength, but I must watch proceedings within the royal family closely," I said.

"Now you must make yourself ready, Smenkhkare, for my father wishes to greet you formally. I will return in a short while to collect you and in the meantime the servants will give you all you need."

He left me in the care of numerous servants who seemed to have been allocated to me. I bathed, ridding myself of the desert dust, and dressed myself in some of the fine clothes provided. Kirta returned soon after I had performed my ablutions and dressed.

"Taduheppa is already with my father. He is a happy man for not only is his health returning but his beloved daughter has returned," he informed me as I followed him down the corridor.

"He is very fond of her then," I offered.

"As am I for we were both reluctant to let her go to Thebes, but diplomacy and the good of our country had to come first."

"I was just a boy when she arrived in Thebes," I sighed.

"But more of a man now, I suspect," he smiled. "I am a few years older than you, Smenkhkare, but I too had to grow up quickly. We should be friends for, who knows, one day we might both lead our countries."

"We must be friends," I agreed, for I knew it would be good to have a companion again for most of my past friends had been murdered back in Thebes.

"We are here," he said. We were standing outside a large and decorated wooden door. He pushed the door open and indicated I should enter. I walked into a luxurious room befitting the chambers of a great monarch and I looked around me taking in the exotic surroundings. Kirta followed me in. "Malkata is not the only sumptuous palace," he whispered.

Sitting on a large plush chair was Shatuarra, father of Kirta and Taduheppa and king of all the lands of the Mitanni. Taduheppa sat next to him holding his hand and being the dutiful daughter as she listened intently to all he was saying.

He stopped talking and looked up. "Smenkhkare, my new son, welcome to Washukanni." He stood up and walked towards me. "Greetings, my boy, greetings," he enthused.

I had not expected such a warm welcome. I bowed and replied: "Thank you, your majesty, for your great hospitality and for receiving your son-in-law in such a kindly manner. I am most grateful to you."

He grinned: "Now we have got the formalities out of the way we must have a good chat. Come and sit with me Smenkhkare and partake of some nourishment." Kirta opened the door and several servants entered carrying trays of food and drink. I sat down with the king and his daughter and Kirta joined us. The food was placed on a table before us and I waited for Shatuarra to begin the conversation.

"It is good to have my daughter and her husband in Washukanni. Kirta has been a great help to me during my illness. I thought I was going to die but now I grow stronger day by day. Kirta will, of course, succeed me but he is not yet married, which is a situation we must soon remedy."

"I have not thought about marriage," said Kirta.

"Then it is time you did, my son, but in the meantime a grandchild would be most welcome." He looked at me and Taduheppa. Such a child would help draw the Egyptians and the Mitanni even closer and would bring me much joy in my advanced years."

"You have many years left, father," said Taduheppa.

He turned to me. "You are welcome to stay in Washukanni as long as you wish, Smenkhkare. If I were selfish I would say the longer the better for then I would get to see more of my daughter."

"That could be for some time because of the present situation in Egypt," I remarked.

"I am aware of the situation in Egypt and how you have made an enemy of the chief vizier, Ay, who wields considerable power at Thebes even though he is subordinate to the pharaoh."

"Or should be subordinate," I added. "And he made an enemy of me when he tried to murder me."

Shatuarra sighed. "My daughter has brought me up to date on all that has recently happened in Thebes and the evil of this man Ay. As long as he poses a threat to your life, Smenkhkare, then you must stay in Washukanni, but situations inevitably change. When that happens and it is safe for you to return to Egypt it may even be to claim the throne with my daughter as your queen."

I nodded. "I wish fervently for the downfall of Ay but I wish my brother well. There is conflict ahead and I must bide my time and wait to see what develops."

"In the meantime enjoy our hospitality and live like a prince in comfortable exile. You have your wife at your side and my son Kirta as a devoted friend. Welcome to the land of the Mitanni."

Kirta smiled. "I welcome you too, Smenkhkare."

Taduheppa also smiled. "We have faced many dangers and many hardships but we have survived and so it will be good to enjoy safety and comfort for a change."

"I must thank you King Shatuarra and you Prince Kirta for your kindness and for making me feel so welcome. What my wife says is true."

"Then relax and eat and drink," said the king and I took him up on his kind offer.

****

I returned to my apartment after a veritable feast. The court at Washukanni seemed very different to the court at Malkata. The royal family here was much smaller and there were not the tensions that I had become used to in my own family. I felt able to relax completely for the first time for a very long time, but I could not help wondering about my status with the Mitanni princess. I sighed for this was my first night in the Mitanni capital and so all I could do was wait and see what developed but I knew I could not be patient for much longer. Once again I remembered the advice of my brother, Thutmose, and smiled. I had done my best to follow his advice.

The night was still young when Rana, the servant of Taduheppa, came to call. I beckoned her into my room and waited to hear her message. "Taduheppa asks that you follow me back to her apartment."

"Of course," I said.

I followed Rana along the corridors of the vast Mitanni palace until we reached the apartment of the princess. The servant pushed the door open. "You may go in," she said.

I entered Taduheppa's opulent apartment and my beautiful wife was waiting for me. She placed a drink in my hand. "We have gone through much together, husband."

The use of the word 'husband' excited me and I felt a tingle of anticipation. Was the moment I had been waiting for so long about to arrive? She must have sensed my hopeful expectation and smiled as she sipped from her own cup. "Come with me," she invited and I followed her into her bedchamber. She sat on the large inviting bed. "My father seems quite taken with you," she said.

"He has been most kind," I replied. Her bedchamber was an impressive room. I looked at the view of lesser buildings from her large window and then my greedy eyes returned to Taduheppa and were captured by her beauty.

"You will be like a second son and you can assist Kirta in running the state now that my father is no longer able to perform all the duties that he once managed. He is getting old and this illness has been a setback for him."

"I will do what I can." Did she just call me into her bedchamber because she wanted to talk about affairs of state?

"He has already told you your first duty, Smenkhkare."

"What is that?" I was feeling impatient and showed it.

She laughed at my frustration. "We are to provide him with a grandchild."

"Is that why we are in your bedchamber?" I asked, but now I was grinning and feeling so happy.

"Come and sit with me on the bed," she invited. I sat next to her on the comfortable bed which was hung with green and gold silk and was decorated with a lion at the feet of a Mitanni maiden. "I thought you might be curious to see where I slept," she added.

"You are right and I feel like that lion," I said.

"Why is that?" she asked.

"As always I am at your mercy, Taduheppa."

"I do believe you are, Smenkhkare," she said teasingly. "I also believe my young husband is now a man or will be by the time we are concluded here."

Her words excited me, and by way of answer I leaned across and kissed her lips softly and tenderly. The kiss did not remain soft for long as I hungrily gave in to the pent up passion that had built up and tortured me for so long. I hastily unfastened the clasp of her robe which glided to the floor and then she helped me out of my tunic. The perfection of her body was breathtaking and I could hear my heart beating for this was the moment that I had waited for ever since I had first cast eyes on her. I kissed her neck and inhaled the fragrance of her skin and she moaned slightly giving into the pleasure of my touch. She guided my hand to where she wanted it and I surrendered control for I had much to learn. The lovemaking was bliss and Taduheppa was at last truly my wife as she met my passion with her own.

When it was over we looked into each other's eyes with intense wonderment for we had lost track of time, such was the continuous pleasure. I kissed her again and then we snuggled into a warm embrace. The past disagreements and difficulties at Malkata were forgotten and so were the dangers we had faced together in the desert. Even the evil machinations of Ay were forgotten in the overwhelming desire that enveloped me. Washukanni was my new home and there was every prospect that I would be most happy in the land of the Mitanni.

Epilogue

"Enter," I called in response to the loud knock on my apartment door.

Kirta, king of the Mitanni, entered my chamber dressed in humble attire rather than his royal regalia.

"Smenkhkare, two scrolls have arrived for you from Thebes. I thought I would deliver them to you myself and remind you that later we are going hunting with some of my courtiers."

"I have not forgotten," I replied. "It seems strange to receive two messages at once. I have received precious few messages from Egypt over the years."

"That is why I brought them to you promptly and because they also look important. I will leave you to read them and I will see you later."

"Indeed," I said thoughtfully. I had lived in Washukanni for nearly 30 years and the only person who had written to me from Egypt in all that time was my sister, Iset. Her letters had been irregular but they did at least keep me reasonably up to date with affairs in Egypt. Even my mother did not write though I had written to her. I think she had never forgiven me for the plot against my brother.

It seemed I had been almost forgotten after Akhenamun and Ay had reached an agreement early in my exile. Akhenamun had moved his capital from Thebes to Amarna and had abandoned the old gods. Now Egyptians were required to worship Aten, the sun god, and Akhenamun had even changed his name to Akhenaten. To enable him to concentrate his time on his new religious obsession and his brand new capital he allowed Ay to govern in his name which gave Ay all the power he yearned for. It was an agreement which suited both of them and left me in the cold though life in Washukanni was a comfortable exile. Horemheb continued as the general of the Egyptian army and had amassed a huge reputation as a great commander. There was no place left for me in Egypt.

However, over the years a lot of my family had died. In Washukanni my wife Taduheppa had died in childbirth two years after we had arrived in the Mitanni capital. She had given me the two most wonderful years of my life and she would live forever in my heart as long as I walked the earth. I hoped with all my heart that Osiris would see fit to reunite us in the afterlife. I see her even now after all these years in my mind's eye, and her beauty and my memories never fade even though I age. The child also died and so I have no offspring and I have never married again though Kirta has suggested it many times. How could I, for there would never be another Taduheppa? Shatuarra died a year after Taduheppa and Kirta become king of the Mitanni and has remained my greatest friend throughout the years.

In Thebes many of my family have also died and many have been born over the past 30 years. Sitamun and Nebetah have both died and I sometimes think with regret about my sister, Nebetah. She had been such a good friend to me in our youth and I often wish that we had been truly reconciled. Iset still lived and I often thought that it would be good to see her again. In Amarna, Nefertiti had also died and this had apparently, for a while, broken the heart of my brother. Nefertiti had been an amazing and beautiful woman and I had owed her much for the help she had given to me and Taduheppa when death threatened me and misery threatened Taduheppa.

Most remarkable was that my mother Tiye still lived. She was apparently in good health even though she had reached the unthinkable age of 74. She still had some measure of control over her family and was respected not only by Akhenamun and Iset but also by her grandchildren. She was the grand old lady of Thebes. Akhenamun and Nefertiti had given Tiye many grandchildren, but with the exception of the youngest they were all girls. The youngest was a small and weak boy called Tutankhamun. The description that Iset had sent of him reminded me of myself when I was his age. That was now a very long time ago.

All these thoughts and memories were in my mind when I broke the seal and opened the first scroll. It was from Horemheb. I gasped with disbelief for I had not heard from him since we parted company on the desert battlefield after the great defeat of the army of Kush.

Greetings, Prince Smenkhkare

I hope you are in good health as am I even though we are both getting no younger. I have to inform you of the death of your brother Akhenamun and the remarkable events that have transpired since his death. His eldest daughter, Meritaten, with my help has seized power and sent the tyrant Ay into exile. She has moved the capital from Amarna back to Thebes and is beginning the process of restoring the old gods back to prominence. She is a woman and therefore cannot be pharaoh, and so the royal family have decreed that you should return to Thebes and marry Meritaten and become our new pharaoh. Akhenamun's only son Tutankhamun is a sickly boy of eight years and therefore not able to assume power. I remember saying to you last time we spoke, so many years ago, that perhaps one day I would invite you back to Egypt to become pharaoh. I did not realise it would take so long but that day has now come. Return to Thebes immediately from Washukanni to become pharaoh of Upper and Lower Egypt and claim your inheritance.

Your general

Horemheb.

I gasped again with disbelief as I read his words. I was to become pharaoh and marry my niece who I had never met. After all these years I was to rejoin my family at Malkata and become pharaoh. It was almost inconceivable but there it was written on the scroll from Horemheb, Egypt's greatest general. My hand was shaking as I opened the second scroll.

Greetings from your last surviving sister, Iset.

How is my little brother? I had given up ever seeing you again but now it looks like I will. We are now the only two left, you and me, though mother goes on forever. Your brother, Akhenamun, or Akhenaten as he insisted on being known, died in his bed last month. It is rumoured Ay had him poisoned but it is only a rumour and I think he probably died of natural causes following an illness. So much has happened since his death. Meritaten with the help of Horemheb has grasped power and sent Ay into exile. She has already insisted on a return of the capital to Thebes and a return to the old gods. She is quite a remarkable young woman and you are to marry her. Do not get alarmed, little brother, for I think you will find her more than pleasing to the eye. Mother still makes decisions pertaining to the family and she has decided that you are to return to Thebes to marry your niece and become pharaoh. How about that for surprising news? Please do as she requires for I long to see you again. We were getting on so well when you had to flee and I was always on your side. You may ask what about Tutankhamun, but he is of little consequence in the scheme of things, for he is a sickly boy of eight years who will probably not survive for many more years such is his bad health. Do you still hate Ay? If you do then you can have him hunted down and executed for all the wrongs that he has done you and our family. I would like that, for I can never forget that he had Thutmose murdered even though it was so long ago. Please hurry back to Malkata and become pharaoh. Meritaten has accepted the situation and will become your great royal wife and a good wife she will be for you, though I warn you she has loads of energy. Once again hurry back to Thebes.

Love from your big sister Iset.

I sat staring at the two letters for a long passage of time. Did I want to be pharaoh? Did I want to marry Meritaten? I was no longer a young man and not as ambitious as I once was. I had spent many happy years in Washukanni and once I had, to some degree, recovered from the terrible blow of Taduheppa's death they had been good years. Did I wish to spend my remaining years in Washukanni with time passing me by as it had been for many years? I thought not and I knew what I had to do.

There was a knock at the door and Kirta entered. "Are you ready for the hunting trip?"

"I have too much on my mind," I replied.

"Is it those letters?" he asked.

I nodded. "Read them," I said, passing the letters to my good friend.

He perused the letters for some time. "I will miss you, Smenkhkare, but you must go. Together, as leaders of our countries, we can face the Hittite threat which will surely one day become much more than just a threat."

"I know I must go and I will miss you, my friend" I said. "But no woman will ever replace your sister."

****

It was many months later that I rode into the city of Thebes at the head of a small Mitanni caravan. I had bid Kirta a fond farewell and I had left the city of Washukanni with some regret because it held many wonderful memories for me. Most magical of all were the two years of bliss I had spent there with Taduheppa as my wife. Now I was soon to have a new wife and a new life. I seemed to be old at 44 years to now become pharaoh, but I reminded myself of the longevity of my mother and even Ay was much older than me and Horemheb was also a little older. The people were on the streets of the city to welcome their new pharaoh and I waved and showed them my pleasure to once again be among them. They were also no doubt happy to have their city restored to the role of capital of the empire.

We left the throngs behind and entered the palace of Malkata. Memories both good and bad came flooding back to me. The gardens and the lake built by my father had been restored in quick time back to the majesty of the past after years of neglect. Meritaten had done a good job and the gardens that I had once loved to stroll through looked as exotic as they had done in my youth. I gulped in the good Egyptian air and braced myself for meeting my family, both old members and new.

They were lined up outside the palace to greet me and Horemheb was with them also. I smiled and waved and most of them waved back. I looked down the line and tried to decide who each of them was. On one side of the line was the great general and next to him was my mother Tiye looking very ancient indeed. She was being supported by an attractive young woman who I would find out later was Ankhesenamun, third daughter of Akhenamun. Next to her was a small, weak-looking boy who I knew must be Tutankhamun, and then came four more of my brother's daughters all of different sizes and height. Next came my sister, Iset, who had aged but then, I guessed, so had I. Then at the end of the line came a young woman dressed more grandly than any of her sisters and I knew this must be Meritaten, my new wife-to-be. This was now my family and I would have to get to know them all.

I dismounted from my horse and strode towards my relatives. Meritaten left the line to meet me with her arms outstretched. I took her hands in mine, squeezed them and then released them and bowed for this young woman was already Queen of Egypt. She bowed to me in return for now I would be pharaoh and she would be my great royal wife. I looked into her dark eyes and they switched from brown to green in the same bewitching way her mother's eyes had changed their colour. I smiled at the 19-year-old woman for she was the image of her mother, Nefertiti. The matchless Taduheppa would always be, for me, the personification of beauty but I could not deny that my new young queen was also very beautiful. I felt an intense thrill of excitement at returning to Egypt, of becoming pharaoh and of having a beautiful, new wife. I knew that I had to make up for a lot of lost time.

Author's Notes

Who was Smenkhkare? That is a question that historians and Egyptologists have been asking for many, many years. Was he the youngest son of Amenhotep III and brother to Akhenamun (Akhenaten), or was he the eldest son of Akhenamun and older brother or half brother to Tutankhamun? In my story I have taken the view that he was the son of Amenhotep and the great royal wife Tiye which may or may not have been the case. Evidence suggests that he reigned for just two years with his consort and great royal wife, Meritaten, and then died between 1334 BC and 1332 BC. I have placed his birth at about 1379 BC, which would have put him in his 40s at death.

Very little is known about the Mitanni princess Taduheppa except that she married into the Egyptian royal family during the Amarna period. Some scholars believe that Nefertiti had foreign origins and therefore Taduheppa (Tadukhipa) and Nefertiti are the same person. This theory suggests that Nefertiti's name – 'the beautiful one has come' – refers to Nefertiti's foreign origin as Taduheppa. I have chosen to believe, for the sake of the story and because I think it is more likely, that they were two different women though both extremely beautiful.

All the members of the royal family in the story are historical characters though in most cases very little is known about them. It has been a very difficult task for Egyptologists to place these people in the right time and the correct generation. This has given me free licence to place them as I wish though evidence is strong regarding Amenhotep, his wife Tiye and his first six children all referred to in my story. Smenkhkare in many ways is the odd one out and his place in history is most in doubt. I shall briefly look at some of the evidence for the existence of Smenkhkare.

Very little is known of Smenkhkare for certain because later pharaohs sought to erase the entire Amarna Period from history, but some evidence still remains. Smenkhkare was known as far back as 1845 from the tomb of Meryre II. There he and Meritaten bearing the title great royal wife are shown rewarding the tomb's owner. Aside from the

Meryre tomb depiction, there are several pieces of evidence which establish Smenkhkare as pharaoh.

A calcite 'globular vase' from the tomb of Tutankhamun bears the full double cartouche of Akhenaten alongside the full double cartouche of Smenkhkare. This is the only object to carry both names side by side.

A single wine docket, 'Year 1, wine of the House of Smenkhkare', indicates he probably had a short reign. Another dated to Year 1 from 'The House of Smenkhkare (deceased)' was originally taken to indicate that he died during the harvest of his first year; more recently it has been proposed to mean his estate was still producing wine in the first year of his successor.

Line drawings of a block depicting the nearly complete names of King Smenkhkare and Meritaten as Great Royal Wife were recorded before the block was lost.

A ring bearing his name was found at Malkata in Thebes.

Perhaps the most magnificent evidence was a vast hall more than 125 metres square and including over 500 pillars. This late addition to the central palace has been known as the Hall of Rejoicing, Coronation Hall or simply Smenkhkare Hall.

Several items from the tomb of his successor Tutankhamun bear the name of Smenkhkare: a linen garment decorated with 39 gold daisies along with 47 other sequins bearing the name of Smenkhkare alongside Meritaten's name; also a bow and a shawl both bore his names.

Less certain, but much more impressive, is the second anthropoid coffin containing the mummy of Tutankhamun. The face depicted is much squarer than that of the other coffins and quite unlike the gold mask or other depictions of Tutankhamun. The coffin is Rishi style and inlaid with coloured glass, a feature only found on this coffin and one from KV55, the speculated resting place for the mummy of Smenkhkare. Since both cartouches show signs of being reworked, scholars have concluded that this was most likely originally made for Smenkhkare and re-inscribed for Tutankhamun.

Since the reign of Smenkhkare was brief – and it is possible he may never have been more than co-regent – the evidence for Smenkhkare is not plentiful, but nor is it quite as insubstantial as it is sometimes made out to be. It certainly amounts to more than just a few rings and a wine docket, or that he appears only at the very end of Akhenaten's reign on a few monuments as is too often portrayed. Smenkhkare has also been confused with several female rulers, most notably Nefertiti, Meritaten and Tutankhamun's other sister, Ankhesenamun, who was mentioned at the end of the story. I have discarded these theories and given Smenkhkare the place I believe he deserves because most evidence supports it – male pharaoh of Upper and Lower Egypt for a few brief years during the 18th dynasty.

Perhaps no one from the Amarna period has been the subject of so much speculation as Smenkhkare. There is just enough evidence to say with some certainty that he is an individual, but not enough to decide on a co-regency or a sole reign. As a result, Egyptologists move him about like a pawn as their larger hypotheses require. He can be proposed as any number of people and he can reign for weeks or years. He is a short-lived co-regent with no independent reign or he is Akhenaten's successor, depending on which expert you listen to. My Smenkhkare had a good life for the turbulent times, was a prince for much of his life and then ruled independently for several years.

Finally I should mention two more major characters from my story, Ay and Horemheb. It is generally believed that Meritaten ruled Egypt for a few years after the death of Smenkhkare. She was succeeded by the young Tutankhamun and his great royal wife, his sister, Ankhesenamun. The reign of Tutankhamun, like that of Smenkhkare, was brief but unlike Smenkhkare he was to achieve immortality. Tutankhamun was followed by the aged Ay, the once chief vizier who also reigned for only a few brief years. If he did ever flee into exile then he obviously returned to Thebes to take up the reins of power. Horemheb followed Ay as pharaoh and the great general had a fairly long reign. He achieved legitimacy by marrying into the royal family and he is considered by many Egyptologists as being responsible for erasing the Amarna period and therefore Smenkhkare from history. Why he would have done so I will not speculate except to mention the word 'religion' which was so important in the social order of ancient Egypt.

Once again I must state that this story is a work of fiction and must not be considered as historical fact. My story is the story of Smenkhkare as prince and not as pharaoh and we have no knowledge of his time as pharaoh of Egypt. Having said that, I must say it gave me a great deal of pleasure to write a story about the life of the forgotten pharaoh,

Smenkhkare, ruler of Upper and Lower Egypt for just a short time a long time ago.